Bread from Heaven

Henrietta Buckmaster

(pseud.)

author of

Let My People Go

Deep River

Fire in the Heart

Henkle, Henrietta

"Ah! when shall all men's good
Be each man's rule, and universal Peace
Lie like a shaft of light across the land?"
ALFRED TENNYSON

Bread from Heaven

New York
Random House

First Printing

Published in New York by Random House, Inc.,
and simultaneously in Toronto, Canada, by
Random House of Canada, Limited
Library of Congress Catalog Card Number: 52–8811
Manufactured in the United States of America
by H. Wolff, New York
Designed by Jerome Kuhl

For Evelyn with my love

Bread from Heaven

1

There is a particular moment toward late afternoon when the sun slants on the hillside just west of the town and makes it the most beautiful place in the world. It is an incandescent moment when leaf and bough and underbrush and bird and small running thing become their true and secret selves, and the eye and the heart are deeply stirred. It is a good moment and a fleeting moment, but never one which is lost.

Just beyond the hill, as one turned into the village, was the Roscoe Stillwell house. It was built in 1802 and had the fine touches which wealth gave it and maintained. Two very fine lilac bushes grew on either side of the front door, and when one leaned out the second-floor window, he could, on any May day, bury his nose in the topmost blossoms. The house stood bare and open in the glance of the sun, the fine lines of paint, the irrepressible, joyful, darting, iridescent light on the windowpanes defined a true and potent sensibility, a concept, a dream. All down the village street the lilacs and the lingering forsythia shaped and shared a fact, and a whole became most significantly discerned in its separate parts. It was a time of day and a place and a state of mind.

Mrs. Stillwell was in her bedroom, and she saw the sudden light on the leaves of the lilacs and stood by the window considering them. Here at the top the blossoms were thickest. Had the bush been properly pruned through the years, the blossoms would have been more evenly spaced, but it gave her an invariable pleasure whenever she realized that she could touch the lilacs from her bedroom window. A small thing—it did not concern her often—but it was pleasant to think about at moments like this. Some people had wanted to cut down the lilac hedges along the main street, and she had opposed them. She thought about it now with inconsequential anger. Some people will do anything, think anything, disrupt anything, overturn anything—people she knew! She stood there in the window, dressed (all but her hat) to go out to tea, and whipped herself into anger. Since she was growing deaf, she did not mind talking aloud. These were her thoughts, and if people overheard them—well, they were still her thoughts and it was very bad breeding to listen to what you were not intended to hear.

She was standing there in the sunlight, roused, talking to herself, reaching for her hat to put on, when she saw the two figures coming down the road. They were not much to watch, a young man and a child. But the young man carried the child whose legs dangled and hit against his as he walked, and she could see from where she stood that they were talking. This meant that the child could not be asleep. He must be sick. Interested in everything, she continued to watch.

The young man stopped in front of her house and stood the child on his feet. The child staggered slightly as though getting his balance, and looked up the village street. Shabby . . . the sunlight shone on the torn leather jacket of the young man. The child said something swiftly. The young man put his arm around his shoulder and they stood as though making plans, the sunlight on their dark heads.

Mrs. Stillwell, pinning on her hat, watched abstractedly. The child looked at the house. Mrs. Stillwell thought he looked at her, so she responded in kind and examined him with narrowed eyes. A bright face, animated—not sick. But it was plain he did not see her. He was looking toward the lilac bush, and the young man went forward a few steps and picked a lower blossom. Mrs. Stillwell started to speak out, she moved to open the window, but what she saw halted her. The young man held the blossom to the child's nose. He smelt it deeply, with little moves of his head, and then he opened his mouth and seemed to lick at the blossom. Mrs. Stillwell narrowed her eyes more firmly and saw that he was indeed biting the flower, and then she noticed something more. The child had no arms.

It was an odd sensation to stand there in one's own bedroom, in one's own familiar place, and look at a strange child without arms. A little boy, six or seven by the size of him, biting at lilacs because he had no other way to touch them.

Mrs. Stillwell did not know what to do. She wished to do something because she was not a passive woman. She wished to call through the window, say, *I am here . . . What is this?* but she hesitated too long. They went on down the road toward the village. She opened the window and peered after them. The young man took the lilac blossom and stuck it back of the child's ear, and for a moment she saw the child in profile, laughing up at the young man, the purple blossom against his cheek.

Where . . . and who? Mrs. Stillwell picked up her gloves and her purse. All her life, since her girlhood, she had asked questions like these, and seldom had she received answers of value. She had learned Greek and Latin, and had believed in women's rights and being one's brother's keeper, and there were many warm and beautiful things to remember out of the past, but always *where* and *why* and *who* remained unanswered. Perhaps she wanted too much. She had not thought about that and she did not think about it now. Being hard of hearing had an advantage, for she could continue asking questions and not be troubled by foolish replies. When one lived intimately in a small town, this was not without a positive value.

The two boys went down the village street, a lovely street full of its own memories. If left to itself, as on such a spring day or on a snowy day, it was very serene. The older boy was not quite the young man Mrs. Stillwell imagined. He might be no more than nineteen. It was something across his brow, a shadow around the eyes, which said that he was young in one way but not in another. There was a rough kind of youngness about his big body and thick dark hair which fell against his forehead, about the slow loose way he walked, as though conscious of an untested vitality; an oldness about his eyes, expressive, watchful, a little sardonic, and about his large mouth, tightly pressed together. Yet it was a beautiful face, in its own terms, mobile, full of life, a man's face and yet most subtly related to some expectation of boyhood.

The child moved eagerly now, running a little.

"Is this the place?" he asked. "Will we stay here?"

"I think so. I feel this is it." He smiled at the child. "Would that make you happy?" He took a quarter from his pocket and fingered it. "I will buy you a sandwich and an ice-cream cone. Yes?"

"Ice cream!"

As the young man fed the child in the drug store, he

asked the clerk, "What is this town called?" The clerk told him. "Massachusetts?"

The clerk nodded, surprised at such a question, and then he could not contain himself any longer. "What's the matter that you feed him?" he asked impatiently. "Got no arms?"

"Yes."

The clerk was startled. He had not expected such an answer. The child paid little attention. When the clerk had first spoken, the child had lifted his pansy-colored eyes and looked at him, but when the cone was offered him, he turned away. The child finished the sandwich and the young man offered him the cone to finish. As he laid the quarter on the counter, he asked, "Is there a garage here?" And the clerk still without speech, pointed down the road.

He came with them as far as the door, and as they went down the step, he asked, "What happened to him?"

They did not hear him or they chose not to answer.

"Funny thing happened today," said George McVitty at dinner. ". . . I was taken aback. Fellow came and asked for a job. Real good mechanic. I didn't see the child he had with him or I might not have hired him. But I did." He expelled a deep breath and fiddled with his coffee cup. "Child was a sight. Had no arms. What could I do? Two boys . . . had to let them stay in the place over the garage."

"Oh, George."

"What could I do?" Then he leaned back and fixed his eyes on the dark window, and his thin lips smiled just a little. "Some things you have to do though it may not seem right. Anyway, there they are."

Clara McVitty considered him for a moment. "Does the child look badly?"

"Sort of."

"What if customers don't like to see such a child around?"

He stirred a little angrily. "Some things you do and then you have to wait and see."

"What are their names?"

"The big fellow's called Karel, and the little one Nicky. Lindemann."

"Is the child bright?"

"Wouldn't know."

"Oh, George!"

He stood up then. "Dammit," he said, "what kind of a fellow would I look like to myself if I hired a fellow and then fired him because his little brother didn't have two arms? I just told you about it. Now let's forget it."

Clara McVitty rubbed and rubbed one smooth plump arm. You live in a place all your life and you still have to ask those questions. She liked George with gumption. It made her proud of him. A woman had to carry a man so often that it was nice to see him stand up that way. And she was glad that a child had stirred him. It was a good thing for a number of reasons, and she considered them, one by one, to herself.

Karel sat at the scratched and battered table in the pool of light from the electric globe and fed a mouthful of beans to Nicky and then a mouthful to himself. The heat rose from the can and made a sweet tracery in the air. Nicky watched the steam intently, tracing the spiral with his unblinking eyes.

"Now milk," he said, and Karel held the glass to the child's lips, and when the child had finished, drank himself from the glass. The child listened to everything. Between forkfuls of beans he would turn his head and say gleefully, "Another car stopped."

"This is a busy road," Karel answered, digging into the can. "A very fine road." His head turned also when cars stopped and there was a gay and lively expression as though he too expected fine things.

"That car is making a banging noise. Will you go fix that one now?"

"No, not till tomorrow."

Nicky laughed and held onto the fork playfully with his teeth. When he let go, he said through his chewing, "You are the best mechanic in the world. Who will tell me things? Will you tell me things? And then when I get my arms I will be a better mechanic than you."

"Oh, yes," said Karel smiling.

Nicky kicked with his knees against the table and shouted with joy. "I'll be many, many, many times better mechanic than you!"

Karel steadied the dancing glass. "Take care," he said, running his hand over the scratched table. "This is a very fine table. We must look after it."

"It is ours?" Nicky asked, and when Karel nodded, he laid his cheek against it and stroked his cheek back and forth.

The lilacs were very fragrant in the early morning. May flowers were blossoming all along the streets, and Karel permitted his heart to open a little way.

But the effect was suffocating. Sentimental and reminiscent . . . It asked him where he had come from and why he had come here. He had walked down the main street in the early morning and now he walked back it, fifteen minutes later, his hands in his pockets, his head lowered, seeing each stick and stone, each cultivated grass plot, his eyes selecting, observing—the dog which lay on the sidewalk and thumped his tail but did not move out of the way, the tricycle which had been forgotten half in and out of a gate, the woman who stood in her doorway staring raptly at her wisteria vine, two milk bottles clasped to her bosom, all the splendid importance of trivial things against which he measured his own experience.

It was a brooding questioning pilgrimage, half a mile down and half a mile back with a pause to lean against a tree. For those five minutes of leaning against the tree, he lived in a world which contained only himself, awful, immense, without the dignity of what we term place or time. He was swept by a terrible belief in what he must disbelieve, the houses all so shining white with green shutters or black shutters, so perfect in line and symmetry and way of living and state of mind—one sensed their sufficiency—with the deep green lawns and the neatly balanced old trees and the air of self-preservation as though all the turmoil and the tossing of human intransigence could be resisted with only the slightest quiver of doubt. They were all so abstract and far away that he was swept with dismay. He felt himself a helpless child again, washed by darkness, clamoring for love.

Perhaps this was too much. Perhaps he had demanded too much of himself and of Nicky. Perhaps the place was too peaceful. Perhaps they should move on. Perhaps the details of personal perplexity might be lost only in the larger perplexities of a rougher town with none of the soft demands of this place. He could not be sure. He had been sure before, even in the darkest moments, of a next step, but now he could not think.

Yet there had to be a stillness. Somewhere in his life there had to be a small life, a little core of unimportant happenings. To study, to go to work, to have a home, to have a wife, to have a neighbor . . . this had all the quality of a dream, like this town . . . yet the pavements of this town were solid, the people were of flesh and blood.

He might watch a merging—himself and this town—it might be. He did not dare to be certain.

He had left the child sleeping, but as he came the last hundred yards, he heard the little voice screaming his name and he saw the thin shirtless little figure standing in the window. He should not have left him to waken in a strange place. His name, in the quietness of the morning, was piercing, and he broke into a run.

"Be quiet, little chicken, I am coming!"

"He's coming—see, I said he'd come," the Negro man who stood below the window called gaily. "See, nothing to worry about, like I said." He watched Karel, smiling a little under a gray mustache. "He was hollering as I came down the road, but I talked quiet to him."

"It is bad to stir people up when we are strangers!"

The man shrugged. "Know worse things," he said, and went on down the road.

"There is nothing to be afraid of," Karel said, holding the child in his arms. "Nothing. Do you understand that? If we belong in a place, we belong, and we behave as though we belong. You must not scream for me. I will never be far away. That man who spoke was a friend, and you must not be afraid of friends."

"His face was black!"

"What is wrong with black? This is a good place and you will grow to know things and you must not be afraid. There will never be any reason to scream. Do you understand?"

Nicky listened, his face lifted away from Karel, the perspiration standing on his lip and forehead. Karel wiped his face and kissed him. Then Nicky said softly, "I want our breakfast." And then, "Where is Bertha?"

"Do you want Bertha?"

He hesitated, and then said, "No," for he sensed that

that was what Karel wished him to say. But he added in a whisper, "She let me sit on her lap whenever I wanted."

George McVitty stood over Karel during a slack moment, watching him change some spark plugs. "Where did you say you came from?"

"New York."

"Never been to New York. Best I can manage is Boston. Wife once got me to go to the Symphony in Boston. Like music?"

Karel wiped his hands with a rag. "When I was a child . . ." Then he stopped.

George waited, but he did not look at Karel for he always tried to mind his own business. At length he said, "When I was a kid I thought I got enough too."

Karel put his head under the hood of the car. "It would be nice to listen again."

A car came in for gasoline. George adjusted his cap against the sun. "What did you say was the matter with the little fellow?"

Karel's head was far under the hood. George waited for a moment, and then he went over to the gas pump.

Miss Nolle, who lived next door, was talking to Nicky, over the fence. ". . . Indians lived here once."

"Indians!"

Miss Nolle told him what she knew, embellishing a little for she was a kind woman and, she said later, the child's face wrung her heart. Such big black eyes, such a nervous little face, such a way he had of trying to express himself . . . The Indians became fierce and gentle all at one time; they hopped about on one foot and uttered strange cries with their fingers beating their lips, Miss Nolle demonstrating.

"And where's your mother and daddy, Nicky? Where's your home?"

He looked at her with expressionless eyes: "Dead. Where is an Indian? Let me see him."

"At the library are pictures of Indians. Miss Purvis will show you, if you are very quiet and make no noise. Where was your home?"

He stared at her for a moment. He said craftily, jerking his head, "There . . . *I do not know.*"

Miss Nolle had a kind persistent mind, like a little tap dripping. It meant no harm; dripping was natural to it. "What's the language you and your brother talk together?"

"Ours. *I don't know.*"

"Of course you know! Now run along. I'm busy."

He told Karel repeatedly about the Indians at the library, and when Karel had an hour free, he took the child down the street.

"Marilyn said there were no Indians," Nicky said shrilly. "Only baseball players. I told her she lied. I'll tell her again."

Karel answered sharply, "She will find out for herself. Forget Marilyn."

Nicky did not seem to notice the tone. He said, "Where is the flower tree we saw yesterday?"

"Around the corner, I imagine. But there are other flower trees all along the street."

"Pick me then a flower!"

Karel said slowly, "I think it is probably time for you to learn to say Please. I have not asked it of you before, but you will have to learn sooner or later. It would be a beginning."

"Begin what?"

"We should say Please. Shall I pick you a flower?"

Nicky laughed.

"Shall I?"

"Yes!"

"Shall I pick you a flower?"

"Please!"

They went through the door of the white clapboard library with a lilac blossom in Nicky's buttonhole.

Miss Purvis was a plump lady in a black dress, the sleeves of which came three-quarters of the way down her arms showing her fat wrists and forearms. She smiled at them in the impersonal way of her calling, and Karel explained their needs. She soon laid a book on Indians on a table and lighted a lamp. Karel turned the pages for Nicky and whispered what the text said.

"Why are you whispering?" Nicky demanded. "Why is he whispering?" he turned to Miss Purvis.

"It is the custom in a library," she whispered.

"Are we afraid of something?" he asked Karel.

"No, we are not afraid."

After a few moments, Miss Purvis whispered, "Would you like me to show you some arrowheads and some Indian beadwork?"

"What are they? What are they?"

Karel sat quietly, hearing the high little voice receding into another room. Since she would not let him handle things, perhaps she would not question his armlessness. He sat there, suddenly weak. He longed for something so inexpressibly that he felt all the world could not contain his longing. It was beyond speech, beyond the confines of brain and body. It had no name. It swept like an icy wind. It made him giddy.

His knuckles shone on the table and he waited for the terrible thing to pass. It was strange to question and doubt at this time. He was stripped and very young, and it is a sad and hard thing to be young with no youth, and imagine you are facing some kind of death while sitting in the quiet library of a quiet town.

He whispered involuntarily, "*Life . . . life . . . I do*

not doubt my own existence. There is no need to run here and there looking for it. I am alive. I believe in life."

Presently the need for movement brought him to his feet. He stood before a shelf of books. He looked at the titles but he did not read them. There was no communication from the titles. He walked slowly along the shelves simply looking at this dimensional thing, a book. His father had many books arranged like these. Here the language was not the same, and that gave an alien feeling. But the shape was the same, and gave the sensation of home. He took down a book and looked at one page and then at another.

"*Over the carnage rose prophetic a voice, Be not disheartened, affection shall solve the problems of freedom yet. Those who love each other shall become invincible. Were you looking to be held together by lawyers? Or by an agreement on paper? or by arms? Nay, nor the world, nor any living thing, shall so cohere!*"

The tears filled his eyes. He had longed to have this said to him, and it had come now without warning. He sat looking at the words with their wonderful vivacity, piercing out of some darkness at the moment when he needed them deeply. He put his finger between the pages of this book and stood up to speak to Miss Purvis as she returned with Nicky. Nicky was talking fast and loudly, making associations which she could not understand, and Karel cut through his voice.

"Thank you," he said. "Thank you very much for showing him things. Now will you please tell me who wrote these words?"

She glanced at the front of the book. "Walt Whitman."

"Yes. But who is he, I mean to say?"

She sat down at her desk, looking at him with a sudden regard.

"A poet."

"Not a Secretary of State or a Defense Minister?"

She hesitated. She picked up her pen. For a moment there was something bare and arrested in her look. Then she blinked her eyes.

"If you are living here, you may use the library at any time. Two fiction, two non-fiction." And then, "What are you interested in?"

He hesitated for a moment, looking at the book in his hand. "I wish to be a doctor," he said. "Are there books on medicine?"

"There are some books about doctors. You may have one of them."

. . . "I wanted to do something more. I didn't know what." Miss Purvis' intensity made her blink her eyes rapidly. "He was such a grown-up, quiet-looking boy. And so nice with the little fellow. You don't get many young people coming in asking for serious books. And reading Walt Whitman. I think I'll speak to Dr. Jarman. Am I meddling?" She stirred her coffee sternly, not really wishing an answer.

Mrs. Stillwell asked, "Was it a dark young man and a little fellow without arms?"

Miss Purvis put down her spoon abruptly. "Without arms! Yes—why did I think only of the older boy?"

Mrs. Stillwell said, "When I realized about the child I can't tell you how I felt. I tried to get Roscoe interested, but he didn't see what should be done." Roscoe did not lift his head from his dinner, but continued with his dessert, a spare man, whittled down to accommodate only so much and no more. "But," she added passionately, in her high toneless voice, "I can never feel indifferent. Why are we here in this world? What is it for if we are not going to help people?"

Roscoe said drily, "I recall some people who did not want your help, or anyone's."

"Well, there are ignorant people and people I misjudged, but that does not say that we should not try to help." His wife trembled a little. "I think that I will talk to Clara McVitty."

Roscoe sighed and his wife heard him, as he intended.

"A child without arms," Miss Purvis was saying. "What would a child like that be doing in this town? That doesn't seem logical. If I speak to Dr. Jarman . . ."

Roscoe Stillwell gave her a quizzical look.

2

Events were all so small, so unpremeditated. The very smallest occurrences were not readily discernible, and their shiftings into proper place went by unobserved in the natural course of events. The lilacs faded and changed the look of the street; peonies began to swell on bushes near the houses; the library opened and closed at its regular hours, as did the garage; definitions of life and of living were exchanged at the post office, the church, and the dinner tables; old Dr. Jarman went about in his 1939 Buick and knew that a younger man would soon have to take his place. Not years but the spirit . . . something had happened to his spirit. Modern hucksters said you should know your limitations and be satisfied. He said to hell with all hucksters. Who put limits on a man but himself? He felt his spirit brace up, but not wholly.

The days lengthened, summer came, farmers began to think of their hay-cutting, and people measured the swiftness of brooks to determine whether it would be a wet or a dry summer. Mrs. Stillwell grew to know the boys well. She invited them to dinner and she took them for rides in her car. She thought about them intensely. She asked them endless questions, interrupting herself only long enough to call attention to some sight which they should admire. She seemed unperturbed by their lack of answers. She wished to enter their lives but she found this hard to do. Well, she would persist.

The Thursday Club met for the last time in June and Mrs. McVitty was elected treasurer for the next year and Mrs. Stillwell corresponding secretary. Mrs. McVitty and Mrs. Stillwell had lately become friends. They had lived in the same town all their lives, but the two boys had brought them together. Odd. They both felt (although they could not say why) that their interest in the boys justified something in themselves. They could not say what. It was not even a thought. It was merely a feeling.

Some time before, Mrs. McVitty had told George that she was glad he had obeyed his best impulse—it was always the right thing to do—and given those boys a home. They were fine boys and they needed a home, and people were even becoming interested in Nicky. It seemed as though something surely could be done for him. She repeated this conviction to Mrs. Stillwell when they sat next each other at the last club meeting, and Mrs. Stillwell looked at her almost indignantly. "Of course!"

Mrs. Stillwell made a motion that afternoon to explore ways and means of helping the little boy.

There was a marked hesitation.

"*Where do they come from? What is their accent?* . . . What does it matter? . . . *It matters a little. One doesn't rush in unless one knows something about people.* . . . *They seem nice boys. But we have our own, right here, we should care for* . . . *Who are they—just wandering into this town?* . . . *You can't just help carelessly.* . . . *Let's discuss it next meeting when we know more.* . . .

It did not occur to Mrs. Stillwell to be cross at herself

for being too impulsive. She was cross with the others for being so cautious.

A few who came to the garage became friendly with Karel and called him by name. Others saw him regularly at the store buying food, a few saw him on the side roads and lanes walking with the child. They all spoke to him. He was something new which had come into the village. A little eddy opened and closed over him and that was the end of it. But the small pieces were shifting nonetheless, and one night or one morning, or some time in between, a personal recognition would take place, limited perhaps, but palpable; judgments would no longer be abstract. In a measure, the two would belong.

Dr. Jarman saw Karel walking on a back road one day and hailed him from his car.

"You the boy who wants books on medicine?"

"Yes, sir."

"Why?"

"I would like to be a doctor."

"Liking and being are two different things."

"Yes. But I must begin to find out."

"You can read my books, as far as I'm concerned. But there are no mail-order doctors." He threw in the clutch. "Trivial intentions aren't worth my time, but come to my office if you want to. That your brother? Bring him along."

The doctor frowned deeply as he drove away, digging an old wedge between his brows. Would the fellow come? And then he weighed the next question. Why did he want him to come? He wondered for the space of that moment if he had ever met anything objectively. New things fed his spirit and it was insatiable.

All these were small things, all forming a pattern.

The boys came tentatively one evening to the doctor's house.

When he opened the door he saw them in the half-light, and he had a vivid impression of two abstract figures, good and evil, right and wrong, the tall and the short, the left and the right. It made him snap, "Well, come in!"

In the lighted room—that was better.

He said, "Sit down," and himself sat in the old mohair rocker, his elbows on its arms, his hands clasped together. The child stood between the young man's knees, watchful, distrusting, the dark eyes preternatural in the small face. The doctor had his impression of the young man as well—a powerful fellow, a manly face, not crude at all though strong and rough-featured . . . with the most watchful eyes he thought he had ever beheld. He noticed the way his large hands touched the child, very gentle and quiet. He liked that. Those things made an impression on a man who had seen most things in his lifetime.

He said abruptly to Karel, "How old's the child?"

"He is eight."

"Good God, I would have thought he was six. What'd you do—starve him?" Karel did not answer. "What's his name?"

"Nikalaus."

"Brother?"

"My brother."

The doctor sat regarding them, his rather watery eyes half-closed behind his spectacles, the rocker moving slightly. "How old are you?"

"I am nineteen."

"*You* look older."

The doctor continued to rock in silence and examine them. And they continued steadily to look at him.

"You want to be a doctor?" He did not wait for an answer. "I see young ones get born in this town and quit it and come back, and what do they make of themselves? What's wrong with young fellows? You want to be a doctor, but how do you know what it means? How do you know whether you're willing to give up your life to it? Kids all full of big words and no experience. Why do you think you want to be a doctor?"

Karel did not answer immediately. He lifted the child to his lap, and he ran his hand abstractedly up and down the child's leg and seemed disinclined to look at the doctor. The child watched the boy's hand, and the child and the boy appeared to withdraw into a world of their own. At length Karel said, without lifting his head, "It seems to me there are a great many things to be made well in the world."

"How do you know?"

The dark eyes lifted swiftly, then the glance returned to the child's knees and he resumed the slow stroking. He merely said, "Isn't that so?"

The doctor groaned and rocked hard for a minute. "Sometimes I wonder. I make a man well. Why? So he can make a fool of himself."

"And yet you continue to be a doctor. It must be worth something." Karel hesitated, and then he made a swift nervous gesture of running his fingers through his thick hair. "Since I want to be a doctor, will you lend me books?"

"Take 'em all, as far as I'm concerned. But do you think books will cure?"

"I think if I know enough I will be able to cure."

The doctor sat very still, his hands on his knees looking at the dark square of window behind Karel's head.

"Maybe you're different from everyone else. Maybe you're a genius. But I recommend to you an undeviating skepticism. It'll never let you down." Karel did not answer, but he seemed suddenly aware of the doctor in highly personal terms, of a man sitting in a creaking chair, beset, it seemed, by a lifetime. He looked at him with something like affection. The doctor was saying, "Believe nothing, fear nothing, and you will reach the end of your life surprised by nothing. What branch of this uncertain science are you interested in?"

"Surgery."

"Why?"

There was a trace of impatience in Karel's shrug. "Should not the injured be helped?"

The doctor started, and he turned his eyes quickly to Nicky who was sitting rigid and very quiet, his black eyes fixed on the doctor.

"Come here," he said to the child. The child frowned and did not move. Karel stood him on his feet and whispered to him.

"No," said Nicky. Then Karel spoke aloud. "Do not be afraid. Remember, you are not to be afraid. This is a friend."

The child went to the doctor, wary, his brows drawn together. The two considered each other for a moment with the equality of suspicion. Then the doctor smiled briefly and gently unfastened the child's shirt. The child submitted, but he reserved a part of himself, the right to protest, in the arch of his brows and the watchfulness of his eyes.

The thin stripped beauty of a little boy's body was disclosed, the shadow of ribs, the bony frame of shoulders, the narrow little chest and the quick rise of breathing. What was truncated, cut off, did not strike you until you examined appearances in the light of convention, for the child wished you only to see what he saw, and he saw himself whole.

The doctor examined him closely, touching the remnants of arms.

"What happened?"

Karel said, "An accident."

"How?"

"An explosion."

"For God's sake, where?"

"An explosion."

The doctor stared at him, and Karel kept his eyes on him and did not look away.

Nicky said angrily, "You will give me arms?"

"What!"

The child was impatient. "I want some arms!"

The doctor leaned back in his chair and regarded them both in silence. "God damn it," he said. "Who do you think you are and what do you think life is? 'Give me arms!' " and he laughed abruptly. Then he looked at the child frowning, and suddenly put out a hand and drew him to him. The child stood in his embrace. " 'Give me arms . . .' Has someone promised you arms?"

The child nodded. "They . . ." But Karel said sharply, "No promise was made unless I made it." The child looked at him, close to tears. "I promised, did I not?"

The doctor considered, his fingers drumming on his knee, and said quietly, "The one arm's cut off too close to the shoulder and we can't do anything about that. Can you move the other, sonny?"

Nicky demonstrated quickly.

The doctor turned away. "Put on his shirt."

"You watched?" Nicky cried.

"I watched. Fine!"

Karel buttoned the shirt, saying quietly, "For my brother I wish everything. He is intelligent and quick and must be like other boys."

"You want me to get him an arm?"

Karel did not answer. He was tucking in the child's shirt. The doctor said abruptly, "Where do you come from?"

"New York."

"Before that?"

"New York."

"I don't believe you. What are you trying to cover up?"

Karel looked at him in sudden despair. His face was white and he started to speak, but he shook his head instead.

The doctor said very slowly, "I don't understand what you want to cover up. I don't understand. Has it something to do with the child?"

Karel shook his head.

"Is it you?"

"He is my brother. I could not do without him. We have suffered. Please let it go at that."

The doctor could not take away his eyes.

"I don't understand why . . ." Then he turned away sharply. "Take the books you want."

The Negro, Vree Dunnigan, stood in the sun by the garage door the next Sunday. His cap was pulled low and his pipe was between his teeth. He listened with a slight smile to the noise of the radio.

"It saves your soul every quarter of an hour on Sunday. Sure makes it sound easy. I can remember when there wasn't any radio and your soul just limped along."

Karel examined the tire. "They praise so many things. All things you can't do without." He looked at Vree and laughed. "I could do without them. Let me have a home and a job and Dr. Jarman's books—and I will do without them."

"Boy," Vree said gaily, "what's the good of being alive if you can't have an automobile and a trip to Florida and a television set? You're not grown-up."

Karel looked up quickly, and then he laughed. "It is hard to know sometimes when people are joking."

"Oh, I'm not joking." Vree propped one large foot against the other and considered the pair. "Some folks would die—I've seen 'em, in this town—without the extras. And if you don't want 'em they'll say you haven't got ambition—because you *haven't*. Not for a television set." He grinned.

Karel sat on his heels, the tire between his hands. "They have never gone without—or been frightened."

"Oh, sure they have. Been shoeless poor, some. We've got that kind here. And scared whether they can hold onto their first job, or their second."

Karel looked at him. "Maybe it depends on what you have been afraid of."

Vree eased his pipe to the side of his mouth. "Maybe." After a moment he knocked out his pipe. "Rain or snow or shine, every Sunday afternoon I go for a walk. Helps me commune with my equals. Would Nicky like to go along?"

"He is—his balance is not always good."

"I know. I'll keep a hold on his shirt."

Nicky was palely intense. "Will we go up on the hill?" he asked Vree Dunnigan. "Will we see any animals? Will I know my way back if you get lost?"

Vree Dunnigan broke a candy bar in two and put half to Nicky's lips. "Little boys that ask questions always get answers. Just you wait and see."

Nicky said to Karel, "Fasten on my watch," and Vree was attentive as Karel pinned a heavy old-fashioned watch with Roman numerals to the child's suspenders.

Karel sat back on his heels and watched them go, and he tried for the moment to see Nicky as another would see him. It was impossible, for he could not afford to see him except with his own loving and expectant eyes.

"What beats me," said McVitty, standing behind him in the garage door, "is the way that little fellow trusts people so quick. Scared one minute, trusting the next." His soft face was passive, but his voice was alive. "I like courage." For a moment he seemed confused, then he straightened his back against the door, and leaned stiffly, his hands in his pockets. "My Grandma McVitty went straight into a burning barn one time when none of the men would rescue a sick horse. What do you think of that?" He pushed open the office door with his foot. "I tell you," he said, "you can live in a little town like this and see *everything*. You don't have to leave it to see *everything*. I never ask a man his business because I don't like him to ask me mine, but sooner or later you see everything. That little fellow now—I never would have thought I'd see him."

Karel held the tire tube between his hands, clutching the rubber. "Why do you admire courage?" he asked suddenly.

McVitty was embarrassed. "Never thought," he said. "Don't see why you have to know why, if you do."

Karel asked softly, not looking up from the tire, "Would you go into a burning barn to rescue a sick horse?"

"Well—it depends. You don't know till the time comes. Depends on your feelings. Might not be a burning barn for me." Then he looked down at Karel briefly, his blue eyes sharp and reflective. "My wife wants to know if you need anything. Another cup and saucer, maybe, or some more towels."

"Another towel would be fine," Karel answered. "Nicky likes very much to have a clean one each day. Thank you very much."

3

It was Sunday and the bells were ringing. The hawks were wheeling. In the farther pastures and the ridges of the hills the mists were rising. In the nearer pastures the cows were moving like slow water. The little river wandered between its ragged banks. Inevitable movement flowed and circled and replenished itself and went on. The sun mounted higher.

John Murray lay for this interlude on the hillside. The cows belonged to his mother. The pasture beyond was his mother's. The far ragged bank of the little river was his mother's. He lay now in a little space he had made for himself, a space as long as his tall body, as wide as the reach of his arms.

He was a farmer. He considered this thing as he had considered it many times before. And then he thought wryly, Thoreau had been a farmer, and Alcott, and Rousseau had been a farmer, and Phoebus Apollo had tilled some earthbound fields. They—*they* had made poetry of it. He smiled tightly. Some way had been open. The sun lay on his brown hair, and its benignness lay on his bare arms and the fine brown hollows of his cheeks, the broad forehead, the finely tempered eyelids. It was a moment when time stood very still, but it was a moment also when the submerged nature of time flayed the will and tormented the purpose.

He was a farmer. He had himself milked the twelve cows at five in the morning. He had sprayed them, and sterilized all the equipment, and loaded the cans on the truck before he had had breakfast. He had taken the milk to the platform, and joked and exchanged gossip with other farmers waiting there. He had repaired a broken stretch of fence, and then, because it was Sunday, he had allowed himself this free time on the hillside.

But why, why, why, when time merely waited to engulf you!

As a boy he had gone out to the barn with his father in the early morning when he was still heavy with sleep, and sometimes he had dozed against the flank of a cow. This life of a farm was not a selected part of himself. When he could decently leave it he had done so. For twelve years he had not been a farmer. For twelve years he had been a student, a writer, a soldier, a husband. And then he had come back.

There was no tidy completion of a circle in this. There was despair. Many men have little relation to their time or their circumstances; they are strangers adrift, not from recalcitrance so much as from an enlarged sense of something which fits them in neither here nor there. They have seen events and themselves neither wholly nor very well; they have seen some spaciousness, some freedom, but their spirits have found no familiar place. The larger thing has carried them away. But where is *away?*

He lay there, and what he had was merely an instinct. He wished to give a name to despair and bring it into an orderly fold, but it was not orderly, its character changed.

John thought so often, entangled and webbed in his thoughts, of how things might have been if the world had been different, the world, the world, the world of time and outer events. Coming out of the army before the war was over, he had felt a splendid hope. In the world things would change. The outworn was surely exposed. This was the moment in history when men would be freer. He had felt a common enough dismay when old stereotypes, bland and assured, had slipped into their old places again. Gradually it came upon him that all the things which held meaning for him were in great danger, the life of his mind, his spirit, his heart, that time moved faster than hope.

When one cannot wholly define the meaningful thing, when one knows only that the elegiac things of the individuality have no voice or tongue, when life might have meant a thousand things but now means none, when the submerged desires are unrelated to the functional demands of the times, then what is the language of communication? A man belongs to his age and yet cannot reconcile himself to the world about him. *Cannot?* John did not use that word. Yet he did not know a common denominator. He could not move in any direction. In a gray flat way, he knew that all his strength must now be concentrated on breaking through.

The impalpable . . . how did one endure it? The stiflement . . . how did one gather his breath? The desperate search for the satisfied spirit . . . how could one know what was true when the mind tossed in every direction?

He looked up and saw Megan, his wife, coming along the bank of the river, their lunch basket in her hand. She was tall and slender and her hair was blue-black in the sunlight and she walked with a light confident possession of herself. He watched her darkly, his gaze half-lowered. When she came to him he smiled, but not as he had once smiled at her, with joy. He did not greet her. He sat very still, his arms crooked over his bent knees.

Since he loved his wife quite subjectively, that sensitive and instant part of himself was suffering a peculiarly violent dislocation. For he intended to leave her. He was fully resolved, and no arguments would sway him, and no despair would reach him, and for the sake of both he would leave no opportunity for choice. What he said would be contained in a sentence. He would leave her and this place, and with nothing to bind him, he would cut down clean to himself. Perhaps he would return to his writing. Perhaps he would merely search until he found some meaning for himself. It was a kind of love. He was giving her nothing. He would be taking nothing away. She too would be free.

She was smiling, happy with the day and the climbing, and her dark eyes had a gay and vivid life. She stood for a moment looking off across the valley as though she had never seen it before. John did not look up. He wished to blot out how she looked and how she stood and what he had loved about her, and let feeling slip away. There must come a time when he would forget whether she was tall or short, dark or fair, gentle or restless. As one forgets something of oneself, some dream, some ardor.

Here to all appearances was a vigorous handsome calm man, sitting on his hillside, but he was in reality one of those who draw to themselves the ancient curse to look on death and stumble in the shadows while searching for a path of life.

Megan loved him. Sitting beside him, she loved the things that their eyes had always seen together, she loved the dearest thing of marriage, the shared intuitions, the searchings, the trust. Her searchings might not be touched with doubt, yet all he longed for, all the intimation, the power, the sweetness were a part of her relation to him. They might live in their own time, they might wear the clothes and speak the language and feel the force and respond to the impact of their time, but there remained the timeless thing over and beyond the present and the future.

Megan took out the thermos of soup and the sandwiches, and she handed his to him as she said, "Every time I come here it seems new. It seems like the first time we came." And then she said, smiling, "I see it with you."

He did not answer, and she glanced at him, and then she turned away, her eyes filled with tears. He said passionately to himself that she was holding him, that she had him tight latched with her spirit and her devotion. He could not temporize with it, he could not mislead her. If he did he would be lost all over again.

She sat a little apart from him, her hands in her lap, her face turned away, deeply sentient, not confident of her powers of waiting.

"What shall be done," she said sadly, "to make you happy again?"

He answered after a moment, with an effort, "There's no time for anything. I am tired."

Her head turned away, her fingers tight together, she said, "How dearly, dearly loved you are."

She had chosen the impersonal way of saying it. He did not answer. He stirred a little, and his hands, clasped between his knees, grew tighter with tension.

"But that is not what you want to hear now, is it?" Then she asked, closer to tears, "What have I done or not done?"

He did not answer for a long time. "It is not you. You are you. In a way you and I are inextricable. This is something that is bigger than that, bigger than I . . ."

"No," she said quickly, "I don't believe that is ever true—the way that you mean it, helpless."

"I am quite isolated," he said stiffly, not wanting to hear her voice. "I am—nothing is real."

"You are real, I am real," she said urgently.

"I do not know that," he said quietly.

"You knew it. You *know* it!"

"No. Not any more."

She whispered, "What has happened?"

He folded his arms across his waist and leaned forward against them as though in pain. "If things outside had been different, everything would have been different."

"Thousands have come out of the army," she said, "and found themselves again."

"Came out into the same miserable slogging world where nothing has changed." He turned to her suddenly, his gray eyes filled with distress, his face strained. "It seems as though everything which means anything to me is in terrible danger—that only the things which are utterly commonplace are really safe. I feel as though everything about me is in danger, and that until that is safe nothing else matters to me." She sat there, very white, her hands moving over the stubbly grass. He was watching her tensely as though she might still offer a way for him. A woman dearly loved yet a ghost in a world of shades.

"No," she said at length. "You're safe. You must hold on to that faith."

He turned away and his head was so far lowered that his brown hair fell like a curtain across his forehead. Who he was might never be disclosed. So deep was his uncertainty that no one other person existed in his world at that moment. Time and fear and lonely man melted into one.

She said, "I feel as though I may not talk about myself in this . . ."

"No."

"Why not?" she asked with sudden spirit.

He put his face in his hands and drew up his knees, huddled there. His voice was muffled and his words came unevenly. He made the effort in a kind of panicked loyalty to her.

"I came back here to the farm thinking that if I was responsible for something then time would take care of the other things. But it hasn't—it hasn't . . . And I can't think about you. I can't even let myself consider what it may mean to you, because then I'll be—really lost. I'm thirty-six—and I'm—and I'm afraid."

She turned to him swiftly and put her hands on either side of his face and kissed him. For a moment, only a moment, he seemed to relax, but then the slow stiffening rose in his chest, his shoulders, and he drew away.

She said, "What do you want me to do, my dearest?"

Then he said what he had planned for so long. "Let me go."

He could barely hear her reply. "How can I hold you? There must be some way."

He said, "I've tried. But I've failed at everything—do you know that? I don't want to fail. The only time I was ever a success was when I was a student. But a writer—who ever read what I wrote? And a soldier—I guess I was proud not being a good soldier." He laughed a little, a jerked sound without merriment. "A real success as a failure."

She said staunchly, "You haven't failed as a husband."

"Oh, yes," he said, smiling slightly. "I've failed everywhere. I did a thorough job. Now I've got to find out if I can start again."

"John!"

He stood with his hands in his pockets, his tall slender body held straight by an effort, and he looked away from her. His eyes were without expression. "I'll tell Mother she's got to find someone to take my place." In a moment he stepped across the sandwiches he had not eaten and the bowl of soup he had barely tasted. "It was nice to eat here by the river," he said. "Thanks." And he touched her hair.

She sat there, cold in the sunlight, her heart knotted as she watched him walk down the hill toward the footbridge and the barn. She saw Vree Dunnigan standing on the footbridge with a little boy, and John stop beside them. Later the three moved together across the road and the field, male figures, and she wondered at how much sorrow always came by this division, man pulling, woman holding. She had never believed that this would happen—not John and she, not *they*, out of all the world.

Karel began to relax. He began to look about him. A sense of belonging stole over him so imperceptibly that at first he was hardly aware of it. He began to wonder about people. He began to look at them with inquiring eyes. He began to wonder what they thought—about the changing world, about events and circumstances.

He thought about events and circumstances as deeply as he thought about himself or Nicky, for he had seen enough of them to be passionately convinced of certain things. And he wanted to know what others thought of these circumstances, and the events which followed out from them. Now that he was a little relaxed, had a job and a home, his curiosity put out tentative inquiries. What did people think? He ventured cautiously.

Life had demanded so much of him that he had no narrow corridors for cramped speculations.

The days fell into a certain routine. He kept one of Dr. Jarman's books in the garage office and, during the lax periods, he studied the pictures and read the text, reading one paragraph again and again until he understood it as well as he could. Each day he bought a newspaper, and he read it with an avid curiosity. Much was incomprehensible, not because of the references but because of something which Karel transposed and translated in his own mind. But each day he read it, and each day he commented on it to McVitty. A small comment, incredulous or admiring or confused, but demanding a reply. McVitty did not necessarily have a reply. Some things he had not thought about. If he generalized, Karel asked him further questions. So on the whole McVitty kept silent, or he dug a small mole-hole of jokes and scurried into it when danger came too close.

Frequently in the evening, when Nicky was asleep, Karel went to the library. The shelves of books there represented in themselves—without even taking one down—a power beyond full comprehension. As a child he had read books, he had accepted them as a matter of course. They were a part of his life, as natural as his father, as familiar as his father reading to him or reading silently by the lamp on the table. An educated man was the assumed position for his father's son. His father had said that the mind was a noble instrument, admirable in its flexibility, powerful in its scope, responsible in its accomplishments. Now he sometimes sat in the library merely to look about him. Lost time had moved so much faster than books . . . lost time.

At first he opened books simply to open them, and read a paragraph here and there. But then as the life within himself became neither challengeable nor appeased, he tried to read to find answers. This simple town, so far away, so remote by every rule of probability, made adjustment neither swift nor simple. For everything about it was sentimental and reminiscent, and when he was unguarded it made him uneasy. And yet the roots, the little tendrils, were searching, searching for a place to cling.

Miss Purvis was sympathetic to what she saw and understood—an intelligent boy seeking information. She had her own private interests—milk glass, the history of the New England seacoast. And then, deep, concealed, intimate—all the reform movements of the nineteenth century, emancipation for women and slaves, communal experiments, prison and hospital reform, free thought and free love, spiritualism and Amelia Bloomer.

But this was a questionable kind of mental passion. It did not move smoothly in and out of conversations. Ten years ago a professor of economics had lived in the village for a short time, and they had had intense, intimate conversations about these things almost every day. But since then the winds which had blown up from her forebears had been all tamed, all confined to the hidden wind-tunnels of her most private life.

Yet to the boy she mentioned some of this . . . because he had memorized that poem of Walt Whitman.

She suggested certain books for him to read, guiding him with a deep excitement which was never revealed, opening up something valiant and rebellious of American history, moral issues to be judged by their own strength and urgency.

He was enthralled, and happiness glowed in a pinpoint behind her glasses. But she could only proceed with him for a short way, for his questions bred other questions, and his interests bred other interests, and he sat in the drowsy library in the somnolent town and asked her with the persistence of a steel drill why there were so many contradictions in the United States, why there were so many big words used and so many small actions to show for them.

He brought her newspaper clippings to which McVitty had given him no answer, and he leaned across her desk, his finger, from which he could never wholly remove the grease, pointing out an incongruity in human behavior—in American behavior, for that matter. And when she could not answer, he turned away too absorbed to be impatient, trying to formulate the same question in another way.

She interrupted him once. "Of course you're *not* an

American?" The question put solid ground under her feet at a time when she badly needed it.

He was halted and frowned a little. The question was mechanical and he answered it mechanically. "No." She wanted to go on from there, pulling aside a little, peering in. But he shut her out. He closed the door.

He had lost time to regain, and he had the immense and swelling anomalies of this slide-rule, high-sounding, deceptive life to comprehend. He had grown fond of the plump face and the shapeless nose of Miss Purvis, her amiable fleshiness, her pink flush. They had exchanged friendships, in a manner, with reservations—and he said now in his clear swift voice, making a gesture which carried him in a semicircle, "I think I know more than all these books and these newspapers. But do I? How do I know?"

She said with a slight touch of pique, "Well, young men are always big talkers."

"But I . . ." and then he stopped so abruptly that her curiosity was roused.

"But you?"

He looked at her, and he straightened up away from the table. He continued to look at her, his dark eyes full of speech. Then he turned away, for there was something avid in her gaze. He felt cramped, he wished to speak without words, overwhelmed by the ambiguities and by the truths which he knew.

A girl had come in, and Miss Purvis got up to attend to her. He turned around abruptly and faced them where they stood by a shelf and said eagerly, "Do not people realize that terrible things have taken place in the world—that we must change?

Miss Purvis was startled and the girl stared at him. He came and stood by the shelf, compelled to finish what he had to say however odd the place and the time. "History does not wait for anyone to catch up with it. Some people know that without being told."

Miss Purvis laughed a little nervously, and then she frowned, and she and the girl looked at each other. "We will all try to do our part," she said, and laughed at the girl. ". . . be historical characters." Then she looked hard at him. "Are you taking a book?"

"Yes," he said and drew back.

That kind of thing was disturbing. Miss Purvis did not repeat it—except a fragment which she could not take from her mind and needed to share with Mrs. Stillwell.

Dr. Jarman repeated nothing of the sudden questions which were deposited in his keeping for the first time in his life. McVitty did not attempt to probe Karel's meanings, for he wished no answer outside the limits of his own comprehension, and he believed in each man having the right to his own opinions.

But he found himself thinking often of his grandmother, and of his great-grandmother who had shot straight at a man who was abusing a child. That was the story told in the family, and it dignified each one who heard it. Why were things as they are? Politics had something to do with it . . . Democrats in seats of power . . . But he knew that to answer this way was to evade the question he had not asked himself, the question he had no inclination to face. Seeing, feeling, hearing were enough for him. He wished no vicarious experiences, no theoretic inquiries. He felt an awed and sudden flooding in his heart like fright . . . like the time when as a youth he discovered that the girl he loved was artistic and his soul was filled with anguish when he first listened to a symphony with her and felt nothing, nothing.

He remembered it now with the thudding heart. Nothing really came to an end, no matter how deeply laid away. Change coming from within or without was the same thing. Yet a man surely had a defense against it, and a choice. He drew a deep sigh.

But very far away, very deeply, something stirred. There was no quiescence for the human soul until all questions had been answered, all hope defined, all stirrings given reality. The wonder stirred far away . . . like a faint lonely sound on a dark night which scarcely breaks one's sleep.

Nicky had a friend, a thin-faced humorous little boy named Tommy, who lived two houses from the garage. Tommy was a year older and he guided Nicky through the intricacies of going to the drug store for ice-cream cones or watching a ball game.

To Tommy there seemed nothing odd in having two cones in his hands, and he held Nicky's cone in the correct position without being told. He had once asked Nicky matter-of-factly about having no arms, and Nicky had said they got blown away. Since Tommy could relate this to no experience of his own, he asked no further questions. He once examined the stumps with care, but after that he seemed unaware of any difference.

It was a child's friendship entered into at a given moment and place, weighed down with no preconceptions or memories. They liked to sit silently on the curbstone watching the cars go by, a Buick, a Ford, a Cadillac, and if Tommy made a mistake in identification, Nicky was not aware of it. Since Tommy was in the third grade he read aloud now and then, giving the same value to all words, but in some fashion imparting the required vividness to stories or comic strips. When Tommy played baseball with his other friends, Nicky watched. He learned the rules. One day he was allowed to call the game. The other boys did not accept him with the same effortlessness as Tommy. They wondered. They were disquieted. They were unkind. But one day he was allowed to be umpire.

In late June when the peas and beans had taken over the garden, Tommy rigged up a tray which he slung over Nicky's shoulders and balanced against his ribs. They sold vegetables to the neighbors. Since Tommy was the producer and salesman, he made six cents to Nicky's four.

Nicky was Tommy's responsibility. Neither Tommy nor his mother nor Nicky understood why this was so. Only Tommy's mother wondered aloud.

On rainy days they turned on the radio which Miss Nolle had lent. They were especially fond of instructions—how to cook pot roasts, how to prepare a house for the summer months, how to plant iris, and they liked to learn songs. Two treble voices would float out onto the road, and people stopping for gas would look up in amazement.

The terror was leaving Nicky's life. Karel felt a tight hand uncoil within himself.

When his day's work was finished, Karel would often take Nicky down the back road past the small river to the little hill beyond it. They sat on the slope and discussed the farmhouse at the end of the meadow beyond the river, and they watched the cows move slow as water from one cropping to another. From here they could see an edge of the village down beyond the stream in the curve of the valley. The dark mass of trees outlined the main street, and beyond the street a few white and gray houses climbed up the slope. Gray stone fences framed the lower end of the village, and the white steeple of a church rose above the trees at the far end. Nicky wished to know if all towns were the same. He wearied of nothing until he had exhausted its possibilities. He was insatiable. Sometimes Karel wondered if it were he or Nicky who craved and questioned the most.

For Nicky a flower must be plucked and laid against his knee, and he must examine it with tongue and nose and eyes until he was satisfied with each component part. He repeated to Karel all that Vree told him, and each time they came to a certain footbridge over the river, he said, "This is the place where the man played."

"What man?" Karel had asked the first time.

"*The man* . . . the man with the harmonica. Vree's friend. I stood beside him and he held it to my mouth and he told me to blow. I blew. It made a sound. He played a tune. John Murray. He said he would bring me one, but the second time I saw him, he said he had forgotten. Tell him—find out where he is—tell him to give me two—one for Tommy. I want my harmonica."

I want . . . I want . . .

Yet in some fashion it was a positive thing, not greedy and grasping.

When Tommy's inventiveness flagged, they too went to the library and waited with unfaltering patience for Miss Purvis to show them things, any things, shells or coins or arrowheads or old firearms. Nicky at first made Miss Purvis uneasy. She was glad when no one came into the library while the child was there to see the armless, insatiable, unchildlike little creature. But she had a good conscience, and it told her what she should do.

She was devoured with the desire to ask him questions. Some day they would spring from her like wild little beasts and she would be mortified and greatly relieved. It is true that if one listened carefully enough, added a disconnected word to an unrelated sentence, one sometimes did not need to ask so many questions, and that was better, for one's own inhibitions were less offended.

"The doctor will give me an arm," Nicky told her one day as he and his friend were leaving, "and then I will turn the pages of books myself." He spoke loudly so that the lady who passed him at the door would know that he was really a competent boy. And Tommy said, "He'll take it on and off like a shoe."

The lady looked after them. "So that is the one," she said to Miss Purvis. "That is the child I have heard about." She stood in the doorway watching the children go down the street. She watched for some time, frowning to focus her gaze, and at length she turned into the library and stood by Miss Purvis' desk. She was handsome and slim, her hair white, her complexion and eyes like a girl's.

"Isn't it strange not to know who they really are? What does Mr. McVitty say about the older boy?"

Miss Purvis did not like questions put to her in this manner and she stiffened.

"No one says anything, Katherine," she replied. "I do not quite understand why some people are disturbed. It seems as though two strangers could come into a town this size . . ."

The lady named Mrs. Wright sat down. "It seems to me that we have a right to be interested in strangers who settle in our home town. Don't you think so, Blanche?"

"Isn't there room . . . ?" Miss Purvis was not sure that she meant this. The words and the sentiment were unfamiliar.

Mrs. Wright drummed her knuckles softly on the desk, and she pondered her answer as she watched her own slender hand.

"And, besides, these are children. They—they are *children*."

Mrs. Wright considered the matter for a moment longer. Then she said, "I will ask my husband. He is always very concerned about the legal protection of children. Don't you think it would be wise—and kind?"

Miss Purvis said, "That would be fine. He is always so generous," and she did indeed feel a kind of relief.

. . . But she wished the Wrights did not always offer. It would be a nice change if the village could make its own mistakes and not always be held to account by certain outsiders. Mr. Wright, for example.

4

Mrs. Wright was knowingly aware of the fine day. As an expert gardener she had a detailed understanding of the weather, catalogued it promptly and sensitively, and was able with an almost embarrassing intimacy to discern the condition of her seeds underground. A fine day was therefore not a mysterious distillation of heart and mind, a subjective essence which might lead to heaven-knows-what. To her, a fine day meant a light-weight dress or a heavy-weight dress, it meant a little extra thought about her lupin and larkspur, and a possible new florist with more satisfactory seedlings next year.

She drove down the main street and, without volition, turned away her eyes from the dead lime trees in front of old Mr. Finch's. They were an incident which still embarrassed her. Mr. Finch had known her since she was a child, and he should not have confused their motives when she and Cecil asked to replace them at their own expense. And she should not have been dismayed at his temper. The dead trees were unsightly. She was proud of her village. She had been born here, as well as her parents and grandparents. Because Cecil was an outsider she was sometimes treated as though she did not belong.

Yet Cecil had tactfully associated himself with the village. He had been willing to serve on any committee, willing to give sound legal advice without a fee, tireless in appreciating the somnolent charm of the village, though many men would have been impatient.

More than once she had talked aloud to herself: *Because my husband is rich this should not shut us off. A little thing here and there for the village—an anonymous little thing if that would make you happier*—but always she saw before her eyes in plain lower-case letters: *independence.* It had a reassuring simplicity. She did not pause to consider that there was also something unfathomed in this independence; that there was no magic in a lone word.

Wine bottles need to be turned every now and then, but in another world . . . not here, not in this sunny town where even dead trees were accorded such dignity.

As for the strange things which come into a town, they are never stronger than the combined character of a place. It was important to remember that. Cecil said as long as those boys were law-abiding and not public charges, no one should interfere. She knew that the whole town would watch them, for the shrill armless little creature alone would drive off inertia. What her apprehensions were she did not know. She had faith in order, in kindness and intelligence.

The hills above the village were lovely, so innocently holding up the sky. She smiled at the child-thought, and felt freshened for thinking it. Her life was good. She was a good woman and lived in a good town. She had every reason to be proud and satisfied.

She turned in at McVitty's garage and pressed her horn.

When no one came readily, she honked again. Presently Karel appeared on the run, drying his hands on the sides of his trousers. She spoke to him pleasantly but watched him curiously as he did the things which she asked.

She studied him through the mirror. She had seen him many times but had never spoken to him, and now she tried to frame a sentence and found it difficult. What she said should be friendly and casual. Her mouth felt dry and she was amazed at some strange perversity which held her. She prepared herself to speak when he came to the window with her credit slip. "Isn't it a lovely day? We're proud of our spring. It's—What is that!"

Her finger jerked out involuntarily.

Karel dropped the slip and the pencil and clapped his hand to his bare arm. Then he looked at her with desperate dark eyes. He found that she was merely bewildered and that her face showed nothing but amazement at his action. He picked up his pencil with a trembling hand.

She signed, but she made no move to leave. Her voice was calm when she said, "What is it? You had better tell me. I believed there was something wrong. What do those numbers on your arm mean? Have you been in prison?"

He stood looking at her and his face was stripped of age or of youth. It had no identification with any recognizable expression, and even the eyes were veiled. His skin was gray and the sweat stood on his forehead and lip. "It means I have been in a concentration camp."

She gasped a little, and sat for a moment blinking at the bright June sun. She tried, in a great lunge, to encompass a world so remote that she had no measurement for it, a world she had half-disbelieved in, since nothing so alien could be creditable. She sat thus for only a moment, but it seemed a long groping time. He turned and walked away, and she called after him, "I'm so sorry. So sorry!"

She could not think of anything else to say, so she repeated to the back of his head, "I'm really so sorry!"

It rang in the air *so sorry so sorry*, disembodied and at length meaningless. Karel stumbled over the doorsill. He went out into the area behind the garage where the used cars were for sale, and sat down on a running board. He sat with his head between his hands.

The hot sun came on his head, but he did not move. The wind blew and lifted his hair, the cat came and rubbed against the wheel of the car and lashed his leg with her tail. Away, remotely, part of air and space, a car horn blew and blew again, two crows circled above his head uttering their hoarse laden cries, a grackle made a small commotion landing on a bush close by the car, and still he did not move.

But all the small natural sounds combined at length to reach him and communicate some movement to him. He stirred and sat up and went swiftly into the garage and up the stairs.

Nicky wished to talk, but he did not answer and went to lie down on the bed. Nicky continued to chatter, then he picked up a paint brush between his teeth. The brush fell to the table after a while, and Nicky slithered over to the bed and crept up beside Karel. Karel's arm held him painfully and the little boy's teeth dug into his lower lip, but he did not try to free himself.

Why was he so terrified? Why—why? The numbers on his arm were an honor. Why was he so terrified?

He knew why. He knew the complexity of his fear, and in a sense he knew its illogic. That it was buttressed by events and time gave it its intensity.

Their whole future might depend on Mrs. Wright's whim or fancy. How and why he did not know; it was enough to be afraid. They were no longer anonymous and safe. The well into which they had dropped was not as deep as he imagined.

If for some reason they took the child from him he could not live. Ever since he had found the child under the dead body of the mother, the child had been his proof of a future. It was the child who had drawn all his demonstrable faith into a single point and held it there. In that world where all doubts and despairs had been formed, there were two forces, the impersonal, the organized, with power to take away, and his own dogged God-sense which was convinced that what was alive could not be defeated. He had tasted them both. Both were very powerful. Both were as powerful in the United States as in Europe.

. . . When Bertha Young had set out that morning last April for the Relief Committee, Karel had not had a moment's doubt. She intended to tell what she believed to be true—that Nicky was not his brother. Organized power would be set in motion again, and he was too experienced to wait for its inevitable ways. They would have to leave before she returned.

Boys who had survived through their own powers of endurance did not pause to arbitrate with the enemy.

Nicky and Marilyn Young had sat on the bed and watched him pack the rucksack. Thin gawky children, they had sat as silent and solemn as death. Marilyn had leaned uneasily against the sloping side of the mattress, her thin legs braced stiffly, her thin freckled face tense, her eyes unblinking. Nicky had sat erect, holding his breath, his eyes wide. He had wished to touch his friend, Marilyn, and he rubbed his shoe over hers. She had said, "Stop that!" and then to Karel, "What are you doing? Where are you going?"

Karel had given no sign of hearing her. Marilyn had screamed, "Where, where, why?" and Nicky had screamed also and clattered his feet on the floor. "*Why!*"

Marilyn had shrilled, "He's not your brother—he's not your brother. Mom'll send the police after you!"

Karel had turned white and lifted his arm. "That is a lie," he had said, and Nicky had butted her in the shoulder with his head. Karel had snatched away the child and put on his coat while Nicky was screaming, "Liar!" Marilyn had stared at him and burst into tears.

Karel had put on the rucksack, and Nicky had suddenly cried, "My watch! My watch!" Karel found the huge old timepiece and fastened it with a safety pin to the child's jacket. Then he had opened the door and pushed Nicky before him down the stairs. On the street, Karel had not paused. But he had glanced back and seen Marilyn standing in the window watching them, malevolent and threatening to his watchful heart.

That was that. It was flight. In a concentration camp reason had been no protection; only some compound of heart and instinct had kept them alive. It was a lesson well learned.

They had taken a bus to Springfield, Massachusetts. There they had taken another bus westward, had hitchhiked and walked twenty miles in one day, and come to this town, seen at a distance, calm and shining against the hillside. Mrs. Stillwell's house, where the high lilac bushes grew, had resembled a picture which his mother had shown him in his childhood. He had recognized it instantly, and that is why they had gone no farther.

When evening came, he went down to the garage. Very well, he was still afraid. They had not walked far enough. Perhaps they could never walk far enough. Yet with the next thought he told himself that tomorrow he and Nicky would leave. There are times when you do not examine your fear. You are simply afraid.

Mrs. Wright had gone home and she had telephoned Mrs. Stillwell. Mrs. Stillwell had cried out over the telephone when she learned of the numbers on Karel's arm, and she had called Mrs. McVitty. Mrs. Wright had also called Miss Purvis who had gasped and been silent. For a short space it was intensely dramatic. Something had come into their midst from a world more alien than the moon.

But the conversations had turned to other subjects before they had put up their phones. The crux of the matter could only be assimilated over a period of time. The war had ended nearly two years before. This belonged to the war and even further back than that. How, in the end, could one really understand these things; how could one believe in them either? Yet Mrs. Wright had seen small blue numerals with her own eyes. It was not something she had been told about. It was something she herself had seen. On a boy, not yet twenty.

And yet she looked up sharply at her husband and daughter as they sat at dinner.

"Since there is nothing dishonorable about it, why did he try to cover it up? Why was he so upset?"

Karel sat in the office waiting stolidly for nine o'clock when he would lock up. He turned on McVitty's radio and half-listened, leaning with his elbows on his knees. Shortly before nine George McVitty came in.

Karel wished that he had not come. It would have been easier to create confidence for himself and leave the next day if he did not have to consider someone else. He watched McVitty guardedly. George made a note of the money in the cash register and locked it up. Then he sat down and listened to the radio for a minute, and then he sat listening to nothing in particular. Five or ten minutes later he stood up and looked down at Karel.

"My wife just wanted me to tell you that we're glad you're here. And maybe you and the boy better come over for dinner tomorrow." He glanced obliquely toward Karel's arm. "I sometimes wondered why you always had adhesive tape on your arm. Wouldn't seem like you needed to wear it. Among friends, anyway." Then he went out.

Nothing was altered, life was exactly as it had been, but he sat with his head on the desk and the tears ran down the side of his nose. Over and over again in the last six years he had had hope, and over and over again it had been broken. Yet apparently nothing is so durable as hope, nothing else has the same power to live again.

5

Something subtle happened. Karel wished certain things now, he wished a different relationship with those around him. *I wish, I want.*

He had wanted the sense of belonging when he was with the Youngs. Now he wanted it again for himself and the child, the affection and the understanding which the young and the old must have, but more than that he felt a fierce yearning for justice. Something new, something wordless, for to say *justice* is to say something poorly defined. But that is what he wanted—the past wiped out, *justice.* All things were possible, yet he had lived many generations beyond his nineteen years, and he had seen how hard it was to reach the possible.

Among the subtle things was the village. Hardly a man or a woman had a sense of what "concentration camp" meant, but it had an association with suffering and pity. Many people who had not noticed him before nodded in a friendly way, and Nicky was, once or twice, bought a lollipop. Tommy made some inquiries of Nicky, and Nicky asked Karel to show Tommy the numerals on his arm. One afternoon they wrote numbers on themselves, on forehead, legs, Tommy's arms, with a fountain pen, but the game made Nicky uneasy.

Friends asked a few explosive questions as though one or two things had been bottled up for too long. "How did it happen?" the doctor demanded, jerking his head at Nicky.

"An Allied bomb."

"Why did you make such a mystery of it?"

"I cannot explain. I did not want anyone to know anything about us. I felt safer that way."

"How did you get to the United States?"

"Properly. Legally."

"Well, *excuse* me for asking."

The doctor pulled Nicky to him and opened his shirt. "This job'll have to be cleaned up before an arm can be fitted."

Nicky trembled. "You promised. *You promised.*"

The doctor looked at him, frowning. "Aren't I doing my very best?"

But in a little town like this, how long could this kind of sympathy and consternation be kept alive? If a Mrs. Stillwell kept something churning that was one thing; a kindness could be extended, a warmth distilled which could become habitual if exercised often enough; an occasional reference could be made, but that was all. In the long view of things this was both enough and not enough.

For Mrs. Stillwell it was not enough.

"It is the *shock* of mutilation which should make a lasting impression. We can *see* it."

"Well?" the doctor said.

"And perhaps it was an American bomb."

"So?"

"What do you mean?"

"*Shock of mutilation.* It should shock you. And then what? Are they going to grow up to be strong boys on the strength of your nerve-titillation?"

She looked at him coolly, very impassive behind her round unblinking eyes, sitting within her squat unbeautiful body, waiting for something.

"*I'm* not the one in this town you say 'And then what?' to, Lem Jarman."

He did not smile. He looked at her with a half-frown.

"Agnes Do-gooder. Just be sure that this time you get to the right place at the right time with the right remedy."

"Oh, my goodness," she said and looked at him indignantly.

He said again, "Well?"

"What I had in mind," she answered stiffly, "was a fund for the child."

He looked at her with respect. "For his arm, you mean?"

"Yes. And then I will have the older boy speak before the Thursday Club and perhaps Mr. Brown will let him speak from the pulpit Sunday after next. We will rouse and stir."

"What?"

"People—make them think."

"Anyone can think! What do they do with their thinking?"

Mrs. Stillwell smoothed and smoothed her gloves, straightened out a finger, smoothed. Being a little hard of hearing, she could shut out certain words. But she was flushed and her lips were pressed together and she looked at the doctor with flashing eyes.

"*Think!*" she said. "There is *nothing* more important in life, Lem Jarman. My dearest mamma taught me that there is only one thing important—especially for a woman.

To think! Separate right from wrong and then do something about it. Be bold." Her voice rang and her eyes were shiny with tears.

The doctor rubbed his face, pushing up his glasses onto his forehead.

"All right," he said, at length. "Be bold. Don't trouble about details—when to be bold and when to be artful. Just be bold, but spare my two boys any pain."

Now she was truly angry, flushed and bedewed, even her hat and the unconfining hair net agitated and protesting. "Your boys! *Your boys.* What about *my* boys—*my* conscience! I haven't lived in this village all my life for nothing. Haven't I struggled, year in and year out, to make people face right and wrong, and *act*? Your boys!"

"You saw them first," he said ironically.

"I did! The first day they came into this town. I'm not half so interested in getting that little boy his arm as I am in making this town see—in making this town *see* . . ." She could not go on but sat there, the tears running down her cheeks.

He was very silent, his stubby fingers braced against his mouth. At last, he said, wry and weary, "Mrs. Stillwell's War. For forty years I've rolled up heavy artillery for you, Agnes. Well—why should I stop now?" He looked at her, smiling a little. "But remember, if either boy is nicked, he will bleed. If either sneezes you will hear a sound. They're real. They have to go to the bathroom. They sleep and eat."

She turned away, her cheeks shiny with tears. "Who cares about making this town think or see—but me?"

"No one," he said gently.

She looked at him, beset. "Not even you, Lem?"

He leaned his head back against the worn leather of his chair and closed his eyes. He said after a while, his lips scarcely moving, "I've told you, over and over, I am a disbeliever. Maybe it'll kill me, but if it does I'll have died true to myself."

"What foolishness," she said softly.

He quickly opened his eyes.

"Foolish? I just want to be shown." He closed his eyes again. "For forty years I've been waiting, hoping you'd show me how to make people better. I *wanted* to be shown." He added as an afterthought ". . . be content with life as you find it. Don't aspire to anything more . . . I wanted you to show me that that was a devil's doctrine—that anything was possible, the world could be remade. I'll go on waiting. I've nothing to lose."

"I don't want to remake the world, Lem," she said thinly. "I just want this town to learn what is right—and to care."

He stood up abruptly. "Talk about the world," he said. "*Talk about the world!* It's the same thing!"

Mrs. Stillwell saw the fund as the first need. Touch their hearts and then you touch their purse strings and then they think, *I am doing something fine,* and that *something* takes root.

"Maybe," Mrs. Wright said, "maybe that is the way it happens. I don't know, Agnes. I'm not sure about myself. I ask, Who are those boys? I saw those numbers on his arm but what do we know? Who has told us anything? How did they get there? Why? I want to know. I have a right not to be fooled."

"Fooled!" The round wattled chin lifted abruptly. "Can't you just be sorry and do something, Katherine? We can always use some Christianity in this town!"

Mrs. Wright was plainly disturbed, the fineness of her face immaculate in her distress. "I have written out many checks in my time, Agnes—many checks. I have contributed to every fund in this town."

"And so you should, Katherine!"

Mrs. Wright considered her for a moment with the reticence of a self-controlled woman. "I know my obligation to my town without being told, Agnes. I do not yet see any obligation to these boys."

Mrs. Stillwell sat, opening and closing her purse. "I don't understand things," she said at length bitterly. "What happens to people who have a little money to give away?"

Mrs. Wright was not a woman to be offended easily by her friends. "Agnes, you have led me down some very peculiar paths in the past. And you have left me or someone else to make sense out of them when you flew off to something else. I'll give you five dollars for your fund, and I'll have this older boy to lunch and will talk to him. But I am not convinced. They're strangers. How do we know what kind of thing is pushing in?"

Mrs. Stillwell shut the clasps of her purse and left it shut. "I'll come to lunch with him, Katherine. I'm uneasy too, but for different reasons. I thank you, with reservations, for the five dollars."

Karel said to Mrs. Stillwell that he had no proper clothes to go to lunch. Proper clothes were important to him for in the normal world they were indispensable. Also he did not like to leave Nicky.

McVitty said he would lend him a shirt and a jacket. The offer came unexpectedly, for McVitty had been exceedingly careful in his detachment. He made the offer and then he thought a good deal about the choice he would make of shirt and jacket. When a man commits himself it must be whole-hearted, though nothing of this might show on his face. A man committed was a man morally obligated, although he could not ponder on this too long if he were to avoid deep waters. He doubted if his great-grandmother Saunders had pondered long before she shot that man for abusing a child. Your commitment had to be swift and decisive and submerged, if you wanted to remain free.

Vree Dunnigan took Nicky upstairs over Mr. Fitch's shed where he lived, and showed him the valley and the world spread out before him.

"I got three windows," he said. "See—east, west, north. Wherever the view's prettiest for the time of day, I take Billy, that old kerosene stove there, and cook my meals. Noon it's prettiest in the north window, and we'll sit there and have lunch and talk about football maybe, or the new kittens. Or I'll show you some of my pressed flowers and my stuffed birds."

"Yes," said Nicky. "Have you got a football?"

"Not yet," said Vree. "I always hankered for one."

"Red—get a red football," Nicky urged. "I kicked a football a hundred thousand yards the other day. And get me an harmonica! That man promised me one and he never brought it."

"*Please.*"

Nick stared at him. "But he promised it."

Mrs. Wright was a very sincere woman. She gave careful thought to the luncheon food. She dressed herself carefully. She asked her daughter, Julie, to pick flowers for the luncheon table and the drawing room. When Mrs. Stillwell and the boy arrived, she was interested, alert, and in possession of all the kind ways of her world.

She greeted Karel as a friend, introduced him to the small and pretty Julie, stood with him at the window and engaged in the little ritual of pointing out the vista through the trees. Without this ritual, no guest had real identification with the place. When they went in to lunch, she put him at the head of the table where her husband sat.

"My husband is in Boston," she said. "I am so sorry. He has nearly given up his Boston practice, but he finds he still cannot stay away altogether. He has a real feeling for the village, hasn't he, Agnes?" And then she added whimsically, "We native born require that of outsiders."

Karel answered politely. He did not wish to eat for he did not wish to be here. He did not wish to be a stranger any place. With this woman he was terribly strange. He sat staring at his hand and at Mrs. Wright when she spoke, and at each in turn when something was said. No one appeared to notice his diffidence. He did not wish to be uneasy or rude. His glance rested on the tweed sleeve of McVitty's jacket. It had been given him as a frail and precarious bridge between one world and another, and whether he knew it or not, he stood now in the center of that bridge, rocking in a high wind.

He wished to answer as they wished him to answer. Mrs. Stillwell, he knew, wanted the picture to be bright and open. He did not understand the conflict within him, or why it should assail him at this time. He had learned to trust his intuition and only later measure the reasons. Gradually his intuition told him that something must be asked and answered of himself which had not been required before, and that there was some power in this soft and graceful world for which his youth and inexperience had as yet no name. Power? He had known only two kinds of power. This was something which seemed unrelated to either. He wished to be polite. He had great friendliness in his heart.

Mrs. Wright was looking at him but not directly. She would glance at him when another spoke, she would glance at him when the maid came in to serve, she would glance at him—not when he called attention to himself but when she thought she was alone with him. Mrs. Stillwell bore the burden of conversation. It seemed as though she had filled an immense vessel for precaution's sake and opened the spigot for the welfare of all. The atmosphere must be relaxed; it must have no ugly pauses; it must be what they all desired, well ordered and refreshing. She wondered at all the things she found to talk about, things vivacious and interesting—because her heart was so good. She heard what she was saying, and was glad she could be so animated, but she did not always comprehend the answers.

Later they went out on the terrace and sat in fine metal furniture while the maid served them coffee. All but Julie who sat on the grass. The sun lay on the side of Karel's face, and Mrs. Wright urged him to move for she was sure he must be uncomfortable. When he had moved his chair into the shade, she asked him abruptly, "How did you get to this country and where did you come from?"

"If you mean where was my home, it was Czechoslovakia. The North American Committee brought me from Germany—me and my brother."

She studied him now quite unguardedly. "Where did the Committee place you when you came?"

"With a family—with a man who had been a soldier in Europe."

She asked quietly, her nose and chin and eyes and mouth peering at him, "Why are you not there? Why are you all alone in a strange town?"

He said, "I was afraid. They were trying to take my brother away from me. The child was afraid. We came away."

"Came away without telling them?"

He looked at her.

"You have let them know where you are by now?" Mrs. Stillwell said.

Mrs. Wright asked, "What would you be afraid of? A Committee—a family to help you. What was there to be afraid of?"

He looked at her, his speech shut off.

"It is really a very unfortunate thing. You could make a great deal of trouble for yourself that way," she said with kindly firmness.

"My brother and I," he said at last, "stayed alive without help. Everyone tried to kill us, but we did not die. We do not need help."

She said coolly, "You have asked for help by coming here. The child is always asking for help. You ask for things and deny that you are asking. We do not do things like that here."

He stared down at his hands, clasped tightly together. "I am not asking for anything," he said softly, "and if the child asks it is because he is a child." Then he looked at her suddenly. "But I think each person may ask compassion from another. I think that is true, and nothing that is said can make it untrue."

"Oh, that's true!" the girl, Julie, said, the first time she had spoken.

Her mother replied, looking at him with a little smile. "That's rather ornate language. Your brother still needs two arms, doesn't he?"

Karel drew a deep breath. "Yes. Everyone deserves two arms."

She said nothing for a moment, and then she asked quietly, "Are you—are you Jewish?"

He was so startled that he looked at her for some time before he answered. He heard the small agitation of Mrs. Stillwell close at hand, and he frowned.

"Jewish," he said, "what has that to do with it? I do not understand."

"I merely asked you a question."

He continued to look at her for a moment. "No, I am not Jewish. I do not understand why that question is asked. Do you hate Jews?"

Her expression did not alter, but something immaculate and cold confined her.

"Oh," Mrs. Stillwell hurried to say, "why, Katherine Wright could not hate anyone."

But Karel was still considering her, the young face with the grave eyes as requiring and questioning as thought itself. Mrs. Wright did not answer. She turned her head to look out across the lawn, and after a while she said, "Certainly I do not hate anyone. Certainly not. But that does not blind me to certain challenges in the world today."

He wished to leave. He had a great desire to go without any delay. He looked swiftly at Mrs. Stillwell. She was far away, balancing and counterbalancing her thoughts. He wished to get up and he tightened his muscles to rise. Julie, sitting at the edge of the terrace, said suddenly, "Would you like to go swimming?"

He did not see her. She had no face. He stood up speaking to no one. "I have been through a great many things. I do not understand when . . . "

"Yes, indeed," Mrs. Wright said, standing up slowly. "I suppose we have all suffered and want to be happy. Well, it was nice that Mrs. Stillwell brought you. We will have to see what we can do for your brother."

"I do not want . . ." But he did not finish. He went without seeing toward the house and the others trailed after. He shook hands jerkily like a young boy, anxious to be away.

Nicky greeted him, sitting bolt upright in a chair, trying to stroke a squirming kitten with his toes.

"She's mine! Tell her so. Tell her to love me!"

Mrs. Wright spoke on the telephone that evening to Mrs. Stillwell.

"Certainly he's exceptional, if you wish to look at it

from that angle. I can't tell you why I am uneasy. No, I wish I understood it—I did not like it when he said he had suffered. People who have really suffered do not ask for sympathy. No, it was not that alone—no, I cannot say. It's a difference—something that doesn't belong here."

Her thoughts were profoundly disarranged. In her disquiet she thought she could not endure to have him around. Such an extremity of feeling was, of course, impossible. Tomorrow, perhaps tonight, she would telephone Mary Dunn and ask for a donation for Mrs. Stillwell's fund. She said suddenly to Julie, "Of course, you must be kind to him. We must all be kind, but remember there is some kind of difference—some very great difference."

Julie, who had the fine delicate pale features of her mother, looked at her for a moment. "Why is he different? I didn't see much difference."

"Well, there is," her mother said without emotion. "These are things one has to recognize."

In her bed, swaying on the edge of sleep, defenseless, Mrs. Wright's mind said, *Why, I hate him*, and there was nothing to stand between herself and that fact.

Mrs. Stillwell had, for many years, adjusted herself to defeat. She never thought about it as defeat; she thought of it as the hardness, the blindness of others, with which she must quarrel, sometimes in a high voice, oftener in an incredulous unblinking silence. Right strengthened the heart and the liver and the viscera, the eyes, the ears, the tongue. Karel said he would not speak at the Thursday Club or from the church pulpit; the program chairman of the Thursday Club and Mr. Brown, the pastor, also said they would not ask him to speak.

"Why?" she demanded incredulously. "Now, why?"

"Bad taste—and he's too young."

"Are we too proud to learn new things or to hear them from children?"

"My dear," said Mrs. Dunn, "let us see what we can do about the little boy. That would be a very nice thing that I'm sure we could all unite on. If we find, that is, that it's all right to do so."

Mrs. Stillwell was silent for a moment, then she switched on her hearing aid. "I was thinking about our Fourth of July parade. Let us have another float. Let us have Young America—a dozen children surrounding that little boy, all offering him . . ."

"No," Mrs. Dunn said firmly, "that would not do at all."

After a moment, Mrs. Stillwell shut off her hearing aid and sat thoughtfully.

6

Nicky heard the trombone and the fife and he turned in fright to Vree. Vree said, "That just means it's time we got down to see the parade. It's the Fourth of July."

"Soldiers?"

"American soldiers," Karel said, taking down the gas hose for a car which had driven up.

"I do not want to go," Nicky said, squatting down beside his little cat.

"Don't you remember American soldiers gave you your first taste of chocolate?" Karel asked.

"I do not want to go."

"They've got firemen marching in red shirts," Vree said, "and the baseball team."

"Make them stop that music."

Karel hung up the gas hose and collected the money and came to kneel beside Nicky.

"In camp they played music for reasons which hurt. Here it is different. This is friendly music. And this is your birthday."

The cat rubbed against Nicky's bare leg, first one side

of her then the other. Nicky leaned forward in a passion and kissed the cat. He whispered, "She will come too."

"Why, certainly," Vree said. "Why else did you think I made these big pockets?" Nicky still squatted, staring at a patch of cinders, but when he saw the little cat peering out of Vree's pocket he slowly stood up.

That night Mrs. McVitty said they should not miss the fireworks and the dancing. The traffic was detoured, and on the main street the dancing had begun to a guitar and a violin.

The violinist was a middle-aged man, fat, overflowing his belt, hearty, hairy, his foot stamping out the time, calling out to the crowd, experienced at maintaining jollity in a mechanical, good-tempered way. The guitarist was a loose-limbed sandy-haired youth who seldom smiled, who played well and earnestly. He seemed more interested in his music than the crowd, and when he looked at them it was with a nervous air of contempt.

Colored lights were strung in trees. Shadowy, poorly lighted couples circled on the macadam road, a fraternity from all parts of the village, quiet in their merriment. Mrs. McVitty glanced at the boys occasionally—a kind woman who wished to understand. The three stood on the grass of the Common, close to the street. She watched the child and the boy in the glow from the colored lights. In her little eyes set in her heavy face was something very sweet and kind, and when she thought something would make the child laugh, she looked at him quickly, and when he laughed she laughed also. She could not fathom their memories since they were not Americans and because they bore marks which defeated her imagination—but she supposed that all children had common memories at some point. The child, she wondered, the child—perhaps this would be his happiest birthday.

She thought about it for some time. The music intent

and merry in the warm night air, the happy lights, the pretty dresses, the children chasing each other up and down the Common, the comfort, the happiness, friends exchanging greetings, things well ordered and safe, the little boy in shorts and a jersey which she had given him . . . She impulsively opened the box of peppermints which she had brought for she wanted this to be a happy remembrance for both of them, something a child would always have to remember.

The guitar and violin played "Doin' What Comes Natur'lly" and Nicky thrust in the words in a piercing voice which kept time badly to the music. "I learned that on the radio!" he cried.

"Dear Lord," Mrs. McVitty said, "that child tears my heart. He's the spunkiest thing I've ever seen!"

Karel glanced at her. He had heard things like that said before. He continued to look at her, the kind heavy face and the billowy maternal body, and attempted once again to understand what others told him—that many lived through childhood and youth into middle age without special suffering. The tears unaccountably sprang into his eyes. It was a marvel.

The guitar and the violin attempted to ignore the child, but a harmonica, back of them in the shadows, picked up the tune. Nicky flung himself against Karel. "That's the man! Ask him—ask him—where is my harmonica?"

Mrs. McVitty burst out laughing. "That's John Murray. He won't come down. He'll stay up there where it's dark and aggravate his friends."

Now the child ceased to sing. He stood leaning against Karel, looking off into the shadows where the sweet shrill little tune blew on to its end. Above the sound of the music and the shuffling feet sounded the unearthly airiness of a rocket rising above the trees and bursting in a shower of sparks. Nicky buried his head against Karel's side, and

Karel felt him trembling under his hand. The dancers stopped and greeted the rockets with whistles and cheers, and Roman candles went up in a blaze of swift glory.

"Oh," Clara McVitty said, "I used to think the Fourth of July was better than Christmas!" But they did not hear her, for Karel had taken the shaking child back under the trees, and John Murray had come to kneel beside him.

"What's the matter?" he asked.

"Things are exploding over his head."

Karel sat on the grass and held Nicky on his knees, stroking him, and John Murray offered the child the harmonica, pressing it to his lips. In the light from the street lamp there was a quick aliveness and compassion in his deep-set eyes, and in all the shadowed leanness of his face was an intensity of regard.

But Nicky could not blow the harmonica. He did not wish to lift his head from Karel's shoulder, and when a rocket rose hissing from the Common, a shudder convulsed him.

"We will go home," Karel said, "or else he will sleep badly all night." He carried Nicky, who shrank from standing on his own feet and clung with his teeth to Karel's collar. John Murray walked along beside him, and he glanced often at the child with a quick intentness.

"So much damn foolishness," he said. "Crashing and banging around to celebrate something which most people scarcely understand." The lights of houses shone on the road ahead, but the sky was very dark and starry and the hush and movement of a thousand things alive at night came in spite of the sound of their shoes on the road.

"Find the North Star," Karel said to Nicky softly. "Where is it?"

Nicky let his head sink against Karel's shoulder. "I do not see it," he whispered.

"Why did you bring him?" John Murray asked sharply.

"I did not know," Karel answered. "And how can I always shield him? Would that be good?"

"I don't know. Don't ask me. But it seems as though he has a bigger load than most people."

"The only thing in the world he wants is to be like other boys. He does not see any difference."

"But there is."

"No!"

In the dim light, in the starry night, John Murray glanced at Karel. He could only tell vaguely where the outline of the little boy became the outline of Karel. Something cold ran through him. Something very cold, extremely personal. Something very wary.

They came to a fork in the road and John Murray stopped. He put the harmonica in Karel's hand. "Wash it off and give it to him." He had a low grave voice. The little boy was listening, black eyes wide and watchful in the dark, but he spoke as though the child were not there. If he gave him this harmonica then something would be finished cleanly as all disturbing things should be. "Good night."

But before he could move on the sound of running feet behind them in the dark could be heard, and a white figure came through the darkness, calling his name. She came up to them, but Karel could not see her well enough to identify her.

"Mrs. McVitty said this was the little boy's birthday. Nicky—is that your name? Wouldn't it be nice, John, if Nicky and his brother came with us and had this ice cream which I bought?"

How silently they greeted her, and no one really understood the reason for the other's silence. After the strange heavy silence of the minute, the girl said, "I'm Megan Murray, John's wife," and there was something smiling about the way she said it although it was too dark to see her features. When a car's lights fell upon them she held up the container of ice cream for Nicky to see, and Karel looked down at Nicky. After a moment Nicky nodded and then he laughed a little and when they had walked a few yards up the fork of the road he stiffened himself and wished to walk.

"He would like to come," Karel said with a laugh of relief.

John Murray still walked in silence. Karel thought for a moment, with an expanding heart, of something tender and comforting in the night. He understood what it was and yet he could not wholly identify it. It had to do with the sound of other steps, but it was more than that also; it was something he had learned, not by heart or by reason but by the spirit, something of the nature of all men's need for each other and the principle determining the need. He thought perhaps he had learned it in the darkness, and that is why the darkness so often gave it back to him. Megan was saying, "I have spoken to you often in the village. Perhaps you'll recognize me when we come into the light."

He was a little embarrassed and he laughed.

"We live on a farm," she said. "John is a farmer and I am a farmer's wife."

"You don't speak like a farmer's wife," Karel said suddenly.

"Should a farmer's wife speak a certain way?"

"I don't know," he laughed, again ashamed but happy.

"Shall we go to our house or to mother's?" she asked her husband and, after a moment, he said, "Go to mother's. I have work to do. I'll . . ."

"It's his birthday," Megan said, but he turned and started rapidly up the road, and presently the footsteps quickened as though he were running.

Megan did not apologize or explain and Karel did not

wonder, for amenities were something he knew little about. They turned in the lane of the farmhouse and went around to the back door, for a light burned in the kitchen.

They came into the light of the big kitchen. The lamp in the window stood on a round table covered with a checkered cloth. The moths flattened themselves against the screens, giant white moths and small gray moths, and tiny winged insects with a day-span of life which came through the mesh and perished sooner than they needed against the globe of the lamp.

Megan went to the hall door and called "Mother," and a voice answered her. Presently a large woman with beautiful eyes and hair like John Murray's came into the room.

"This is my mother-in-law," Megan said, and she greeted them and exclaimed over a boy's birthday and the ice cream.

Karel sat down where he was told, and he looked with a sudden great curiosity at these people. He felt more curiosity than he had felt toward anyone in this town. He did not know why or search for the reason, but he did not take his eyes from one or the other. He watched the dishes being laid out and the ice cream dug from the box, he watched the milk and the cold drinks being taken from the pantry and Nicky leaning against the table silent and smiling, missing nothing. Something was stirring at a level of memory, but whether it was a good memory or a sad one he did not know. Something was in abeyance. He had no desire to think or to move from this place.

When he was told to come to the table he came gladly. A mile away the sound of the fireworks could be heard, but less distinctly than the sound of the cicadas and the whirr of the moths against the screen.

"Now do you remember me?" Megan said smiling, and he nodded. She had spoken to him many times in the village. He continued to watch her as they ate the ice cream. She was not a pretty girl, but he liked her face. It was vivid and frank, and there was something very pleasant about her mouth and eyes. He was not accustomed to looking at people externally. He knew how he felt about them, he understood them well in relation to himself—that was enough. This young woman and this older one had a kind of grace. He felt it in his swelling heart, in the suffusion of joy, as he sat eating their birthday gift to a strange little boy. As he sat there, large, rather awkward, holding his plate, he smiled and continued to smile at the look on Nicky's face. After the first spoonful given him by Karel he had wanted one from Megan, and now she made a game of it, eating from his plate while he ate from hers.

He felt very shy, he did not know what to say to them. There was nothing one could really say when the links between them were so tenuous. He made associations in his mind. In the summer house in Slovakia, there had been a room painted in red and yellow with round buxom figures painted on the closet door and the bureau, a blue porcelain stove, far older than he, in a corner where his mother kept a copper kettle always humming. The room had been his own. It had a bolt on the door, bright yellow but scarred with opening and closing—but his own bolt, his own room, his own view through the window, his own comfort, his own security, his own questions and answers. This older woman made him think of the comfort which had come over him when he went into this room and shut the door.

She was telling Nicky a story now. Nicky did not understand all the story about another little boy and his birthday party, but he watched her face intently, and it was so expressive that he shrieked with pleasure and stamped his foot and mimicked her mimicry until he lost control of himself. Then Karel came to him hastily, kneeling beside his chair and speaking to him in Czech.

Megan said to Karel, "He will never be passive or indifferent to things."

"I know that."

Mrs. Murray lifted the child into her lap and showed him a magazine.

"Did you know that Mrs. Stillwell is raising money for him?" Megan asked.

"I know."

Megan looked at him smiling. "You don't think that is unusual?"

He turned his eyes toward her, frowning a little. Then he raised himself from his knees and sat in Nicky's chair. "The child needs something . . ." he said.

She was still smiling a little. "Will he ever understand what all this giving means?"

He considered her intently. "I don't understand what you mean. He suffered a great deal and he refused to give in. I think the people who did not suffer owe him something."

She rested her chin in her hand and studied the checks of the tablecloth. "I think all we owe is to be kind to one another." She looked at him obliquely. "You're frowning."

He did not answer but he still considered her intently. She said rather sadly, "I said what I meant to say and yet it sounds very cold." She leaned her elbows on the table and put her fingers against her temples; her face was half-hidden by her hair. "Why did you come to this special town?"

"Why not?"

She smiled a little, studiously tracing a whorl of wood with her fingernail. "It's one small town out of so many."

"Well," he said, watching her diffidently, "perhaps we will not stay."

"Oh, stay," she said, her eyes raised suddenly. "If you've selected it, that means you should stay."

"Does it?" and he smiled at her, amused.

"Do you—do you ever talk about yourself? I don't mean to be curious, but I would like to be friends."

The heat of the night was heavy and he felt the heat on his forehead and the palms of his hands. He considered her for a moment, the high cheekbones and the deep-set eyes and the aliveness with which she regarded him. His lips tightened and he watched her as he shook his head.

"No. It happened so long ago and so far away, even kind people do not understand it."

Her studious preoccupation with the grain of wood continued. "Yes, but I think most suffering is—suffering. And with a good heart one can understand a universal thing. And friends can often understand . . . particular things."

He smiled at her slightly. "You use the word 'friend' so often."

She was startled and flushed. "Isn't it a good word?"

"Oh, a very good word. We had some friends last year . . ." She was a young woman, he supposed, but the women he had known since he was a child had been mostly beyond age, neither young nor old.

Perhaps Megan was twenty-nine. He did not know whether she had any children. She was very nearly as tall as he, as tall as her husband. She had dark eyes, bright and warm, and a frequent smile which changed her expression. For when she was not smiling she seemed proud and the corners of her lips turned down a little in a way which held his attention. Her dark hair, as dark as his, framed and accented her face. He liked something about her which he could not name—the pride and the straight way she carried herself and the contradiction of her mouth—downgoing might mean sadness, and yet when she smiled she seemed very happy.

Across the table Mrs. Murray was still showing pictures to Nicky and prompting him to laugh often. They were a wonderfully smiling family, Karel thought. John with the grave lighting smile and Mrs. Murray with her bright blue eyes asking questions gaily and accepting answers with a merry doubt.

This kitchen room was nice; the lamp in the window, the round table with the fruit in the center, the black square of night beyond the open door were nice. The whole, the room and the women in it, was comforting. He sighed deeply and consolingly and reached for his glass of milk.

"Thank you," he said. "We're friends."

He wanted very much to have friends. It was a great and deep need.

This young woman became suddenly quite beautiful to him. When his eyes were lowered he still saw her. Up to the age of thirteen, women had been his mother or his aunts or his schoolteachers. For the next six years they had been participants, without sex, in the business of staying alive. Megan had grace and ardor, and he responded without identifying her special appeal.

After a time John came in. He came in very quietly; he stood by the door for a moment, neither here nor there. He refused the cake and the cold drink, and he sat down as though against his will. There was something wholly tentative about his being there, but he seemed to listen carefully, although he was very withdrawn. His eyes were alert, although he kept them lowered most of the time.

Karel watched John intently. The husband of his friend. He was suddenly alive with curiosity. He had not seen John clearly before. In the darkness he had been aware merely of a voice and a smile.

He did not know how old John was—perhaps fourteen or fifteen years older than him. And he did not know what lay behind the serious, responsive face, which was so agreeable to look at, nor why the expression of his eyes was veiled, as when he came in, and piercing now, when the attention was away from him.

Karel was young, and that is why he sensed withdrawals more keenly than others. He looked at Megan. She was sitting in front of John, at the table, but her head was turned often toward John. Karel thought that she loved him. He knew the feeling in his own heart, and he believed that if one could see the feeling it would look the way Megan looked when she was turned toward John.

And John? There was restlessness in his tall body and his movements, and the being here and not being here which seemed to explain his silence. He was sitting very low in his chair, and his chin rested on his clasped hands.

In his mind Karel went back and forth tirelessly between his friends. He said suddenly to John, "Is this really a farm, and do you really farm it?"

John hesitated. Mrs. Murray laughed. "For three generations it's been a farm." John did not speak. He sank deeper into his chair and smiled a little.

Nicky had edged near to John, his dark eyes accusing. Twice he tried to interrupt and at length he succeeded. He said, "You took back my harmonica."

"No, I didn't," John answered. "Your brother put it in his pocket."

Karel put the instrument on the table, and Nicky said, "Hold it—no, she will hold it—*please*," and Nicky leaned back toward Mrs. Murray.

"What will you play?" Mrs. Murray asked when the child leaned against her, and she put her arm around his shoulders so that she could hold the instrument as he wanted it.

" 'Rudolph the Red-nosed Reindeer.' " He blew happily but too hard, and John came to lean over him and show him how it should be done. He tried again patiently and they all applauded. But the tune was not the tune of the song and he knew it. He held the harmonica with his teeth so that it could not be taken from him until he had tried again. Megan looked at the narrow face with the sucked-in cheeks and thought that the beauty of a little boy was timeless, and for that reason her heart swelled. John looked at Nicky and at Karel with his deep gray eyes and he looked away, drawing in more narrowly his world which must not be invaded or challenged or enlarged until he had learned its topography, its storms and stresses and himself in the dead center. There was room for no one, no stranger. In the dead center was room only for himself. He did not wish to say why he had come back here tonight. He knew only that he had felt a loneliness deeper than his need for solitude, and that he could not stay alone reading in his own house any longer.

At least that is what he said to himself in the endless colloquy between John and himself.

He fixed his gaze on the edge of the hearth and tried to close his ears and the pores of his skin.

But why was he here if he did that?

The fits and starts of music went on, Mrs. Murray taking the instrument away occasionally to wipe it, and then holding it carefully in the position she was learning. At length the child struck a tune and held to it note by note. His eyes were happy. He looked about him, his glance swift and proud above the instrument, his lips straight and hard with blowing. It was weird and distracting music. He made a mistake but he rectified it immediately, and he came to the end triumphantly while the others clapped.

"That was fine," Mrs. Murray said, "but it was sad."

"Sad?" Nicky looked at Karel. "It is our Treblinka song."

"It is sad," Karel said, "but you played it very well."

Megan said, frowning, "That is terrible music. What can it mean to a child?"

Karel did not answer directly. He sat hunched by the table studying his hands. To Nicky he said suddenly, "Shall we sing the song?" and Nicky turned smiling to Mrs. Murray.

> "Not far from here at the shunting yard
> The people are crowding round the cattle trucks.
> The piteous cry of a child is heard calling to his mother,
> Don't leave me here alone. You will never come back again!
> For Treblinka is a grave for everyone,
> Whoever goes there remains there;
> From there, there is no return.
>
> My heart breaks
> When I think of the poor friends who there met a violent death . . ."

Megan said, "No—no—don't sing any more. It's not good!" But Karel only glanced at her and Nicky did not heed her in any way. He was smiling at Mrs. Murray and rubbed his head against her shoulder. Sometimes he lost the pitch, but when he did so he picked it up a syllable later from Karel.

> "My heart breaks
> When I remember that there my brothers and sisters perished.
> My heart breaks
> When I remember that there my mother and father were murdered,
> And I join the others at the shunting site,
> Sobbing bitterly with them and crying
> Don't leave me here alone!"

John sat utterly still. There were patches of white about his nostrils. Megan did not speak. Her brows were drawn tightly together and she did not look at Nicky or Karel. Nicky put his head back against Mrs. Murray's shoulder and very gently touched her necklace with the tip of his tongue. Then he whispered to her and she reached forward and fetched him a piece of cake. Karel stood up.

"It is time to go home," he said to Nicky. "Do your friends know how much you liked your birthday party?"

Nicky rubbed his cheeks against Mrs. Murray's cheek and said, "May I have another piece of cake tomorrow?"

Megan burst out, "It is a terrible song. What does it mean to him—and to you?"

"What it says," Karel answered after a pause. "To him, it was a song. We sang it when we all thought we would die. Just to sing was reassuring."

Megan asked passionately, "What are you like to be able to sing this so calmly now? What are you feeling?"

John said sharply, "Megan!" But she turned distractedly to her mother-in-law and to Karel.

Karel stood like a self-conscious nineteen-year-old boy, uneasy with his height, his long legs, uneasy with the sharp questions. The illusion would have been perfect had it not been for the suddenly sardonic expression of his eyes. He turned a man's sardonic eyes on Megan and did not let her turn away.

"How do I seem? Different from you? How is *he* different? He needs affection. Your mother is giving it to him. He will want to come back. I will want to know if he is welcome as he is. That is what *I* will be feeling—in spite of your wish to be friends."

Mrs. Murray brushed back the hair from the child's forehead. "He knows he is welcome. *He* does not have to ask."

"He has not seen the things I have seen. That is why I must ask."

Megan asked softly, "Is it pride? Is it self-protection? Is it fear? Why did you sing that song?"

Karel sat down suddenly as though his knees had failed him. He felt the dull and terrible ache he had felt in the flat in Queens with the child Marilyn and her parents—human relationships all awry. It went over him like the wash of a sea, and when it left him he was cold and weakened. The need to communicate and to be understood was as imperative as the need for food. He sat silent for a moment, frowning.

He abruptly unbuttoned his sleeve and exposed the numbers on his arm.

"There is that," he said directly to her. But that was inadequate. He stood up abruptly and went to Nicky, lifting him off Mrs. Murray's lap and standing him on his feet. "You ask for words. Perhaps there are words, but I have not found them. You ask questions . . . and there's no way to answer them. He stayed alive and I stayed alive, and I know that that is the answer. That is all I know. I am alive and I wish to be alive and I wish others to be alive and I will help them when I can because I know none of us can do the work of life more than that. You ask me to use words and I can only *be alive.*"

He had not taken his eyes from her. John continued to stare at the hearthstone, but he had sunk into his chair so that his body rested on his spine. His eyes were wet. The depth of his silence created a kind of invisibility behind which a world lay. *Be alive.*

Nicky's head rested against Karel's chest and he stared up at Karel sleepily. Karel put his hand over his eyes and closed them. "The child feels the tension. That is not good for him."

"Even so," Megan said urgently. "You can't go now. Certain things have been said and felt which can't be left that way."

Karel put his hand under the child's knees and drew him up onto his lap. "If I could show you a film or a negative on which things were printed—but there are not words."

Mrs. Murray said, "I don't know why we need words. We're all people with hearts."

7

It is what one remembers, I suppose . . . not whether one remembers it correctly. The first camp was terribly evil. It was down a dirt road, flat, in a plain. There was barbed wire and dogs on chains and whips at the guards' belts. Our heads were shaved, our clothes taken away from us. Only my handkerchief I kept which my grandmother had hemmed. Can one put into words how one feels?

They taught us to mend roads, and we worked without rest and, as far as my stomach knew, without food. For the first time in my life I was hungry, and my hunger lasted for three years. In a little time I did not think of anything but how to get more turnip soup, more rutabaga, more bread. I cleaned boots for the SS, ran errands for them. I remember things about that camp that I do not remember about any other. I remember smells. The smell of decay which is like wax in your nostrils, so solid you cannot breathe. And the smell of foulness. The filthy blankets and our foul bodies which smelled of excrement and disease. It was a constant sweetish smell, and there was also the terrible smell of the crematorium when the wind blew over the camp. And the smell of decomposing bodies waiting to be burned. The smoke and the smell filled your hair. Even when you were in the fields or working on the road away from the smoke, you still had the smell in your mind.

There were many more camps. There was one where the commandant was of the Organisation-Todt—the organization-death—and wore always a huge whip at his belt. There the beatings never let up. One was beaten for everything—for stepping off the path or speaking to your neighbor or asking for water, or one was beaten to see how much dust was on your clothes.

They wanted us killed quick and cheaply. If we died without causing them trouble, then we saved the Reich money; we aided the great war effort. When we learned that, many determined to stay alive by every trick they knew.

First you destroy the man's spirit. When that is destroyed, then the body is nothing and quickly goes away. That is why they made us stand naked in the heat or the snow or the rain for a whole day, why they shaved all the hair from our heads and our bodies—piling it up to send into Germany for mattress stuffings—why they gave us trousers that would not fasten or shirts that fitted a small man like a tent. I have seen women dressed only in a jacket—that was all they had on—or in a torn satin evening gown with only a few shreds of bodice left, their heads shaven.

At three in the morning we stood by the thousands for roll-call. One OT man would shoot his revolver from the end of the line to make sure it was straight. A man might lose an arm that way or get a belly wound, but he lay on the ground for two hours until the roll-call was over. In the snow we have knelt for the whole day, rocks in our upstretched hands as punishment for some one man's act of compassion. One hid one's heart, if one was wise.

Always the orchestra was playing waltzes or marches

or sentimental songs when we marched out the gates to the fields or the quarries or the factories, and we had to sing. The dogs were there to attack us if we fell down or faltered. For the women in their camp it was the same, but it was harder. Only some did not say so, they did not want to believe in anything worse.

A man is degraded if he does not have enough food. None of us—not one of us—had a moment's freedom from hunger or thirst. But to get food, to appease hunger and thirst, was to fight the enemy. It was patriotic. It was for humanity, even when you thought only of yourself.

Yet with all the will, all the stubbornness to defeat them, a link in your resolve was broken here and there, and you gave in to something. Perhaps you had to in order to keep any part of yourself. You looked about you for response and you did not find it. Each one was thinking of himself. You developed prison eyes—no expression, no giving, no sharing. You lost your self-control—you never thought a moment existed beyond the present moment. That made you cruel to others. It made you forget who you were. Now and then I would say to myself, "You are Karel Lindemann," and it stiffened me a little. Karel Lindemann was a boy with a family, with a home and parents and a friendly spirit toward others. But one day I said, "So you are Karel Lindemann—so what is that? A number tattooed on your arm." After that I found that I behaved differently. I ate up all my bread instead of hiding some in my shirt, and then when my hunger was too big I stole and was beaten. I did not wash any more; it was too great an effort. I did not fight the lice. I let them swarm over me. I did not go to the latrine. I said I was becoming like an animal—and it satisfied me. So then I began to die. My legs swelled up. I took beatings rather than work. Only then, when I did not care, did I begin to lose my strength.

A little fellow from Poland tried to talk to me, but I

looked at the professional men in the camp, the intellectuals like my father, and I thought, When they talk to me, then I will listen. I will not listen to this carpenter.

But the little fellow talked to me every night, even though I turned my back. He talked to others as well. Something tingled in me and ran down my spine without warning when he was talking. He was talking about life, that it was up to us, we had a choice. This was funny, for the death selections took place every morning, and your familiar friend was taken without warning out of your life and at night you saw his smoke going up from the chimneys. But he said it was our choice of what we believed in most, and I guess that he proved it. Twice he was selected for extermination, and twice he came back to answer the roll-call that night. Not like the dead did, who were carted back in wheelbarrows from the fields where their suffering had ended and propped up against the barrack walls at evening roll-call so that the Nazis might keep their day's records in order. No, he came back alive. He would not say how he had done it, but two or three others he saved in some fashion I do not know how.

The politicals and some of the religious men—they were our souls. They did not give up their humanity. Inside themselves they did not bow down. They opened up a little window on hope and you did not wish to close it again. They talked of life, when each man had justice and a fair share of happiness and prosperity. They said it would not come to us if we were apathetic. It must be born of our resolution and faith. They compelled half-dead men to work, for unless they did they went to the gas chambers. Somehow they kept a life of the mind and spirit alive. The carpenter said you must believe that each one had a good important future. Some of these decayed, terrible creatures who had ceased to be men made one turn aside, but he said one had to love them. He said there was no choice.

They had to be loved and kept alive in spite of the way we saw them.

To kill men like him you had to shoot them. When one was shot he seemed to reappear in another man.

But these were my days of doubt. What entered my mind to comfort me must have entered by instinct alone. I was fourteen, fifteen, a boy growing to be a man but not in a normal way.

I had pneumonia, but one did not go to the infirmary unless one wished to die. When my fever was high, I tried to steal a bottle to hold water and the block chief beat me until I lost consciousness. Then I went to the infirmary. For days I was unconscious, and the doctor told me later that I was twice selected for the crematorium. When I became conscious again, something had happened, something small, patient, as though I had come back from the dead. For a day or two I did nothing but lie there staring at the top of the bunk, moving when my bed-mates needed to move, but not speaking, even my thinking so far away it had no contact with those around me.

I lay there, and the morning and the noon and the night passed, and I did nothing but think. I had never thought so much and so long in my life. When I came back out of death I was not a child any longer. I thought of my family, the love that had bound us, the power that made me a man, able to feel. . . . All that the religious men and the political men had said, and to which I had not listened, was there word for word, truth for truth. That was real, that seemed to me *power*, not the SS guards who had to stay drunk to endure the world in which they lived.

I can only say it the way I feel it, and I do not really care if anyone understands me or not: I suddenly understood life, the business of being alive. I would not die here. I did not know why, but I believed in some fashion that death was the only language and the only power my enemies understood, and I meant to fight them by staying alive. There and then I believed in God, in something stronger than evil. It is growing up. . . .

When I left the infirmary I would sometimes steal potatoes or an extra roll of sausage, and my friends and I would cook them in secret at night. Everything to resist, to give the mind hope and occupation—perhaps a problem in mathematics or a small plan built around your work or, with me, repeating English phrases I had learned in school. Each time you came safely through another trap laid by death, when you could do something, even a little thing in a normal way, it gave you great strength. Some men planted wild lupin back of a barracks. Many stole out at great risk each day to look at it.

I felt less weak and confused when I took an interest in others and helped them stay alive. At those times you say to yourself, "I will positively live for a month," and then, "positively until spring, and my friend will also live that long." Sometimes a break comes in your resolution, and then you build up again or you do not. There is no in-between. There came the terrible days and nights when all your faith and hope collapsed and you felt that you were a giant fool and that what you must be prepared for was the inescapable. You were ashamed you were a fool. Hope was the cruelest thing that could be asked of you. Then—something would happen. You had to hope again.

They hanged a Jewish boy my age who had stolen dynamite. He did not die quietly. He shouted, "Lift up your heads! You will live again!" That is what I called bread from heaven. When we went to cut his body down the next morning someone had thrown some flowers at his feet.

The squads which worked in the crematoriums were destroyed and replaced every three months. Many went insane first. I was sent there in December, 1944, while the camp was already preparing for evacuation. My father wanted me to be a doctor. I tried to look at cadavers with the eyes of a doctor, for those are the ways one saved his heart. Night and day I planned to be a doctor. I let nothing else enter my mind.

We burned bodies at the rate of seven hundred and twenty an hour. They were also being piled up in pits in the woods and burned with kerosene. The smell of the burnings never left you. The Nazis wished to liquidate the camp, but they did not.

By January the Russians were coming very close, wave after wave of planes. They bombed the crematorium and it burned all night. By the end of the month, ten thousand prisoners were started on a march westward. It was bitter and terrible. Behind us we could hear the Russian artillery, and yet we could not remain. Many were sick with disappointment and despair. We slept in fields or in barns, the dead left unburied the next morning. If they had not succeeded in exterminating the prisoners nature would do it. They gave out no water. Some of us tried to dig with our hands for water through the frozen ground, or some drank their urine and died. There were five hundred women and young children with us. All the children died—all of them.

Some of us who were healthy were loaded into boxcars and sent farther west. It was March and the spring was coming. I stood on a strut in the boxcar and looked out a window near the top. We passed through little villages. People were walking along with their bicycles and women were standing in the middle of streets talking, and young girls, with kerchiefs round their heads, were going into stores. What did they think of these cars? Did they think? Outside, in the beautiful country, people must have seen these endless boxcars going past, and in the moonlight they must have seen them pass. Could they imagine, did they know what was in the cars? Did they know and pretend they did not?

In Buchenwald I found my brother. We were there only three days, and I saw the American planes, so beautiful. Then they loaded us, ninety men, into a boxcar. In some fashion I got the child on as well, and no one betrayed him. They opened the car the next day to distribute bread. They had distributed to the first eight cars when the Americans began to bomb the train. I did not say, "Oh, my God, the poor wounded!" Or, "oh, my God, where is my brother?" I said, "Oh, God, I didn't get food!"

For the first time I cried. We were so near to the end, and this happened. The Nazis did not bother to kill those badly wounded, and after a while I and a friend could not stand the crying. We crawled out to see what could be done and to look for the child. I found him just as the planes went away. The child, my brother. His arms were as you see them. We dragged him away and we hid under the car. A guard saw us and beat on the soles of our feet to come out. I came out the other side and I killed him. Then we escaped.

How can I say it? *We escaped.* With a mutilated child. There were no antiseptics. We boiled water in a tin can. We made tourniquets. We carried him for three days. Then my friend said we were insane not to leave the child at some farmhouse. We separated, for the child was absolutely necessary to me. The child did not complain, he did not cry out. He suffered and he suffered, but when we told him he must be silent, he was silent. He was unconscious but he rallied. When we found water he did not ask for more than his share. Perhaps the shock of freedom would have made me do reckless things if it had not been for him. I had to have him. I could not be without him. He was the absolutely necessary proof to me that there was a future.

No one would give us any help, but I felt very healthy. This wild life, stealing milk from the cows at night—no one to help you and no one to hinder you—suited me. But the child was my care. Dozens and dozens of people in concentration-camp rags filled the roads, escaping like me without direction, everyone looking out for himself. Three days, four days, I do not remember, the guns never silent, the confusion terrible. I came from a woods and stood on a slope and there were the Americans, a big convoy.

They were exactly as I had imagined. There they were, a mile long, just waiting, for some reason. I was glad I could speak in American. They came to look at the child, and a sergeant told a soldier to bring a medic. So I sat in a jeep with the child on my lap as I had known that I would sometime do.

They cared for the child, my brother, and they gave me army clothes and I ate with them. When I found they did not demand work before I ate, I said that I wished to work. Later we were moved to a children's center. I was sixteen, nearly seventeen, and the child was six, very small.

We were the cared-for now. The ladies at the children's center did not know what we would do. You could see it in their eyes. Our heads were covered with scabies. New children were picked each day, and they could not guess their ages except by their voices, they were so small. Some children said, "May we do anything?" and the UNRRA ladies said "Yes," and for three days they screamed. The Nazis had struck them if they spoke or made a noise. Now they screamed for three days and no one struck them or even complained.

I wanted to talk; every one of us wanted to talk. The

grown-ups listened whenever we wanted to tell them what had happened. When I talked a stone seemed to leave my heart. But it would come back, and then I would have to talk again.

We wanted only justice, nothing else. If our families were lost we wanted new families. We wanted to learn things and be independent. Is it hard to understand the little child for whom a piece of bread is the symbol of safety, who cannot sleep at night for fear of waking in a world of hunger unless a piece of bread is under his pillow? I was not a little child, but I carried a slice of bread in my shirt until I was made to understand that there was enough, and my brother had to have a piece of bread where he could touch it with his cheek every night.

It is hard to stay in one place when one remembers all the time that has been wasted. Yet it is fearful to leave and go off into the unfamiliar. But I knew that the child and I had to find something new, made by ourselves. I wished to go away where I did not hear German spoken. They let us come here. We are here. They let us come because I insisted on certain things for the child and myself. I was only asking for justice.

8

In the darkness, in the night, in the farmhouse kitchen, in the ears of friends, his sorrows found expression. Stretched thin, vaporous, they had ceased to be the things of fear. Now he talked aloud in the dark, the sleepy child (who was not really his brother, though closer than his own) moaning delicately against his shoulder. He had emptied the seamless, cavernous bags of sorrow into the night. Strewn out, they would not be seen in the morning. How tenderly he had carried the wretched things, how heavy their weight had been.

There were things he had not told Megan—for it was to Megan he had talked. He had not told her the truth about the child or how he had come to the United States or why he had not yet found what he needed. These things stood in his mind like geometric symbols; a small memory stood for a large memory; out of the symbols a close and intricate meaning could be made. He thought again step by step of how he and Nicky had been bound together; of the day in late February, 1945, when heavy snow-filled clouds seemed to hang as low as chimneys of the camp, and the transport from the south rolled into the concentration camp; of the strange mother who had been killed there and then on the railway siding by the air strafing, and the strange child he had pulled out from under her body and, in the excitement, concealed.

It was a profound moral victory. One small life which would have been automatically sacrificed in the gas chambers—he setting himself against the murder and succeeding.

A half-dozen men set themselves to protect the child. They all stole food for him, they all helped to conceal him at roll-call, but it was Karel the child trusted, Karel the child looked for when other faces came near him. The pinched little face with the immense black eyes, the endless inquiries for "Mama," the weeping for "Mama," the talk of home, the swift familiar flow of Czech which looped and webbed two spirits. He trained the child to think of him as his brother, he made him repeat the name Lindemann again and again. At night, in the darkness, when Nicky was convulsed by the sirens and the planes overhead, the child would whisper, "You are my brother, brother, brother, brother . . ." And then, "You will look after me?"

The brightness of this New England night kept the dogs wakeful. Far off one would bay tentatively and nearer at hand another would answer. An old bullfrog sounded in the marshy strip by the road, one calm expulsion of air, and the smell of the hay came as sure and arresting as sound.

Sounds and smells come steeply when one is deeply moved. As he and the child had reached the edge of the woods that spring day in Germany, he had a swift sharp sense of smell, of the bursting earth. Everything was pungent, everything was alive. A moment later they came out onto a sloping meadow above the road and saw the convoy.

He had been at first afraid, then curious, then skeptical. He had stood on the slope above it, the child on his back, staring for some minutes at the inert, waiting convoy, stretching out as far as he could see in both directions, white stars on the vehicles. He stood there for some time before anyone noticed him, and even when he was seen, the soldiers and he remained apathetic, making no move. An event of profound significance, a climax, was no more than a weary exchange between tired people. And all the while he was aware of sound and smell, birds' songs, the smell of the machines.

Then the soldiers saw the child and a young fellow lifted him off Karel's back. German farm laborers and men and women in the rags of concentration camps crowded around the trucks but they gave the child and him only fleeting surly looks. A sergeant sent for a medic, and the medic gave Nicky a shot of morphine, and when he saw the limp and truncated piece of humanity which was the child, he asked the sergeant to send a jeep back to battalion aid.

"How many days you been carrying him?" the medic asked, squinting at Karel.

"Three days."

"Jesus, God!"

Someone broke open a K-ration and gave it to him. The hungry ones who leaned against the trucks set up a cry, and a few other rations were stealthily distributed. The medical officer returned in the jeep and looked at the child lying on the floor of a truck.

"Sure he needs a hospital," he said to the medic, "but I can't release any damned ambulance for a civilian." The medic said something and the officer shrugged. "Sure, take him along. I don't know what good it'll do, but maybe there's a hospital up the road."

The medic, who was relieved that Karel spoke English and who told him his name was Perry Young, said to

Karel, "Don't worry. We'll figure out some way. Doesn't look like any blood poisoning's set in, but there ought to be a clean amputation. Don't worry—just *don't worry*."

He could not say that he was not worrying, that he had no reaction. He had sat there in the German spring and felt nothing, not even fatigue. He had struggled to draw a deep breath, and had coughed and could not stop coughing. Perry Young had given him water out of his canteen. The simple action of Perry Young giving him water was unnerving. They sat under the hot spring sun while Karel gasped for his breath and vomited up the water and saw in a blind way the sum of strength and anchor of hope in the worried face of Private Young.

Solicitude and affection were too strong a draught. He thought in an odd far-off panic that this might be the end for him. He could have struggled on, hidden, improvised, carried the child, demanded food as a miracle and seen it fall from heaven, but solicitude came too unpreparedly. He was a child and he needed love and he had forgotten how it was experienced in its natural state. He loved this American. He loved Perry Young as Nicky loved Karel, with despair and wonder and, within a short time, he was terrified if Perry Young was out of his sight.

He did not know how he looked to others. It was fortunate he did not. He was nearly six feet tall, but he weighed eighty pounds and his head was covered with scabies.

That first night Karel slept for twelve hours, although he had watched Perry go in a panic. After that he subdued his great fatigue and made himself indispensable. Because he spoke German and English he was in demand. Perry was his close and dear friend. Only at night he wakened screaming, and the child shifted and moaned beside him.

In the minds of the indestructibles, the future had been easily defined. It would be the period when the world paid what it owed them, and paid meticulously the last coin. The survivor would demand, and be given—because the world owed it to him—home, family, education, opportunity.

When he had first been offered a plate of stew, he had not moved. Instead, he had asked sharply, "What do I have to do in exchange?"

"Do?" the mess sergeant shouted, handing on his plate to someone else, "eat it, dope!"

Karel wished all who came from the outside world of healthy people to declare themselves. He wanted all of the untouched to make their attitudes plain to the survivor. He wanted to be perfectly sure what power men in uniform had. Yet he needed these men. But not if they gave and asked anything in return. They must give; then he would accept. It equalized an unbalance, it steadied the years.

Never for a moment did he forget Perry. Perry needed him too, it appeared, to shape some overturning emotion within himself. Perry was past thirty, with a wife and child in Queens, a man who frowned when he talked as though the effect of all he had seen was more than he could apprehend.

Perry would sit and look at him, the kind, shapeless worry on his freckled face, the fathomless perplexity in his knitted brows. He was not a wordy man, but Karel believed that Perry Young considered them bound together by something which went beyond words.

The poor corrugated brow, the fumbling hands said that a bond of some common experience held them together. To Karel it was like having a family.

The moving, crashing world outside, the world of war and armies moving, of monstrous collapse and the lives of a hundred million caught in events of death and life came to Karel narrowed and muffled. It was not that he wished it that way, but he was too young and beset to range widely, to understand the complex and artificial. Often he held a newspaper in his hands and stared at the information and read here and there, for he remembered the upsurge which he had felt in the camp when the narrowness opened, and a glimpse of the world had come through.

But what must a boy do, what must a boy do, he sometimes cried out to himself when the terrible ambiguity of being sixteen years old and filled with present passion and past remembrances came too steeply upon him? The present passion was to catch up to life without a moment's delay, to gallop backwards and forwards with time till it delivered to him all that it had had and would have, with no trustworthy evaluation except his own staggering and formless assumption of life.

At the end of five days, the battalion moved on, and the boys went with it, inconspicuously riding a truck. Because they now had friends, they continued in this way for two weeks. Then the first sergeant said that word had come that all displaced, unaccompanied children, under a certain age, were being gathered into centers. If he was interested, he and Nicky could go back on the mail truck.

Perry Young said, "This is your chance. You can't go on with us any more. Take the chance. I won't worry so much."

Karel said tensely, "You won't leave us completely? You'll come back when you can?"

"Jesus, what do you think I'm doing—walking out on you?"

"No."

"Well, then, say so."

He gave Karel his APO number, shook hands again and again, and tried to say something more. But when Karel climbed into the mail truck, and Perry handed him the child, Perry merely said, "Be seeing you," and Karel nodded.

In the late summer, Perry Young stopped by the Children's Center. He expected to be home in Sunnyside, Queens, within six weeks. He learned that Nicky wanted a watch above everything else, a large watch which he could pin at his belt and have handy for someone to tell him the time. He went away and he returned with a great embossed watch, liberated with its chain, with thin Roman numerals and a resolute tick. He brought Karel a shaving kit, a gesture, a thing from man to man, although Karel showed no need to shave; such delays happened in concentration camps.

Perry Young had a week's leave. He spent it here, and the two walked along the road which ran among the hills, the boy carrying the child. Germany would have been a beautiful country had it not been German, Karel said.

Perry talked a great deal. The wordless man found his tongue. He told about his wife, Bertha, and his little girl, Marilyn, and his job with the electric company, but he did it with a frown as though all that was another matter. He wanted to know what Karel had been thinking. It was evident that he believed Karel would have fixed ideas about the future of himself and the child.

"Two kids need a family," he said. "You've got ambitions. There's no chance for you here. Bertha and I'll go bond for you, *adopt* you both, see that you get a home and a chance." Perry was talking devotedly, finding words and fluency. "Back home—there's a lot wrong and a lot right. But people wouldn't ask questions, and school's free, and most folks like kids and you'd have a chance to catch your breath. Bertha knows about you. We got a nice place, fixed up nice. We don't need the dining room, and we'd fix it up like a bedroom. You'd have somebody who'd care if you got knocked down by a cab or if you met a nice girl or if you made a home run." He laughed abruptly. "They'd fix Nicky up with new arms. They make fine arms now. I guess you can use them for everything."

Karel drew in his breath and moved slowly from his cramped position. He pushed back the hair from his forehead and looked off across the little valley. "Why do you want us to be part of your family?" he asked, deeply moved.

Perry did not answer for some time.

"Aw . . . Europe stinks. But you hit me where I felt it. That's important to me."

Karel thought of America in terms which were his own. Each child who thought of America (and most had stopped thinking of home) gave it shape in his own terms. The terms were narrow, confined to a street, to a school or a house or a faceless adult, and himself larger than any external thing—until loneliness struck him down again.

Karel thought now of America constantly, of being a part of Perry's family. It was in his dreams, in his daytime appraisals, in his questions. It shaped his apprehensions, determined the value he put on the close and the far.

Nicky had picked up English words, but now Karel taught him English; he insisted that Nicky must speak only English. It was an obsession shared by many of the polyglot children who wished no longer to speak in German, who would not learn German songs, and who believed that America was a bright and shining beginning, an *All.*

Perry had gone on to Paris, and in due time to demobilization in New York. He had made inquiries, filled out questionnaires; he needed certain information from Karel; they had to come in on a quota, so such-and-such had to be done from both ends. For both: father and mother's names, birth date, place of birth, and so on and so on. At the end of the letter he had scrawled in pencil in his childish hand, "Is he your brother?"

Karel sat staring at the penciled words. *Is he your brother?* Someone doubted it. He stood in the hall of the administration building where he had opened the letter, the institutionalized white walls about him, the children running back and forth and up the steep stairs. *Brother . . . brother*, something which even the blood could not define.

He crumpled the letter in his pocket and he went and sat outside the window of the room where the Czech children were having their lesson in arithmetic. Who did this child belong to but him? What cold kind of questions could make realities where nothing was real? Until something better was seen, no cold questions, no authority could change that fact. He could not make himself go deeper and find the words which would say the final thing: that the fraternity of a death camp made a bond stronger than blood. And in his future he must be needed—must be needed.

The days were swallowed up. Karel studied everything he could lay his hands upon. Very deep, very faraway, self-protection demanded that one know everything so that one would never be taken by surprise.

He talked to everyone who would talk to him. Adults liked him because he was quiet, smiling, intelligent, spoke good English. They said in his hearing that the children had given them deep faith that the human spirit could remain intact. The sardonic eyes of the children answered this. . . . Adults, relieved that children did not cause trouble, relieved that accepted standards had proved durable.

The day came in the spring when he and Nicky and forty-five other children with American relatives went up the gangplank of the ship at Bremen. They had rucksacks on their backs which held their belongings. They watched the docks and the islands and the city draw away from them. It was a bright German-blue day, and even the dirty waters of the harbor shimmered with spring. Not one called back *Good-bye* or waved. All of them, children and adults, leaned against the rail, staring, eyelids still. They stared until the city was a rim against the blue tender sky.

9

When New York came into sight under a hot sun, when a hundred thousand windows gleamed with light and steel pylons gleamed like fire and the long shrill whistles of passing ships greeted them, then something beyond reality had to be grasped. What was America? It was an idea, a state of mind, and those who wept and sang and shouted proclaimed this fact.

When the tugs eased the ship into the pier, a thousand stood on the upper and lower levels of the pier, shouting, screaming names, holding up signs which bore the names of those they were seeking: *Gilinsky—Faske—Husek—* the lands and people of Europe. Those on the ship who recognized their names uttered shriek upon shriek and leaned far over the rails which separated them from home.

He searched the crowd for Perry Young. Nicky leaned back against Karel, frightened, confused, sobbing a little, forgetting all his English and whispering in Czech, "*Where are we going? I don't want to go there.*"

Karel said, "We are going home. Watch for Perry."

They went down the gangplank, the children and the

babies in arms, Karel steadying Nicky ahead of him, his hands on his shoulders. The gangplank stirred and excited each child. It was his lonely venture, his proof that the impossible was possible, his maturity.

They stood by the charted buses, silent children, deeply unsure. Ladies with arm bands urged them to find seats. One obeyed because there was never a choice, but one was never deceived by appearances. How would one ever know about adults in authority, ever, as long as one lived?

Karel sat at a bus window, Nicky on his lap, and then he saw Perry Young. Perry was running down the pier, waving, and the tears sprang into Karel's eyes. He could hear the sound of Perry's shoes beating against the pier, and some of the other children who also knew Perry began to shout and to wave.

"God Almighty!" Perry panted, bracing himself with one hand against the bus. "Hello, kids! Kiss your old man, Nicky!" for Nicky was wailing, "Let me kiss him—let me kiss him!—Hello, Luba, Wanda, Pepi, Georgie!"

"We come now with you?" Karel said urgently.

"Tomorrow," Perry said. "I'll be there at five-thirty—soon as work's over. Tomorrow—sure as shooting!"

Bertha Young was strong and blonde, and hearty and quick to exclaim. When she heard Perry at the door with the children, she ran out of the kitchen, wearing a pretty plastic apron, with a dishcloth in her hand. She held out her arms, but no one knew exactly who she meant to embrace. Marilyn was sure it was not she, Karel was sure it was not he, Nicky stared at her. Then, to clarify it for herself and the others, she called, "Nicky!" and the child went, hesitant, stumbling, and then in a rush. She hugged and embraced him and sank to her knees. Karel was astonished at the child's expression when he turned, beaming and joyous, still in her arms, to look at them.

She shook hands with Karel and then she abruptly drew down his head and kissed him. He needed that. He smiled slowly. Perry was talking at the same time that she talked, unwrapping a cigar, laughing, showing them the radio and record player, the view out of the window, the ash tray which Marilyn had made in school.

They were shown their room while Marilyn swung from her father's arm. Two beds and a bureau and a chair had been put in the dining room, and a curtain hung in the doorway. The window had the same view as in the living room, across the low roof of another orange building and away into the sky.

When they sat down at the dinner table, which had been moved into the living room, Perry and Bertha Young showed their happiness. Perry set out three bottles of beer, the children had milk, but they all lifted their glasses to "Being here." Then Bertha sat for a moment longer, red suffusing her eyes, and lifted her glass with a tender intense gaze, "To our sons."

Nicky understood only an emotion which sent through him a blissful warmth. *To our sons*. Karel felt a faint panic. What did that mean? He had yearned to belong to Perry's family, yet in his heart he belonged to no one. Where he went, how he went, must be the sum of himself. Yet he knew what their hunger was, his and Nicky's, and he could not have stirred from this chair even if he had hated these people. The continuity of things was stretched so thin that he could not cause it anywhere to break, for the rending would be irreparable. As Karel sat eating and laughing and telling his impressions of New York, he did not—now at this moment—want anything more, whatever his caution might say.

He washed the dishes with Bertha, smiling and listening happily to the details she told him endlessly. She wished him to know everything, who the family was and how they had lived, and what Marilyn said when she was two, and what she thought about her Daddy, and what their ambitions were.

Yes, his mind kept saying, *yes, that's a fine life, that's right . . . that's what a person should want . . . That's why we're here.*

In the living room, Marilyn and Nicky sat on the floor and she showed him the comic books which were her favorites. Perry had turned on the radio loudly, but he did not appear to be listening or reading the paper he held in his hand. He was just smiling.

Later some friends came in, a man and his wife named Burnham and her mother, Mrs. Pike. They said, "Well, well, well, we've certainly heard all about you." And Mrs. Burnham said, "My, you've had experiences, haven't you?" and then they sat smiling and waiting. Bertha, in fresh lipstick and straightening her stocking seam, said, "Tell them about it, Karel—about how you got out of that camp."

He tried. He had told it so often. It was like his name. He responded when his name was spoken. He tried, but tonight he failed. Presently he realized that Mrs. Burnham was whispering to Bertha, and that the only ones who were really listening were Perry and the old lady. It was this room, he decided. The room was very strong. It selected with great care what it wished to include or shut out.

Later he put Nicky to bed. The curtains did not shut out sound but still they were isolated. They knew their own hearts and they were secret from everyone else. Karel turned out the light, but the room was not dark. He pinned Nicky's watch to his pillow and then sat beside Nicky's bed for some time, reluctant to go back. The child whispered after a moment, "Tell her—tell the lady—tell *Mom*—to kiss me good night."

The following Saturday he returned to the Committee Center.

He wished to see Miss Speyer but he took no initiative. When she heard that he was in the building, she came down herself and shook hands with him.

"Everything all right?" she asked.

"All right," he answered.

"Come on in and tell me about it."

He sat in her office, running his finger over the scrolls on the chair arm, smiling a little, waiting for her to begin.

"We're here to know and to help if it isn't all right."

"They are kind and Nicky is happy."

"You just came back to see us? Good."

He continued to smile a little, in silence, the scroll work rough under his finger.

"But you understand that I cannot accept anything from strangers."

"It depends a little on how they offer it. Isn't that so?" He hesitated. She added, "Mr. Young isn't a stranger, is he?"

"No. But his wife is." He added with sudden intensity, "She is really a stranger. I should like a job, so that I can pay for the things for the child."

She considered the view outside her window for a moment. "I think you could get a job. You're intelligent, you speak English well. But there are other things you wanted to do. You couldn't do both."

"Why?" he asked, not lifting his eyes.

"Oh, if you worked all day and went to school each night who would care for the child?"

He did not answer.

She considered him for a moment, the bowed dark head, the strong heavy features, the sensitive mouth. "You know," she said, "it's a long way, where you want to go. I suspect you're older than you tell—a year or two," she added hastily at his look, then smiled. "You had to get into the country, didn't you? Eighteen—nineteen—education takes a long time, and specialized education even longer. You want to be a doctor. Why?"

Perry had asked the question once, and he could have answered again in the same words. But he did not, for there could be no glibness in such an answer. The answer was something deeply submerged and organic. One could not take out the heart and examine it, with all its valves and arteries, and expect to learn anything of its feeling. No more could this be taken out.

He shook his head. "Because I want to be."

She looked at him with her little eyes partly closed. "Because you've seen a lot of death?"

He smiled slightly without looking at her. She waited for a moment, and then she said briskly, "Of course there are things that can be gone into, like scholarships. The Committee will help you financially until you're twenty-one; after that free scholarships are hard to find. I don't know how many years that gives you."

He answered quietly, "I will be eighteen in June."

"To be a doctor takes a long pull. You've got plenty of handicaps without wanting to earn your own living as well."

He replied, "I am not saying that we want to leave the Youngs. Perry is my friend. But I do not wish to take things —like money. His wife gave me a dollar this morning."

She asked, "How would you have gotten here on the subway if you had not had some money?"

He was not moved. He said very low, "We got along without money before. We saw how worthless it is."

"That is unrealistic," she said briskly. "Life is giving, taking. Every one of you children here has got to realize that. People want to give to you—and you must learn to take." After a moment she swung her chair around so that she faced him directly. "Karel, I think you face most things straight. I think you will not run away from things. You may have to change and shift and maybe go from one home to another—some of you have already done that, one or two who came before you even want to return to Europe—but how you do it will determine whether that is a natural adjustment or a running away. Most of you are poorly prepared emotionally for failure. Understand what that means, will you? Think hard about this matter of being a doctor. We will help you in every way—but think hard."

"I have," he replied. Then he looked at her wryly. "*I* am one who is not prepared for failure. When I found that I was still alive, I knew there was something I had to do. I do not mean to be emotional," he said, standing up slowly. "I know that people fail. But I cannot think of failing. I see life in different terms. Very—enormous. Very promising. That is what I have to be certain of."

She stood up then too, and came around to him. "All right. I have faith because you have faith. Let's leave it at that."

Bertha Young was hurt because he had returned secretly to the Center. He tried to explain, but she said, "*This* is your home, isn't it? A nice home—not a relief agency! Ask your friends here if you want to."

He looked at her in silence. So simple a thing this woman did not understand. He heard her later that night speaking to Perry about it. Perry understood, he explained, but she said, "He lives with us now. He ought to do things the way we do, out of consideration. Sneaking is bad. He's got to see that it's bad. We're not a family with secrets!"

Perry said soothingly, "He'll tell you next time. Sure he'll tell you next time, when he sees how you feel. That kid's pure gold. He wouldn't hurt a fly."

Karel lay in the semi-dark, his arms behind his head. Evidently a happy home meant to do as the strongest one in it felt to be right. Bertha was plainly the strongest. He wished a happy home.

He had one objective, to be educated as quickly as possible. He and Nicky. Nicky was in a school for disabled children, learning to use a pencil held between his teeth. He talked excitedly of school and of his endless expectations. Karel had been five years out of a schoolroom, but he wished so intensely to close up the gap of those years that he studied all day and all evening. It was simple to do because his whole life depended upon it. Yet it was hard to do because there was no privacy, and the playing and quarreling of the children, and the loud passionate intercession of Bertha filled the world on the other side of the curtain. Sometimes he sat with his arms and his forehead against the books, listening to the noise. Home meant a family and a family meant love . . .

The winter passed, and Karel continued to study, in YMCA classes, in night school. Bertha mused about him and stared at him, getting onto the merry-go-round of her speculations and getting off again at the self-same spot. One day he was, to her, a man, the next day, a boy. It made her uneasy and angry. He was a boy she must guide, explain the ways of a new world to. But when she started to do so, he became a man, and she made a fool of her tongue —for he was after all a boy, was he not?—immensely attractive with some slow peculiar power and an ageless male face.

She turned her anger against the thing she could not understand. She talked on the surface of the matter to everyone. *Gratitude.* There was something about gratitude here always woven into her comments, about being considerate of other people. She was not thinking of herself. She *was* considerate.

She loved Nicky and she would do anything for him. All children were the same. They needed love in great waves, they needed to be taught unselfishness, they needed to obey. Their thoughts were children's thoughts and should remain that way until grown.

She wanted to give. She wanted to give these children everything. When Perry had written her about the children from Germany, and made his proposal, she had hesitated, but not for long. The enormity, the drama, the romance, the tremendous implications had swept over her, and from that moment she had not wavered. Why, her heart was as big as the world. She had room for all homeless children! But from the children she wanted appreciation.

The knowledge of this rose like some small frog from the quiet underwaters of the mind, and it sat croaking its presence at her. Appreciation was natural, it showed co-operation and a right spirit on the part of others. It conformed to all her standards, and it beset her—as she watched Karel coming in and out of the apartment with barely a word, always ducking his head behind a book, always looking at her bewildered when she wished a point of hers carried, always assuming that all this homelike atmosphere was theirs by natural right. It beset her when she considered Nicky who would *not* give up his fears, although she had shown him again and again that one could not love little boys who held on to silly baby-notions, wet their beds, and she overflowed her feelings to Perry.

She wanted thanks for the family unit, for the affection and welcome, the sacrifices which were being made. It was hard on their income; she would not accept help from the Committee, only people on relief went to an agency.

"Why," she said, "I would want this appreciation from

my own child. Why shouldn't I expect it, all the more, from boys who aren't my own? It's only normal. They can't go into life selfish, not considering others."

Perry muttered, "They're grateful. For the love of God, you don't need it in words, I saw what they came out of—*we* ought to be grateful we got 'em."

Perry said, to Karel, "You see how it is—she's sentimental. She thinks you're great kids. She likes to feel you really take in all she's doing. Women are funny. I'd take a poke at you if you thanked me."

Karel said wonderingly, "I try to thank you both by studying hard. By making you proud of me."

Perry kicked at a paper bag. "Sure, sure—it's just for peace," he muttered, "so you can get your schooling and be safe."

It was not a trivial shock. Karel tried conscientiously to match sentiment to sentiment. He felt great affection, he felt gratitude, he paid sudden attention to Nicky's manners so that as many things as possible would conform.

Then one day he spoke jokingly of American habits and ventured to believe that some things might be better in Europe. Bertha went up like a flame.

"That's no way to talk," she cried. "Why, all that America's done for people—people come here and take what they want and then they pay it back in that way."

He looked at her in the slow disturbing way which made her both aggressive and weak as water. "I do not know what you are talking about," he said.

Then, sitting there, she wept, a stout blonde woman of thirty-eight with shoulder-length hair and no beauty. She wept because something was too big for her and she did not understand what it was.

He looked away. Weeping was for the purpose of hopeless mourning and lamentation, and he was bewildered by anything lesser.

"I've given you a mother's love," she wept, pounding on the table beside her, "but you're simply not the sons I dreamed about."

He looked at her with veiled eyes.

"What's the matter with you?" she cried, pounding steadily. "Always thinking of yourself—what *you're* going to do, how *you're* going to get on!"

"What has happened to me and my brother has happened," he said. "It is impossible for anyone who has not lived through it to understand. Why did it happen? Nobody can tell us. We would like to be sons to you and Perry. Our hearts are very warm toward you."

She barely heard what he said. "You're full of self-pity—that's what it is. You think no one has suffered but you."

She sat there sagging, her wet-stained eyes on Karel, as though she did not herself know what she felt about him.

He wished to have no reaction. He felt a great wave of pity, and yet he despised her.

"No," he said. "I did not mean to ask for sympathy. I was trying to find the words to explain."

She stood up distraught, beside herself, and slammed the door of the bedroom.

The child was not a simple part of the picture. The child did not ask often now for his arms, because most of the time he had something downy and yielding to his other demands—Bertha's drenched maternalism which loved him when he was a good boy, a normal boy, a cuddling little fellow. Yet the wild dreams at night, the thrashing of his legs, the moanings and occasionally the screams of his nightmares showed that something was still unsatisfied.

On one of these occasions, Bertha came, white and fierce,

brushing aside the curtain to clasp the child in her arms, to scold him, bid him be a good boy. But he looked at her with wild clouded eyes, tossed his head to be away from her and huddled against Karel.

Karel explained that patience was needed, please, let him think that nothing he does is bad, please do not discipline him sharply. I do not know what the child thinks about or remembers, but I can guess.

Bertha made it clear that she loved the child when he stood pressed against her, needing her. That was natural. But the child who grew dark-browed, struck out, spoke pertly, was his own enemy. Karel said nothing. He hated her at that moment, so he remained silent.

The nightmares increased. Through the screaming, portions of remembered things came out, things that were a part of his own grave-like, suffocating, dismembered dreams. The monstrous unblinking eye, the impression beyond pain, the disembodied shriek which did not vibrate the tranquil air—they were all like a deaf person who smiles through another's cry for help.

Marilyn came in one morning to put on her shoes and stockings with them. She dawdled, fumbling with her shoelaces unnecessarily. "What makes you yell at night?" she asked, her round marble eyes cool. "I used to yell because enormous feet came down on me. Or I got shut in a big beach umbrella and was dying."

"I don't know," Nicky said sullenly.

"Onct I dreamed I was shut in Mom's oven and roasted to death. Onct I . . ."

"Forget it," said Karel sharply. She dropped her cold scrutiny to her shoelaces and found the holes even more slowly.

Then Marilyn had a nightmare. She was a mutilated child, but she could not describe it. Her legs were gone or her arms were gone or only her head remained. A poor head, screaming on the ground with great feet nearby.

In the daytime life was normal. Karel was about to take his first examinations; the clinic report on Nicky would be delivered. But at night there was the dark sea and the two children afloat upon it.

Some nights they would float happily, dreamlessly. But it seemed as though they waited, one for the other, seeing who could endure the unnatural silence the longest. Marilyn waited on Nicky or Nicky on Marilyn. Perry could not sleep, waiting, and remembering certain things of his own. Bertha slept well but claimed that she wakened at the slightest noise. One morning a neighbor clapped a hand to her forehead and said there was nothing more terrifying than hearing a child shriek in such pain. *What was the matter?* Pain! . . . Bertha encased herself in her outrage . . . the landlord would be complaining next.

She wished Nicky to be happy. She loved him. Everyone who heard her say so believed her. Karel believed her as much as he was able . . . But she was going to take him to a doctor. Marilyn was being changed from a nice little girl into a little girl nobody would want around.

The doctor pulled out his file on Nicky and examined him carefully. He mused over his files, and said it had been decided that the child could not be fitted with arms until he had a second operation. For this he must be carefully prepared, physically and emotionally. He was a disturbed child and might need special treatment.

Bertha took him home, looking at him from her own mental distance, far away. From that time on her course was devious and depressing. She told herself it was love which impelled her, love. She loved the child very much, but there were neighbors to think of, and the child's own special, professionally supervised adjustment to life. She told her friends that the child needed very special care. The eddies spread. The centrifugal base became her home. Love was referred to increasingly.

She explained to Perry that the child must be sent away for his sake and Marilyn's. Later, when he was entirely recovered, had had his operation and his arm, then . . .

Perry looked at her long and bitterly. "This wasn't what you figured on. You can't take it."

"Who comes first?" she demanded, "your family or these boys?"

Some fellows would know all the answers, but he did not know a single one. These boys were symbols to him. More than that they represented the moment of his most profound spiritual experience. Some definition of life had come to him when he met them, and he recalled it as the one satisfying moment of his life. It remained. Nothing tangible, nothing he could hold in his hands, it had the nature of integrity. Not to defend them or to challenge what his wife was attempting assaulted a particular and irreplaceable element of his manhood.

He stood up and walked desperately up and down.

"If one goes, they'll both go, and you know it."

After a moment, she nodded.

He sat down abruptly, and put his knuckles against his eyes.

"You're a goddamn bitch," he whispered, "and you've taken my guts away from me."

This was not the time to be offended. After a while she said, "I'll go to the Committee. They'll make it easy."

The next morning Karel said he wished to speak to her.

"You'll be late for your class," she said a little uneasily.

He sat down implacably at the kitchen table. His face was pasty and his expression honed to a fine point.

"Did Nicky tell me the truth last night?"

She was not afraid of anything, of her convulsive sensations, of her rightness, as she stood pressed hard against the stove, a dish towel in her hand.

"What about?"

"He said that Perry and you intended to send him away."

They were harsh words, like an unflattering, incandescent light. She fumbled with them for a moment and then sat down opposite him to put them into a better glow.

"Since we all love Nicky, we should all want . . ." But she was not permitted to make it soft and appealing.

"You are afraid," he said. "This is something too much for you. It is pitiful that you use a child. It is better when one says frankly that something is too much for her."

What he said was quiet and almost gentle, but she was stripped, a poor fleshy woman who did not look well, ungarmented.

"We have tried to give you everything we would give our own children . . ."

"I believe that. But it was too much. Why?"

She wished to keep her voice even. "It has been expensive. We get two extra bottles of milk each day. . . ."

He pressed his hand flat against the table, and stood up abruptly. "You're a very cruel woman," he said sadly. "I—I am very sorry."

Without warning she burst into tears and she struck at him violently with the dishcloth.

"You're a troublemaker," she said. "There hasn't been any peace here since you came! And I think you're a liar. I think you're here under false pretenses! Get out of my kitchen! I asked Nicky if you were his brother—Perry had his doubts!—and he said he didn't know. *Didn't know!* You're a liar and a sneak!"

She retreated out of the kitchen, watching his face. She stood in the hallway and said hysterically, "I am going to the Committee to see your Miss Speyer. I'll tell her everything that's happened—and the things that I think—and we'll do what she says!"

He did not move, but he had turned cold. After that there was nothing but flight.

10

For half the night, he sat by the table in the room over the garage, electric with his remembrances. For the first time, he felt identified. Back there, down the road, was the farmhouse with the lamp on the checkered tablecloth and his friends—and Megan. He felt as though he had at last a name and a place and, at the same time, the anonymity which name and place confer on them who have been accepted as a part of the whole.

He felt free and weightless, his burden shared and dispensed with. He thought of the Youngs with regard and love. He wrote them a letter, there and then, on the old battered table with a dull pencil, before any of the conventional memories reasserted themselves. It was full of the affection and gratitude which Bertha craved. It was a letter they would like to have, especially Perry. It cut nothing off. The continuity which Karel loved became plain again. He would mail it from another town so they would not know his address.

The next morning as he went into the post office to fetch McVitty's mail, he met Mrs. Wright.

"Oh," she said, "I meant to tell you. I wrote to the North American Committee and a reply came a few days ago. They assure us you are bona-fide refugees. That will be one reassurance for your friends." She laughed pleasantly and nodded and went down the steps as though not expecting an answer.

Like that . . . so simple. They knew where to find him now. He remained very still. Vree, who was leaning against the post-office wall, winked at him. He stood beside Vree silently.

"People . . ." Vree said, knocking his old pipe against the wall. "Poor saps . . ."

Karel thought of his new good friends the Murrays many times during that day. He thought about Megan. In one way or another he thought about her all day. She represented something very newly discovered, a femininity which was unmistakable, full of grace and persuasion, older than he, and yet having an appearance he could admire. He felt at ease with her. He felt that commonplace events were not a mystery to her, as they were to him.

One remembers things as a whole—the people in the room last night, how they had sat, how the light had fallen on their faces, how their faces had turned toward him and turned away, how they had responded to each other. He had been very aware of these things because, as he had talked, he had wondered how they could relate themselves to what he was saying—he was acutely sensitive to that—and then he had wondered how they would have borne themselves had they been in those transports which came from all over Europe. One could not tell. That is the strange thing: one could not tell. And he thought about the low-ceilinged kitchen with the red lamp by the window and the round table with the checkered cloth. It was very reminiscent. It connected him with something remembered and loved.

He thought of Mrs. Murray, so calmly doing many things—he filled out her life, cooking and cleaning the house and caring for the chickens and preserving and hanging out wash, and then sitting to talk so responsively to whoever asked her attention. He thought of John, the withdrawn and hidden light which shone out in such flashes, warming suddenly, suddenly a man loving life dearly, wonderfully aware of something, and then withdrawing as though taken unawares. And he thought of Megan who was his friend. *Friend*—a kindling word.

McVitty looked out of the office window when a noisy car retched its way to a standstill.

"You take him," he said. "It's Roi Arnow. Don't let him sign any slips. He's got some money from guitaring last night."

Roi was the straw-headed youth, the boy with the thin skin which had looked sunburned even in the wavering lights of the Common last night, the boy who had been playing the guitar when Nicky started to sing. He said "Hi!" to Karel and stepped over the side of the car, hitching up his trousers as he went around to unscrew the gas cap.

"Boy," he said squatting down, "smell that juice going in. Fill her up. Like to hear her gurgling right to the top. How's your boss? Feelin' all right?"

Karel looked at him, smiling. "Something for nothing?"

"Naw, Something for *something*." He reached into the car and took out his guitar, tuned a string, and then struck a ringing chord and walked toward the office. He played and sang, and Karel watched smiling, but McVitty made an abrupt gesture, an impatient waving away of his hand, with no smile. Amiability was broken off with a snap. Karel saw the boy's expression change. He watched it with interest for a moment and then he dropped his eyes. The expression was raw. There was anger and humiliation so swift and apparent that it was embarrassing to observe. Without a word, the boy looked at the tabulation on the pump, and counted out the money silently into Karel's hand. Then Karel impulsively sat down on the running board and took the guitar in his hands.

"I guess one could be quite a fellow with a musical thing like this," he said warmly. "But it would take a long time to play as you did last night."

Roi put his foot on the running board and picked at his teeth.

"Sure, I'm good at it. Learned fast. I can learn anything fast."

Karel twanged at the strings once, and laughed. Roi took it away. "Like this," he said. He handed it back to Karel.

A car came up to the pump, and Roi took away the guitar and threw it into the car. "Get's you a girl. Boy, how they fall." Then he waved a thin long hand. "Want to learn?"

"Sure," said Karel good-naturedly.

"Be seein' you."

Karel said nothing to McVitty, and McVitty said nothing to him when he rang up the cash register. But as McVitty opened the door to go home for an early dinner, he observed, not unkindly, "That kid's no good. Not his fault. He's just no good."

"What's the matter with him?" asked Karel.

"Maybe the old lady beat him up too much when he was a kid. I don't know, I mind my own business. When you live in a town like this you can know too much and then you want to meddle."

Karel asked, "Why is he no good?"

McVitty stood in the door, pulling at his cap, his face phlegmatic, only his eyes keen as slate. "He doesn't work —just does odd jobs badly. *You can't be shiftless.* Gets people down on you. And what's more you've got to work in the way they think is right. Maybe he would have been a good guitar player. I sometimes wish the kid had the gumption to clear out and go playing that guitar." Since he had said more than he cared to handle, he opened the door abruptly and went out.

A good guitar player. Well, that was one goal in life . . . Karel kicked against the chair for a moment, and then he picked up one of Dr. Jarman's books. But he closed it after a few moments and sat with his cheek against his fist. It was not a good thing to have a person as quickly hurt as that boy was. What the boy wanted was plain. What McVitty wanted was clear. He sighed from his heart and kicked the chair again.

After a while he saw Dr. Jarman drive up. The doctor parked to one side and came into the office. He sat in McVitty's swivel chair. He examined the checks on the desk through his bifocals, swung around to see what the illustrations for August and September were on the calendar, peered intently through the window as Karel waited on a motorist, said, "This is a hell of a place for a conversation. Sit down. This is what I've been thinking about. That Agnes Stillwell—she's working like the devil to raise money. Damnedest woman I ever knew. Town always acts like she was a joke, but I notice they give when she whistles. She's a moral woman. Ever notice that? I just did. I just realized that's what she is—a moral woman, and maybe you pay moral women to stay around for the looks of the thing." He reflected on this and then he laughed shortly as though pleased. "Be that as it may, I hear things. I hear who she's calling up and who she's nailing to their front door. She's saying the little boy needs an arm, and, you know, I honestly believe she doesn't hear when they turn her down. She goes right on talking. It's only when they say Yes that she lets them go. Well, I've been thinking. I don't think they give just to get rid of her. I think something happens. It sounds idiotic, but most human behavior sounds idiotic to me."

He paused for a long time, flipped again through McVitty's checks and paid bills, then looked hard at Karel. "I'll operate on the little boy immediately, and then we'll know exactly where we stand and be all ready when she gets her job done."

Karel felt no struggle, no debilitating moments of emotion. He did not even say Thank you. He searched for words, that is all. At length, he said, "I think that is right. And I will pay you myself to begin with—I have saved twenty dollars."

"Hell," said the doctor softly, "I wouldn't do this for money."

This was a climax. This was a great yearning which was drawing to a close. The child and Karel were one and the same. He knew this, and he knew that it was not good, and, in a fashion, he sensed that if the child were liberated thus far, then his own attachment would be shaken. He wished the child to be whole, and yet whole, the child would not need him so much. And, not needed, there was insecurity.

Yet this was exactly why he had come to America—to find Mrs. Stillwell, to find Dr. Jarman, to find something of the assured faith which is life. For one does not make faith out of wretchedness. One makes faith out of something greater than the thing which confronts him.

When he had locked the door of the garage, he had gone down the road, beating at the grass with a stick, knowing that he could not sit still or listen to Nicky's talk when he returned with Vree. He walked because he felt a terrible swelling restlessness.

He came to Mrs. Murray's house as he half-expected to do. He did not go in. He stood and looked down the sloping meadows into the valley and on toward the hills. The restlessness beat against this strange wall of wide meadows and rolling hills. They knew nothing, they guessed nothing, they *were*. He beat at the grass, but he could not take his eyes from the sloping meadow, the valley, the hills.

Mrs. Murray called him from the house. She was standing in the kitchen door in a blue apron waving to him. He went toward her slowly. The setting sun made the trees on the brow of the hill wonderfully luminous.

She greeted him smilingly. Her young very blue eyes and the vivacity of her face were disarming. She spoke warmly and casually as though they were old friends, and they stood for a few minutes talking in the warm evening light. Then she went in and brought out some glasses of fruit juice, and they sat on the stoop. Silence was fine. It was rich, filled with tenderness.

"This doesn't seem to end a day, does it?" she said quietly. "It seems more like a new day beginning."

He said suddenly, "The doctor is going to operate on Nicky, and Mrs. Stillwell is going to buy him his arm."

There it was, a few words, tangible and comprehensive.

"Oh," she said, and her face slowly lighted, "I'm so glad."

He went on stiffly after a moment. "It will make a great change. It's very fine. He deserves it."

She continued to smile at him for the news had pleased her very much, and she put her hand on his arm. "Now this town will seem like home. This means a lot to me, after what you told us last night. This'll be home, and you have friends and affection."

"Yes." He smiled. He could not talk of it any more. It had already churned and tossed him enough. "Some smoke is going up in the valley."

"No, it is mist. It is very pretty to watch when the trees

seem to hang suspended in the mist. It's also very pretty in the heat of the day when there's a kind of shimmer and everything looks lighted in the dead center. You'll see. You'll be staying!"

He said warmly, "This is your familiar place—from a child?"

"Oh, yes. I've been to Boston four times and once to New York."

His home came back to him with sudden poignancy—the heavy Bohemian furniture, the lace curtains at the windows, the porcelain stove.

"And your father lived here?" he went on, for there was something he wished to fix in his mind—what it might have been to remain and grow up and rear a family in the town of his childhood, where names were familiar, where things were accepted and assimilated naturally.

"Yes," she said, "and my grandfather."

"And they all looked at this same view?"

"Nothing much changes. I expect they did." She sipped at her fruit juice and took a cookie from the plate between them.

This was the familiar place of friends. He wished to know about them. He liked her dog who raked a little at the path and then, his nose twitching, left well enough alone; he liked the stirring of the lower branches of the lilac bush by bees or drifting flies, the rustlings of the tall grass, mole or mouse or bird, and the stately undulation of a caterpillar from the place of rustlings across the dusty path.

She said easily, "John's father once painted a view on the side of that barn which showed the valley and the hills and the trees which he would have liked to see closer up."

"That barn?"

"Yes. But he painted in water color, and after a while the rain washed it away."

"Was he an artist?"

"Oh, no. But he was not a very good farmer. The village said he was an oddity. It always seemed to me he was simply unsettled, that he wanted more things than his environment allowed. It seemed fine to me that he did not sit and mope. When he was hard-pressed he never talked about it. I did not know what went on in his mind. I would see him go out into the barn and after a time come out with a ladder and pails—and sometimes the snow was on the ground—and I would know that this was not the time he wanted his family. Often I've sat in the window and watched him painting things that he had in his mind—a winding river in thick foliage, or strange battlements on a hill, or the things he would like to see in our meadow. I enjoyed watching him. But no one ever talked about it afterwards. We knew it was there, we looked at it, for it would be hard not to see that barn staring you in the face. I think we went where the painting led us, but we never spoke about it. And by the time the spring or the autumn or the winter came, it would be almost too faint to see."

"That is an oddity?" Karel reflected.

"Well," she said, "a name must be given to everything. But I believe that something like oddity gives us our texture. You—your texture is quite different from John's, let's say."

When she did not continue, he said, "Is he your only son?" and she nodded.

He felt suddenly diffident. He would have liked to ask her about her son, he would have liked to tell her about his family, but he did not know how to begin.

She said, "John is no farmer, any more than his father was. He is growing restless already. He tells me he is leaving when the crops are in."

"Then his wife—my friend . . ."

She hesitated. "Oh, you will always have friends."

He asked thoughtfully, "If John is unhappy—with a nice wife and a home—are others, with the same things, unhappy?" It was not as naïve a question as it sounded. He had held normality in front of him like a bright sun, and yet its component parts were very elusive.

Mrs. Murray's sun-weathered face crumpled into little lines of merriment. "Oh, I doubt if there are more than two happy people in this village. And this village—would you say it was different from any other village in the world?"

He was startled. "I would not know how to answer that." He was silent for a moment and then he said suddenly, "I want a home and a wife and children . . ."

"Do you now? Well, I daresay you'll have them."

"Then one like me would be able to say, This is why I stayed alive."

"You will say it for other reasons than that."

He looked at her obliquely and smiled a little. "Will I? I suppose so." Then, "John has no children?"

"No." She stooped down suddenly and pulled out some weeds from between the marigolds. She appeared to be studying how to phrase her thought. "War has broken up old ways of thinking and behaving. It's a crisis, and it brings a shock, and many like John struggle to find out where they belong."

"The war in Europe?" Even though he had seen Perry Young in uniform and had lived with the American Army, he could not accustom himself to thinking of Americans as a part of the thing he had known. She nodded. He lost himself in contemplation of the squares and circles he was tracing with his heel.

She was saying, "And for Megan it may be so too. I've known Megan since she and John were in college, and her life before that and since then has been broken. She questions too but she seems to find some sort of answer. John doesn't seem to find them."

She was silent for some time. There seemed an incongruity between her words and the weathered barns, the Biblical cows, the ruminative fields.

"It is very hard to know what these times mean. To me it seems to mean that people have got to begin to understand what they owe to each other. How else will all of you live together? Megan or John or you or anyone?"

"I ask that question," he replied gravely.

"Well," she said, "just so long as you're not smug or running away, there's hope for you. My father read Emerson, not the Bible. He quoted so often that I remember it well: 'Every true man is a cause, a country, and an age; requires infinite spaces and numbers and time fully to accomplish his design.' Take a person like John. I think he will find what that means, and then he'll be more satisfied. *Infinite*. It does not all have to be done at one time."

He smiled at her. "But I am impatient too."

She looked at him intently, smiling. "Well, then, you must quiet the impatience. Women are the realists in such matters."

"Men or women," he said ingenuously, "I do not know the difference."

She laughed. "It is just that women have not been lords and masters for ten thousand years. It gives us a different point of view. I think we don't try to find so many excuses."

He looked at her, and he continued to regard her reflectively, as she sat on the wooden step with the dark square of the door framing her.

She handed him the plate of cookies. "I do not know why we need shocks. It seems as though we choose it that way. Men do especially." She thought about this for a moment. "Now will you have some more fruit juice?"

"No, thank you. I must go home and give Nicky his dinner."

"Bring him here tomorrow. Let him stay here any time."

"Oh, he would like that."

"Yes," she said looking at him with her bright eyes, "he knows that he's welcome here."

He hesitated for a moment. "Your daughter-in-law said she wanted to be friends. Did she mean it?"

"Oh, yes. She meant it very sincerely. She will be a good friend."

He hesitated again. "And your son . . . ?"

"I imagine he is a little afraid of you. You might involve him in something—into feeling something he doesn't want. Not at this time."

He said nothing for a moment, and then he asked, "Does your son love his wife?"

"I think so."

He had come full circle, and he asked his deeply centered question again. "Then why should he be unhappy?"

She sighed and smiled a little. She picked up the empty plate and stood the two empty glasses on it, and stood looking down the meadow toward the river glinting in the sun. "You'll have to ask him. I couldn't tell you."

He had gone to talk about the child. But the child had been somewhat diminished. For the first time, the child was less than the full thing. If the operation was not successful, and the child did not have his new arm, then what would they do? What would their objectives become? He wanted normality and Nicky wanted to be indistinguishable from every other child—they wanted the same thing. But what was it? An arm—and then what?

By the side of the road he saw a rabbit which had been hit by a car. Its ears twitched, its dark oval eyes struggled with fear to lift itself and be away. He kneeled down beside it and felt of the broken leg, and then he took out his handkerchief to tie the bone into place. It was within the frame of reality that one had to find his greatest satisfaction, but what reality was was not always very clear.

The child was deeply moved by the plight of the rabbit. He sat on his haunches and stared at him. He asked to touch the rabbit's fur, and Karel held the animal to his cheek. He insisted that the rabbit must rest on the table before them as they ate their dinner, and that it must have its lettuce as Nicky had his meatball. He wanted to know why it ate as it did, and if it would lose its leg and if a rabbit had the same thoughts as a cat, and if it was in pain . . . in pain . . . such as a child remembers.

Karel answered as best he could. Then he undressed the child and brushed his teeth and said the prayer which his mother had said for him. The rabbit was bedded close to the child's bed, and the little cat slept at his feet.

When he wakened the next morning, and saw the child, his head dangling over the side of the bed toward the rabbit, the sunlight shining through the lace curtains Mrs. McVitty had hung at their windows, he thought this could be his home, his family, his town. Each piece could fit together. He lay there looking at a patch of sunlight on the ceiling. His patch of sunlight. His road with his sound of cars upon it. His village wakeful and stirring. The little cat was scratching herself and yawning widely. The rabbit was quiet. The child lifted his head and looked at Karel.

"It's a very good thing the rabbit found you," he said. "He's feeling much better."

"Good. Tell him good morning for me."

The child fixed himself to a place like a suction. There were no delicate balancings, no *this* against *that*. Nor for me, after this, Karel said to himself.

When he went to the post office for McVitty's mail, he found a letter for himself. His heart turned over. It was from Miss Speyer of the North American Committee. She said she was glad to find out where he was, through Mrs. Wright; that she wanted him to know that the Committee was his friend and wished him the greatest success, and that if he needed help within the next few months to let her know. And give Nicky her love.

So simple. No need to have run away. His hand shook as he put the letter back in its envelope. He went, unseeing, down the steps and up the street. The fear that had been so large . . . The tears filled his eyes.

11

Roi steamed up that day. He poured water into his radiator as Karel waited on a customer. He helped himself to the Free Air. Then as Karel stood folding the money he had been paid, Roi asked, "Did you really mean you'd like to learn the guitar?"

Perhaps one merely imagined that there was something desperately wistful in the way he tossed out the words. But since Karel wanted the company of his own age, his own wistfulness was caught and held by it.

"Yes," he said. "How much?"

"Three bucks for six lessons. Or free!"

"I've got two dollars," Karel said.

"Okay. Want me to come here?"

Since McVitty did not like the boy, Karel said no, he would come to his house. Roi jumped into his car and opened the cut-out and roared down the road.

At noon Karel took Nicky to Dr. Jarman's where the child had a glass of milk and a sandwich, and the doctor told him matter-of-factly about the operation, which he accepted matter-of-factly. He told the doctor about the rabbit and asked if the rabbit's leg hurt. Then he fell into silence, but it seemed impassive silence.

So that great step was taken. Mrs. Stillwell had been notified and was enthusiastic. Mrs. Dunn had contributed ten dollars more, and she thought they could give a concert and raise the rest.

The day was metallic hot; to touch the gas pump was an ordeal. When a car drove up, Karel looked at the driver, for many faces were becoming familiar. The girl said Hello, but for a moment he did not remember her. Then she said, "I'm Julie Wright."

He was pleased to see her. As he stood alone at the back of the car, he thought about the luncheon at her mother's, and tried to remember her. Something vague was in his own memory, that was all. But this girl was of his age. He liked the thought. When he came back to the side of the car, he looked at her.

She was pretty. Her hair was yellow and drawn away from her face by a barrette. Her complexion was fair. She was small and slender. But she possessed something more which he did not identify—one of those faces of deceptive delicacy, the nose short and very straight, the mouth small and sensitive, all the planes of her face unsweeping and flat to the small whorled ears. A deceptive delicacy because, in spite of all that, and the pale bloom of complexion and pale blue of eyes, there was a tensility about her that sprang from the quick movements of her head and the assured springy movements of her body and from the clear swift way she spoke.

She said to him, "You've never come for a swim. Don't you want to?"

"Oh, yes," he said. "Yes, certainly. Thank you very much."

"When are you coming?"

He looked at her with smiling intentness. "Tomorrow—Sunday?"

"That's good. Come early."

Yes, yes indeed—this was his place, and he belonged here, and such things demonstrated it.

That night the child put his face against the rabbit's fur.

"It hurts, it hurts, it hurts," he whispered. "His leg hurts. My arm hurts. They will cut it off?"

"Cut what off?" Karel asked kneeling beside him.

"His leg. It hurts."

That night he shrieked in his sleep, a thin, piercing cry that went out over the dark road to shake neighbors from their sleep. Karel sat for an hour holding him in his arms. The child pressed against him, saying, "Mama, Mama, Mama," again and again.

The next day Vree took the child and Tommy to hunt for blackberries.

For Karel to be sitting on a springboard swinging his bare legs toward the water, observing Julie's bare brown legs as he did so, was to be aware of a place and a circumstance and a remoteness and a hereness, which was wholly unreal and yet an unreality he would not willingly exchange for the real. He was a boy and yet he had not lived as a boy, and the desire to live as a boy had many anomalies. He wished to sit here in the hot sun, gripping the recognizable shape and hardness of the planks, waiting for something out of the unfamiliar to make the way plain. Every part of him, the roots of his hair, his skin, his listening, his sense of touch, his thoughts, his desire to speak, were aware of this girl, yet he could not look at her or communicate readily with her.

His thoughts kept going to Megan with whom he had not felt this constraint. They were a new thing in his life, these girl-women who moved with such apparent ease through a clear and intelligent world. Megan was older. He was an old man. Between them there was an understandable degree of giving and assurance. With Julie, he did not know what to say.

Julie took the initiative. In a soft eager way she asked questions. She found he could not swim, he could not dance, he could not play tennis, he was not going to college. After the most delicate pause in her mind, she probed further. He was thoughtful, he was different, he was grown-up. Because she was gratefully surprised by many things and endlessly curious and most insatiable to learn, and because she wanted a grown-up young man—not college juniors or football heroes—in her life, this pleased her.

She too fell silent. Her legs swung slower and slower. It was pleasant in the hot sun. It melted through and around, it melted together. It was more communicable than words. She turned on her stomach and lay with her closed eyes toward him.

"*I'll* teach you to swim," she said drowsily.

He did not answer, and she opened her eyes to see if he had heard. He was leaning forward and gazing into the water, and he looked very happy. She pushed herself to her feet and jumped off the board. She demonstrated the basic positions and swam slowly so that he might see the positions of arms, legs and head. Then she stood breast-deep and told him to imitate her. He lowered himself from the board. His mouth filled with water, his legs sank. She shouted at him and he shouted back, and she swam in a circle and dove under him, and both were highly pleased with the complicated threshing and eluding and dexterity required.

At length she climbed upon the pier exhausted, and kicked water at him as he stood with his arms spread out on the surface of the pool. They knew each other now very well. There was no need to bridge something complicated and alien. Everything was open and outgoing. Mrs. Wright, strolling down in due time from the house, a book closed over her index finger, said, "Are you having a nice time?" and they said, "Oh, yes!" together.

Mrs. Wright stood for a few minutes pleasantly surveying them, and they stood fixed in their positions as though compelled to demonstrate the quality of their good time. No one stirred. Then Mrs. Wright turned and said, "When you're hot enough come up to the house for something cool to drink," and went up the sloping lawn, an erect slender figure who stooped once to pull up something from the grass.

He came out of the water and sat on the board. After a few moments, she said, "If you don't go to college, what will you do?"

"I will be a doctor."

"But doctors have to go to medical college."

"I will go anywhere I have to go to find out what I need."

She reflected for a moment. She looked very pretty, pale-brown and gold, her round little breasts and small curved hips disarmingly plain in her white suit. "Yes. You're very intense. Why do you feel that way?"

He looked at her quickly. "Do you not feel intensely?"

She shrugged her small shoulders slightly. "It seems as though everything is set. I'd like to be an archeologist. But I don't feel intensely about it. And I don't think anything will come of it."

"Your father thinks a girl should do so-and-so?"

"I suppose, a little."

He looked at her again. "That is foolish. You should tell him so."

She laughed a little. "Tell him what? He'd like me to do what I want."

"Then why do you not?" He was frowning.

"Because I don't know . . ."

She wished that she could say the formless things which were in her heart and he wished that he could talk. Emotions, intuitions churned inside them and failed to find words. Because he did not look at her or understand the key words which she offered, he was different.

She sat there so small and pretty, eighteen nearly nineteen, all her outer needs satisfied, and yet nothing genuinely fulfilled—neither individuality nor emotion nor passion nor intuition. Why? Some taste, some delicacy, some fear could not find the answer. It was very fine to read books, it was very fine to have vicarious experiences. It gave one a contact with reality, and sometimes that was altogether sufficient. Quite sufficient, in fact, if the confinements were familiar and the behavior fixed.

He knew what he craved—prettiness and softness, easement of mind and spirit in an ordered and recognized world. It had relevance and logic. It answered his questions of neither youth nor age, it answered the deep and illimitable longing, the loneliness, *I want, I want,* and there was a strength in the wanting which wrested the desire into conformity. He could not measure how deeply he was aware of this girl. *A girl.* It was a fact which had no meaning and every meaning. He looked at her, turning his head very slightly, and his heart dissolved. Everything about her was lovely to him, her hair drawn smoothly back so that the sweep of her face was uninterrupted, the good health of her skin—and of this he was especially aware—the exact color and shape of her mouth, the shape of her arms and legs and body, with no heavy fleshy parts, all supple and womanly, the small nails well cared for—all healthy, normal, well-proportioned, all *right.*

She bore no relation whatever to the things he had known or the places he had been. With Megan there was a relation in thought, an awareness which bridged their separate worlds. It was to Megan he had talked the other night; the others had merely been present. With Julie, he had only the impulse to please, to admire, to start forth from this moment. A girl satisfied a deep submerged longing for grace. That was a beginning and end.

They talked for a while longer. They exchanged commonplace words and thoughts. He thought of her so intensely that he did not give her a name. She was she, something in his own heart and mind. He answered diffidently when she asked if he would like to go to the house, and he walked silently beside her up the lawn, listening to her voice but listening to nothing, confused, held in the moment.

He greeted her parents and he drank lemonade, and he smiled as he answered questions, but all the while he thought it was a marvel and very strange . . . there was Julie but who was Julie? And here he was and between them sat nobody—nothing—but their own discovery of each other.

Of course he was mistaken when he said that. The parents *were* somebody, very impressive in the somethingness of their lives.

Her father said, "Nice boy," after he had gone, and her mother said, "Yes, very nice," but behind the reading of the newspaper and the novel moved the slow wash of a thing as strong as the tides—how Mr. and Mrs. Wright had been raised, what they believed in, what position their parents and their own efforts had given them, what convictions, what expectations.

They sat in the late afternoon on the lawn in the lovely New England sunlight with the pool at their feet, and they found it impossible to open their minds to anything as catastrophic as a strange boy from eastern Europe with the mark of hell upon him. One is always polite and kind; their hearts were naturally good, but in the presence of the thing which is fundamentally alien, one must sit very quiet, very estranged, very watchful.

Julie wandered back to the edge of the pool and sat down on the springboard. She was aware of many things, but when your deeper experiences are vicarious, you are afraid to give a name to the sensed. You might be wrong, and there would be no one to tell you.

He could not go home. He went and sat in the meadow above the Murray farm. There was no future, no hour-from-now. There was only an infinite vaporous churning irrepressible *now* without form out of which could emerge nothing or all the world.

He did not ask if the thing which emerged would be recognizable. He did not ask anything. He wanted and, by wanting, he made real.

He sat in the meadow stripping the bark from a broken branch. He raked spirals and whorls on the ground with a sharp stone. He stared for a long time at a bird hopping from branch to branch on a bush. At length he lay down, his arm across his eyes, and remained very still. In time the churning, the passion inside him subsided.

Ants crawled over his hands. In time things would be clear. Now he merely wanted—he did not love or fear or plan. He merely wanted.

After a time, the feeling gave place to thought. He wondered suddenly what Julie thought about him. He went cold. He tried to imagine his appearance, his words and voice. He was a man who had been an adolescent without adolescence, a boy whose voice had changed without notice being taken of it.

He brushed off his clothes thoughtfully. Within him was a sudden clamorous blubbering dispossessed cry. He wanted. And he wanted to give. The fear and the blackness would be terrible if he were denied it. . . . All the fear and all the blackness against which the spirit had tried to arm itself.

Nicky climbed onto his lap, and he held the child tightly, hiding his face against Nicky's hair.

He listened to Nicky's account of the afternoon with Vree. Vree had been teaching Tommy and him to distinguish the barks of trees, opening a world in which a child might move with authority. It would give him a place with other children, it would minimize his strangeness and their curiosity.

Vree had told them stories of Billy, his kerosene stove. Billy was very wise, but now and then he grew frisky. He went with Vree on a camping trip once, and had misbehaved badly, afraid of the dark, refusing to give any light, refusing to cook the food. "Tommy says my rabbit is the best rabbit he's seen. He says even if its leg is cut off, it will be the best rabbit, better than any boy's in the town."

Tommy linked him with the commonplace world. Tommy gave him arms and a place. Tommy was the reciprocal. Julie . . . Julie . . .

After supper he told Nicky they would go down to Roi's. His restlessness still drove him in his search for someone his own age. How he yearned for the thing which was familiar to Roi—whatever it was, whatever it was that led him effortlessly from day to day in a world of small identities.

They went down into the lower part of town, across the little river where houses rented for $15 a month and the plumbing was inadequate. But here was a soft lush beauty and nice old forgotten houses, and the lilac hedges were as tall here as in the other section of town. Roi's house had not been painted for a long time, and there was a broken step going up to the stoop. Roi threw open the door angrily, but his face broke into pleasure, a sudden childlike sunniness as though the punishment was over, the party at hand. He paid no attention to Nicky, but he brought Karel into the house as though he had been long overdue.

It was a house with a musty smell. That, and a tired age pervaded it. A 1936 calendar hung on the wall near the wood heater and it seemed to indicate that apathy had gained the upper hand. The harsh single light in the ceiling made Karel blink and it seemed to him that something cold was in the house, and he grew uneasy as a child is uneasy.

Roi sat astride a chair. He offered cigarettes. He jumped up and fetched two cans of beer. Karel said he had come for a guitar lesson, and Roi put his fingers over his mouth and beat out a cry.

Nicky sat with large angry eyes. It was hard for him to sit at one side and be ignored. Roi was, for a moment, overwhelmed by the unexpected demands of his role. He kidded, he played wildly on the guitar, he made the rocking chair in which he was sitting circle and gyrate. He called Karel names of cheerful obscenity, and then, without warning, he settled down to demonstrate a masterful chord.

After a time, Karel took the guitar, placed his fingers as he was told and, at length, ventured an unsteady chord. Nicky wept and struck his shoulder against Karel's arm. An old woman with a dishcloth and a plate in her hand came to the door on silent carpet slippers and looked in. Karel lifted Nicky onto a sofa by the window. Roi looked at him sullenly, and said harshly to Karel, "Come on. You got fifty cents worth of lesson to use up."

Karel experimented for a little longer, but the pleasure had gone. In his heart he knew that he did not care whether he played a guitar or not. He had come seeking something different, and although Nicky troubled his conscience, he pressed toward the thing he desired.

"If I wished to learn how to dance, what would be the best way to learn?"

"Get a girl," said Roi crisply.

Karel hesitated. "I have a girl," he answered, his voice clutching at him.

Roi paused for only a moment, looking at him through narrowed slits of pale eyes. Then his voice rose. "Well, what's stopping you? Why don't you get busy? What are you waiting for?"

Karel made an effort to answer. He wished to answer in an acceptable way but he was not familiar with the language Roi used.

Roi was stimulated and sure of himself. "What's her name? Boy! Maybe I can give you the low-down!"

Julie . . . and what would that say to Roi? He became embarrassed and withdrawn. He had thought it was he who wished to be with Roi. Now he realized that it was Roi who wished to be with him. The aloneness deepened, for he wished to talk about his girl, but not to Roi.

Roi switched on the radio so loudly that he had to shout above it.

"You get you your girl and I'll get me mine, and we'll blow out some fuses!"

Nicky was pleased with the sound of the radio and went over to stand near it. The old woman appeared again in the doorway, shouting, "Turn down that thing! What do you want to do—blow us out the window?"

Roi made a rude dismissing gesture with his hand, but he turned down the volume. The old woman remained in the doorway eyeing Karel.

"Evening," she said.

Karel stood up and bowed slightly. She had a closed face, brown eyes which in their youth might have had warmth. Now there was a smell and a look of mustiness about her, the smell and look of the house. Roi sat down by the radio and sang and played the music which came over the air. The old woman looked at him scornfully, looked again at Karel. Then she saw Nicky and came into the room. After a moment she marched to the radio and switched it off. Roi cried out angrily, but she said, "What's the matter with that child? Where'd he come from?"

The cry was such an old one that Karel responded automatically. He went to Nicky and lifted him up in his arms and said that they had to go.

Roi cried, "Shut up, Grandma!" and his face was white. "Don't go—don't go!"

There was sudden wildness and despair in the sun-reddened face and the pale eyes, and his long loose fingers searched for something to hold to—the back of a chair, the neck of his guitar, the can of beer.

All this stripped something away from Karel. In the normal contented world around him was fear and loneliness —the Youngs, the doctor, Mrs. Murray's son and daughter-in-law, Roi, Mrs. Stillwell. Only Mrs. Murray and Julie did not seem to toss and seek in this way—and in a vague true fashion he knew that, in reality, when all was plumbed and understood, he too was free in spite of the stir and commotion which beset him.

The turmoil within him subsided. He felt an odd detachment.

Roi shouted at his grandmother, "Get out!" and to Karel, "Sit down! I'll get some more beer!"

Karel said, "No. The child must go to bed." And then he said, "But I will come back. I'll come back sometime soon for a second lesson."

"You'll make a great guitar player!" Roi cried. "You've got class! Boy, what class!"

As Karel went down the road, he heard the radio suddenly tearing up the silence, and then abruptly cut off.

Roi came the next day and leaned against the side of the garage for an hour, smoking and joking and occasionally laughing loudly, although observing a form of deference toward George McVitty.

Karel did not know how to joke with Roi. What Roi talked about meant very little to him, yet Roi standing there in the sunlight, because he wanted to be near him, because some things were understood without exchange when the age is the same, meant a kind of comfort. When Roi finally went away he urged Karel to get his girl and come on a party that night. . . . Julie, whom he thought about with a passionate and exclusive intentness but could make no move, even if his life depended on it, to see again . . . Karel shook his head and laughed and took refuge behind a newly arrived car.

The next day, Roi came again. He stood and joked and smoked cigarettes, and then, because no one had much to say in reply, he disappeared up the stairs. After a time, Karel followed him, wondering.

Roi was sprawled on the bed, his guitar against his chest, teaching Nicky line by line a nasty song. There was no visible love or misplaced kindness in the action, but Nicky, insatiable, was not aware of this. The radio maintained a cacophony at odds with the song.

Karel drank a glass of water and he washed his hands. Then he said to Roi, "Come along," and to Nicky, "Come along. Tommy is waiting."

Roi returned for a time each day, and he would jerk his thumb and say, "Okay?"

When he went upstairs he would turn on the radio, put his guitar against his chest and teach Nicky new lines of a hillbilly song. It was all a mechanical action, wily and lonely, but the child took, with no misgivings.

At no place did the jagged ends fit together. McVitty

who had been plainly uneasy, who frowned whenever he saw Roi, said one day to Karel, "Has that loafer gotten to be a friend of yours?"

Karel hesitated. The hesitation restored McVitty's diffidence. They were both silent, but the silence was edgy. Karel wished to answer "Yes," but he could not, and McVitty did not repeat the question.

Karel, lying on his back under a car, thought of Roi in the German camp. He imagined him arriving with his guitar and his cocky ways, and being broken and crumbled. He thought that if *he* had come with only an old guitar and a harsh grandmother and a musty house to remember he might not have considered life so desirable.

The next time Roi came, he felt awkward, and Roi also lounged awkwardly. McVitty came out and stood in the door of the office and said, "Why don't you get a job? Your grandma could stand some help."

Roi muttered an answer and fumbled for a cigarette and did not find one. There he stood, helpless, his hands idle and fumbling. McVitty stood silently for a moment longer and then turned back into the office. Karel, sitting on his heels as he replaced an inner tube, did not look at Roi. He hated the moment.

After a time, Roi said sullenly, "Coming for your next lesson?" and Karel said Friday night, and they lifted their hands in brief farewells.

McVitty came to stand in the door again as Roi went down the road.

"The kid's no good," he said half-apologetically. "I don't like him hanging around here." Karel did not answer, and McVitty said musingly. "Don't see how it can help you, knowing him. That's a bad family, shiftless." He turned to go in. "The old woman's not bad. Just mean. But you're a nice fellow. Don't waste your time."

Karel nodded and smiled but he did not really answer. He went upstairs later and found Vree reading to Nicky. He was raising his voice above the radio, and Nicky was sitting close to him so that he could hear. Something sick and angry seized Karel. He turned off the radio furiously. Nicky screamed at him in Czech, and kicked him, because he himself could not turn it on again. It was a curious inchoate rage which seized them both, and Vree sat by, with the book on his lap, his knees together, his head bowed over it, but his eyes attentive.

Karel went past Nicky and flung himself on the bed, and Nicky followed him, kicking against the bed since he could not reach Karel, and building his rage higher and higher. Karel looked at him with the dark hot containment of dismay, and Vree at length called Nicky and picked him up as the fury exhausted him.

Vree said nothing to Karel. Holding the child in his arms, he looked at Karel impassively. Karel said after a time, "There is no quiet. Everyone is afraid of silence. And these things—this blaring and blaring and shabbiness and lying—rots you away. Don't you hear it?"

Vree did not answer, and the balefulness of the child's eyes ripened into blackness.

"Can't you hear it?" Karel demanded. "That blaring says people are idiots."

Vree said easily, "Provided you get a good slogan you can sell anything. Just don't knock yourself out over it."

"But Nicky is growing so that he cannot bear silence. He'll get like Roi."

Vree said, "He's lonely."

"I am alone. You are alone. Is loneliness so terrible?"

Vree did not answer immediately. After a while he said, "You're talking foolishness."

Karel banged his fist against the wall. He continued to

beat against the wall with the flat of his hand. Then he said softly, "Why do people hate Roi? Nothing will keep them from hating me if they hate him."

Vree laughed a little. "Oh—hate . . ." A wide smile, without jollity, remained fixed on his face. "They don't hate Roi. They've just got to have a name for their confusion about him. Otherwise they'd have to help make a man of him. They say he comes from a family of bums. So he's a bum. Hallelujah!"

Karel's hand still beat against the wall, his eyes were closed.

"I am hungry," Nicky said carefully to Vree. Vree stroked his little rump absently, and after a moment he went to the icebox and laid out food which he saw there. He looked at cans on the shelf, and he selected and combined and lit the stove, all in silence. Nicky stood by watching him for a moment, the preternaturally vivid face tensed to each movement. Then he glanced at Karel, lying very quiet, the open palm of his hand against the wall. He drew forward a chair with his foot and sat down. He watched Vree intently, and then he turned to look with half-lowered eyes at Karel. After a time, Vree poured out a glass of milk and said, "Food's on."

Karel sat silently at the table, and Nicky whispered to Vree. At length Karel broke the silence.

"There are no in-betweens. You either hit a man or you do not. You either help him or you abandon him." He added reflectively, "There is no way of being just a little bit kind or a little bit killed."

"That's something you had to learn," Vree said. Later he added, "Well, I learned it too. And there may be a way Roi will learn it. Maybe."

Karel had nothing more to say. He had withdrawn. Vree opened a can of peaches, and Nicky looked from one to the other to see who would feed him. He did not intend to do without his peaches. Vree sat down and poured himself more coffee, and reached for a spoon to feed Nicky his peach.

"I used to think a black skin had the most misery. I learned from you that's not necessarily right. They tried to break you one way, they tried to break me another way. They? Who are they?" He pondered and snorted at his question. "I went to school in a one-room building. I knew everybody. It used to be when I saw my old school fellows riding around as the school principal and the president of the bank and the real-estate dealer, I'd call them mister. It set things right for them. They understood that. But it didn't set right on me; they all called me Vree. So one day I just began calling them by their first names in public. It was a big rebellion, and I felt better."

Nicky wished another peach, and Karel fed it to him.

Vree said, "That rebellion came from a lonely thing. They tried to pull my self-respect away from me over and over again, the way they tried to kill you. You get humiliated over and over, and then you finally discover its phony name, and it don't hurt near so much any more. All that hurts is when you're fooled. I don't feel ignorant fear toward anyone. But I did till I saw old George Dillon afraid he might have to ask me to dinner one night. He was so pitiful . . . I've been sort of fond of him ever since."

Karel fed Nicky the last bit of peach and wiped his mouth.

"I wish to be like everyone else," Karel said very low. "Then there is some reconciliation."

Vree looked at him for some time, his eyes warm, his mustache upturned a little. "Reconcile what? You *are* different. Better be glad."

"I do not wish to be different," Karel said passionately.

"I wish only for people to see why this-and-this makes life worth living, and treating you and Roi and . . ." He stopped.

Nicky stood up slowly, and stood by Vree. He said softly, almost in tears, "I wish *someone* would kiss me."

Karel looked at the child. Surely there was reconciliation. Surely the conflict could not be so great in the minds of so many.

12

At mail time, Karel met Dr. Jarman. It was raining hard and they stood under the portico of the post office watching the fine streams of water pouring past them. Many people, crowding under the shelter, spoke to Karel. He was aware of that suddenly. Miss Purvis was there, and Mrs. Ewing, and Mr. Crain, the chairman of the school board, and there were others who nodded in a friendly way, and made a joke in the lexicon of the village which they assumed that he understood. He did not understand the jokes, but he laughed. Evidently they no longer considered him a stranger.

"The operating room's reserved for Thursday at 10 A.M.," the doctor said abruptly. "How's the boy taking it?"

"He does not talk about it," Karel said. "I do not think he understands very much except that you are going to do something for him."

The doctor grunted. Mrs. Stillwell honked the horn of her car and motioned to Karel. He ran through the rain to her, and she said if he would get her mail, she would drive him to the garage. She motioned to the doctor who ran to the opened door.

When Karel returned, the doctor was saying ". . . therapy and exercises. I've found out what that arm will cost."

She nodded jerkily and, as she threw in the clutch and jerked the car forward, she said in her high-pitched monotone, "People seem to think in summer it's an effort to help others. Or they say they've got their own charities to take care of. Their church needs money, or they say, 'Why don't we help our own first?' I tell them we've got to always be thinking of others, always, always."

"Are you going to finish this job, Agnes?"

"People are so hedgy."

"How much have you got?"

"Oh, there'll be money."

"Whose? Roscoe's?"

She chose not to hear. "Even half—that would help the little boy, wouldn't it, Lem?"

He was silent for a moment, and then he said in a carefully chopped-out voice, "Let me tell you something, Agnes. I think you're congenitally unable to finish a thing. Did you hear me? Don't turn off that hearing-battery! You're a fine woman. You're sick to death of the sluggishness of this town. You're always trying to stir it up, but you don't know how to do it, and you make people mad, and you don't see why they get mad. And then you're left to finish alone or in failure. You've seen cause and effect only so far."

He paused and glanced at her. Her face was impassive. Her neck was stretched so that she could see over the steering wheel. He went on grimly, and Karel, sitting in the back seat, was raked with coldness going down the narrow tunnel of this world.

"But you're not dealing with an abstraction now. You've got boys who are looking to you to prove something. That bigger boy, that Karel, knows life better than you or I, but he still needs to be proved right, find a real life, and, by

God, you can't let him down by a mishmash of do-goodism." He paused. "Did you hear me, Agnes?"

Her neck stretched, her eyes darting for converging traffic, she stopped the car at the corner. "I heard you. Here's your corner." She waited impassively while he fumbled out of the car, and she drove off with a jerk before he could start up the path. She said in a high voice, "And a good wetting down will be good for you."

After a moment, Karel said thinly, "I get out here, madame."

She said, "Oh—oh, you're there . . ." and came to an abrupt halt.

Early Thursday morning, Karel took Nicky to the hospital. McVitty had told him to take the day off if he wanted, and Clara McVitty came down the road with a present for the child and kissed him and watched them go down the road. She had said, "I'll be glad to do some school work with Nicky when he gets out. You know—so he can start in school this winter and not feel strange."

Nicky was very silent. Karel told him what would happen, step by step, but he did not know what was taking place behind the child's silence.

When they put him to bed, he screamed, for the bed was not his own. Karel said, "Hush, hush—everyone is your friend here . . ."

The child insisted on wearing his shoes to bed—thus he would be ready to go home instantly—and the elaborate old watch was pinned beside his pillow. When the doctor came for him, Karel went out. He walked whichever way seemed natural, and this brought him back to the garage. He did not speak to McVitty, and McVitty of course did not hazard the emotion of speaking to him, and Karel worked for an hour on the generator of a car.

The child was his own . . . the child was the part of

himself which protested and refused an easy peace. He was disturbed and conscience-ridden that Julie and the idea of Julie had pushed Nicky aside. You did not discard a part of yourself simply because that part moved about on its own power and spoke with a different voice.

He returned to the hospital at noon. Nicky had been brought back to his bed and was lying there, a sheet up to his chin. His black hair was rough against the pillow, his face new-born and beautiful, the eyelashes softly on the cheeks, the mouth relaxed, the flat cool little ears and the tender jawline reflective of that moment when life moves secret and assured. He sat looking at the child who waited now so calmly for life to be renewed and his arm to be made whole.

Then consciousness came back to the child and he moaned and whimpered and screamed for his mother. The cry *mama mama* went out through the corridors, and he did not seem to know Karel. Karel sat on the side of the bed and cooled his forehead with a damp cloth. When the child opened his eyes, he could see in the little boy's leap of expression that for a moment he thought everything had been done, time had been telescoped, he could now get up and go out and be a whole boy. He sank back with a little cry when he found that something impeded him.

Karel sat with the child until the doctor came in. Nicky looked at his watch and rubbed his cheek against it. "It is four o'clock," he said huskily. They gave him a sedative and Karel watched the eyelashes come down on the cheeks again. His love for the child came up like a tide, and he put his head down beside Nicky on the pillow, and he cried.

After dinner, he went to the doctor's house. But first he walked down the dark road, beyond the ridge of the village, where the Wrights lived. He had no intention of going as far as the house. He could have walked up to the door, rung the bell, asked to see Julie, talked to her. He told himself this, and it gave some purpose to this walk in the dark. But he did not want to do more than lean against a tree and watch the lights of the house in the distance. He wished nothing consciously, but all passion and wonder rose up in him.

He wished to excel, to exceed in whatever profession he chose. He wished to plan his life very carefully. Doctoring seemed less important to him now, almost circumscribed. Not far off, not far off at all, was Julie. The length of that field and beyond the next house. He stood for a long time, this close but no closer.

The doctor had not expected to see him, but he showed pleasure. They sat on the front porch in two rocking chairs. After a while Karel stopped his rocking and asked quietly, "Will Nicky really get his arm?"

"Oh, yes," the doctor said, "don't worry." He rocked uninterrupted and a loose board sounded frailly.

"You think that Mrs. Stillwell will accomplish it?"

The doctor rocked steadily, the board creaked, the headlights of an oncoming car shone on the leaves of the lilac bush, transmuting it.

"Oh, yes," he said, "but not perhaps in the way that she'd like."

Karel left the rocking chair and stood rigidly against the upright of the porch. The doctor said to him after a time, "I fed on bitterness. I ate it like pap. But you've got to forget it as much as you can. One or two good people make all the difference. You count on them. And something in yourself."

Karel said, "When you have seen nothing left and you live, you believe there is something—God. I do not know, I can't possibly know what the child suffered today. When he screamed he could have been remembering many things. . . ."

"A cruel God," the doctor said tartly.

"No. That is something else."

The doctor rocked and did not comment. "Don't over-strain yourself, boy," he said at length.

Striking the back of his head against the post, Karel said, "I know what he feels now—and I know what he will feel as he grows older unless he learns what he is—to be physically different, to be crippled, to be looked at, to be treated as though he were set apart—suspicious even when people do kind things. Why do they do them? Because they are sorry for you, or because they love you? Afterward you build a heavy layer of commonplaceness, but you remain suspicious in spite of yourself, always waiting to be denied. What will happen to him in the future unless he understands something more than dependence on good people?"

"Where's your good God?"

Karel looked at him after a moment, and then he said very low, "I do not think any of these things are necessary. That's what I mean. And somehow there is a way to prove that—which is not clear."

The doctor was silent.

Karel went on quietly, "I am talking about what I know—but which I don't altogether understand. We saw through people. We saw what was worthless. We saw what kept life alive. And life was not just the lungs and heart—one could have those and not be alive." Then he added after a long interval, "And we have seen people who were dead by every law and regulation stay alive because some faith, some kindness—some truth—was stronger than anything else."

The doctor was still silent. Karel said formally, "I do not want you to misunderstand me. I am not asking for sympathy. I am not wishing to dramatize hard times in the past. I wish merely to question the things which are not useful or true. This is an important time to me with Nicky getting his arm."

The doctor cleared his throat and Karel was aware again of the frail clamor of the loose board.

"You still want to be a doctor?"

"Maybe."

"There's a lot of training. And a lot of money that'll be needed." Karel did not answer. "I suppose you know that. Will you be able to do it?"

For the first time Karel hesitated. At length he said huskily, "I am trying to weigh all those things."

The doctor continued his rocking, deliberate and heedless of the litle racket of boards. "All right." Then he added after a moment, "You have to be genuinely skeptical. You've got to trust only the things you can handle."

Karel turned his head swiftly and smiled at him.

"Listen, boy, I mean it," he said edgily. "Let's not confuse issues."

Karel replied, "If I were skeptical, I would not know where I am going."

Some anger, some impatience out of proportion to the occasion seized the doctor. He moved his chair back roughly. "You'll learn," he said sharply, "or those notions'll be knocked out of you. You've got day-by-day things to meet. That doesn't take faith. That takes doggedness."

Karel said doggedly, "They are the same."

This fed the doctor's anger. "God damn fool," he said more to himself than to Karel, but with the intention that Karel should hear. Then his anger increased and he repeated more loudly, looking directly at Karel, "Fool, you're old enough . . . !"

Karel did not answer. If he was not a fool then he was very young, and very young meant vulnerable, and yet at the center was this surety. Only at the circumference was pain. Standing on a dark veranda looking into a black night, made more black by the car lights, thinking of the little boy alone in the hospital with his undercurrent of remembrances which must be wiped out, to be called a fool seemed far from the point, seemed wasteful. He turned slowly to the steps of the veranda and went down them. The doctor struck a match fiercely to light his pipe, and Karel, come to himself, said, "Thank you very much for what you did today."

"Glad to," the doctor muttered.

Karel returned to the empty room, empty until he heard the rabbit in his box and the little cat on the balcony outside. He gave them their dinner, and sat leaning forward in his chair, his arms on his knees, watching the cat as she selected her mouthfuls, crouching low over the plate, the white under-fur showing where her shoulders came up like wings. He gave her more food so that he could continue to watch her, for the moment after this one would be lonely and there was a strange dry brittleness inside him as though his thinking was now exhausted.

The cat finished her dinner and sat down to wash herself. There was the child's bed unmade. He made it up carefully, and he straightened the big-paged colored books which Mrs. McVitty had given Nicky and which he could turn with his lips. It was a deep sense of loneliness he felt, broad and long, but outside of it—outside of it—was his life!

Presently he heard footsteps cross the cement yard and then a voice speaking his name. He leaned out the window, and the light fell on McVitty's face tilted to see him.

"The wife wanted me to come and ask how the little boy is."

"The doctor said it went well."

"Glad to hear it. Mom'll be glad."

Karel stood in the window sensing, not seeing, McVitty

go back up the road. Something kindled in the darkness. He watched the black night and the fireflies until he saw the lights go off in the McVitty house. Then he turned out his own light and lay down without undressing. Something came over him like the roar of the sea, and he said Julie's name, muffled and overwhelmed.

The child greeted him silently the next day, and the trouble did not leave his eyes for a few minutes. Then he laughed and wished to be entertained. The next day Vree came and drew comic faces in crayon on large sheets of paper at the child's direction. Many people in the village left him presents, or brought Karel custards or "something my mother used to make." Tommy's mother brought Tommy's comic books. The generosity was spontaneous.

Mrs. Murray came one day when Karel was there, and she kissed the child and sat with her arm on the pillow stroking his cheek. He was very content. He lay without stirring. He cried when she left.

She asked Karel to come for dinner that night. He fed the child his supper and wound his watch for him and kissed him before he left.

On the way two or three people spoke to him, inquiring for Nicky. Miss Purvis stopped him and Mrs. Dunn and the manager of the grocery called out an inquiry. These were the small links, the assurance he needed. He thanked them from his heart. Then as he turned from the main street he met Julie.

He felt the color rush to his face, he felt a thudding in his ears and the palpable collapse of the previous moment when she had merely been in his thoughts. This was real. All the rest, all the dreams he had had of her, all the nameless expectancy he had built, all the calm plans made in the night, existed only in his imagination. They had never been exposed to her physical presence. He had built himself a fine and notable house in which to live and yet it had no foundation. She, incarnate, could topple it over in a minute. His courage deserted him.

She said, "Oh, hello," and she asked how he was, and then she too fell silent. He told her of Nicky, and she said she had heard and meant to take him a present. She asked Karel why he did not come back to swim. Then his words were shaped out of his night visions and his days' restlessness.

"Because it is not good enough. I would like to feel that we have always something to say to each other, and that something important . . ." But this was not it, this was not the summation of his restlessness and desires, why he dreamed, why he walked down the road to her house but did not go in.

She was frowning and looking at him with her clear blue eyes. He shook his head.

"I have thought about you a great deal," he said simply.

She answered calmly, "I've thought about you a great deal. I liked talking to you. Usually conversation isn't interesting."

He hesitated. They stood at the side of the road in positions of surprise and transiency, and the thudding still sounded in his ears.

"I—will you go for a walk with me sometime?"

"Come and go swimming," she answered.

"No," he said, "I would like you to go for a walk."

When she agreed and they arranged for the time, he felt that something had become real again. His blood was beating more quickly but it was no longer erratic, and he looked at her intently for a moment, for he wished to remember exactly how she looked.

They shook hands formally, and he went on down the road. When he had gone a little way he started to run. He ran faster and faster and presently he shouted and when he came to the little river at the edge of Mrs. Murray's property, he was singing.

This-and-this had been said, and she had looked thus-and-so. He submerged himself in it, he sat down by the river and hid his face against his bent knees. He told himself he was in love. Then, alarmed, he said No. He was merely happy.

He was willing to go no further than that.

13

When he reached Mrs. Murray's there was Megan. He saw her instantly, and his happiness was renewed. She was coming up from the chicken house with a basket of eggs. Since seeing Julie he had become very sure of himself.

Megan said, "You look like a different person. What has happened?"

"The child is getting well," Mrs. Murray said, putting her hand on his shoulder.

But Megan stood looking at him and smiling. "No, it is more than that," she said, laughing a little.

"I feel dizzy," he said to her. "I suddenly seem to have no troubles."

"Then we will celebrate."

Mrs. Murray disappeared and returned with a bottle of elderberry wine in one hand and a peach pie in the other. Megan put flowers on the table. He brought out the dinner, and they sat on benches at a table which stood under the linden. Only the three of them.

"Where is your husband?" he asked Megan.

"He—he is not home."

"He has gone to buy a heifer," Mrs. Murray said, after the slightest pause. Then she laughed. "*We* milked the cows tonight."

Happiness could not be dislodged. The linden was throbbing with bees, each white blossom quivering with them as though a wind were in the branches. He could not remember such a moment before. The wonderful country held no desolation. It seemed to need nothing but itself, the small wind stirring, the distance and the closeness, the small cloud which moved past at this moment, content with its high place and its lofty destiny. The haying was almost done. He could see the bundles lying in the field and a tractor near the lane.

Mrs. Murray's supper was splendid. But possibly any supper under the circumstances would have been splendid. He tried to tell them what their kindness meant. He fumbled with the relaxation of this moment, with the joy that was behind him and its continuing sense in his heart. Its alarms were even now negligible. He looked at Mrs. Murray with such happiness that she laughed aloud.

"Come and let me kiss you. You're a great hulking boy but I think you need to be kissed as much as Nicky."

He went almost shyly. He did not remember when he had been kissed this way before . . . when he was a boy of thirteen and had left his mother for the last time. He wanted to do nothing but sit here and watch the present swell and swell to the sound of the bees until it melted into the future.

They sat there as the twilight came down and the sky grew violet around the hills. They sat there even when the night wind came up and a lonely mosquito sang and swooped companionably. Surely, surely, this time must be the stuff of all time, and there was nothing to struggle for or to long for unfulfilled. Everything was possible. He would always remember how he had turned from the main street, all unsuspecting, all wanting, and seen Julie just before him. He would always remember it as a proof that nothing was ever impossible.

Somewhat later, when it was dark, Megan stirred and said that a light had just gone on in her house. John had come back. She began to carry the dishes into the house. It shifted the moment away from the present. He stood up also and helped.

Suddenly he was dismayed. He did not want Megan to go. All through dinner, the fact that Megan was there had given a kind of assurance. When she stood up, something had been broken—the breathless, taut wonderment had moved; it threatened to become indistinguishable from the commonplace things. Julie was suddenly amorphous, a girl whose voice he could not hear, who had said nothing he could remember. He was dismayed. What was permanent if such things could pass away so easily?

Megan stood in the lighted doorway, and she looked no older than Julie. He felt close to something which he needed to understand. He felt older and she looked younger than the ten years which separated them. She washed the dishes and he dried them, and Mrs. Murray put them away, and all the time he was silent. He could not afford to be so shaken, be dislodged so easily. In the commonplace life he could not be so vulnerable. He dried the same dish over and over, not looking at Megan but thinking of her.

Megan washed out the dishpan and hung it up. She washed her hands and put on powder and lipstick, and he was intently aware of her actions. When Megan went toward the door, he stood up quickly, and as Megan kissed Mrs. Murray he kissed her also—swiftly and shyly—without a word to deflect him from going with Megan.

They walked down the dark stretch of road between Mrs.

Murray's house and Megan's. Other lights were shining in her house now, and she started to walk more swiftly.

He said, without warning, "Did you always know that you loved your husband? Were you ever afraid to say so to yourself?"

She looked at him quickly, the glow from her flashlight showing his face. He was watching her with great intentness.

"I was surprised."

He said with a half-frown, "Yet when you knew he was the one you wanted to marry, how did you say to yourself that you knew it? How is one sure of it?"

She answered after a moment, "You trust. You feel completely natural—yourself." She added pleasantly and warmly, "You've got a girl on your mind."

He was silent. Then he said, "You are happy?"

She did not answer for a moment. The shining eyes of a cat watched them from the side of the road, and the cat made a small flurry of departure into the thicket by the road before she replied.

"No," she said, "I am not especially happy. But that is something else again."

He frowned. "Why?"

"Because it doesn't have to do with the main thing."

He said with a flare of anger, "I want to know something very—very—ah, I thought because you were young and married to a young man you'd know what I meant."

She answered quietly, "I'm sorry. Let me try again."

He was silent, and then he said softly, "Did your husband know it too and feel the same way?"

"We were married," she replied. "Isn't that the answer?"

They had nearly reached the walk which led to the house. He stopped and put his hand on her arm so that she also stopped. "I did not ask these things as I would like to.

I'm sorry. Perhaps other boys do ask, are not sure, but I have many reasons for not being sure." He sat back against the bank, and felt in the dark for grass to pluck at. She stood, a light-gowned figure, and the light of the house fell upon her. "I'm not—very little has been natural in my life."

She came and sat on the bank near him. "Ask me anything you like."

The stubbly grass was rough, and he rubbed his hand stiffly against it.

"Most of the things I have seen have been evil in one way or another. It seems that I have to find out what each thing means before I can feel safe with it. If I am in love—in all the ways that you say—then that is what I want. But I do not know. She is a stranger. Her experiences are different. It may only be loneliness or sentimentality. How do I know?" and then he added in a whisper, "I do not want anything that will not mean a home and a family."

She answered quietly, "It is not the thing that a man of your age is usually worried about."

"No." Then he said rather desperately, "There is so much of my life which has never been lived. What can I do about it? I ask myself. Now I have come and I have stayed in one place peacefully for two months, and I am aware of pleasant things, but I have grown into the habit of questioning them coldly. I do not think that is right for all things. But there must be some simple way of knowing."

She stood up and brushed off her dress. "I don't think there is. There is a great deal of ignorance disfiguring things." She smiled at him. "For example, a number of people are afraid of you. They confuse you with their consciences or with what might have happened to them or with the world which doesn't in any way conform to their world. Anything which stirs up makes many people afraid.

But you also make them fond of you. Make them very glad that you're the way you are." She smiled. "*I'm* glad."

He looked at her gravely, and he was still sitting on the bank when she glanced back from the house door.

14

Karel dressed carefully the day he was going to walk with Julie, painstakingly shaving and carefully brushing his hair. He had confided to Vree the evening before that his only trousers were spotted and mussed, and he had sat in his tan coveralls watching Vree fold the trousers on an ironing board, work with his fingernail at certain spots, rub the cloth together, sponge, and at length press.

For the most part, Vree had worked seriously, but now and then the corners of his gray mustache had turned up, and once he had looked slyly at Karel.

"Got a girl," he said, and he seemed pleased.

Karel had answered stiffly, his heart beating wildly, "That is foolish."

"Nice girl," Vree had stated, and Karel had realized that he had spoken as though he knew who she was.

After a moment he had asked him, irresistibly impelled, "Why is she nice?"

"Natural kind of girl. Nice-spoken. Don't put on airs—like her mom does. She needs a chance, like everyone."

"Chance?" He had picked up the word in surprise. "You know who she is?"

"I've known her since she was three years old."

"What kind of chance?" Karel had repeated, his brow furrowed.

"Same as all people. Find out what's really going on."

He thought of this as he dressed. It reassured him. Perhaps Vree had intended that. He hesitated over a tie, but the tie was frayed so he left his shirt collar open. Then because the cuffs were frayed, he rolled up his sleeves carefully. He had a sudden vanity of his brown arms against his white shirt. He was suddenly proud of his masculinity. The number on his arm stood out bluely, but he did not think about it. He was wonderfully glad that he was a man.

She was waiting for him near the driveway leading from her house. She came out of nowhere, and that was the way he liked it. He did not wonder why she waited for him by the roadside.

She was a girl who smiled and laughed often, but it did not seem altogether spontaneous; it seemed more as though the liveliness was a concession to good manners. It was not natural for him, either, to be smiling and laughing all the time.

He thought about himself consciously as they walked down the road. He was much taller than she. Everything was masculine in contrast to her—the size of his hand, the texture of skin, the color of lips, the way of walking, the slope of the shoulders, the quality and tone of voice. He was absurdly pleased with the difference. He felt a potency that he was content to reflect on. It was the kind of confidence that did not make it even necessary to take her hand or touch her arm.

This occasion had a different quality from the time they had sat by the pool. The road was rough, the countryside belonged to all passers-by, the houses were plain and anonymous; in the hills all things belonged to the hills.

Because he knew her so well in his mind, it seemed unnatural to build bridges of idle conversation, and yet because of the shock of finding her walking beside him, as he had imagined, he felt he must say many things. But she took charge of matters.

She wished to go across a pasture to see the foundations of an old burned house where purple loosestrife was swarming. This was the bridge between them, this was the way to do things together. She asked direct questions, "Do you think . . . ? Do you know . . . ? Why do you . . . ?" and it all made it easier. Then she wanted to climb up above a little waterfall to see a view—a child showing her games. He enjoyed these things. He enjoyed having to help her climb the rocks to the view although she knew the way and he did not. He enjoyed finding something she had never observed before when he pointed out a rock which had been split by a growing tree.

Then she wanted him to compare this countryside and these houses with his own country. She asked him to sing a Czech song and was pleased with it, and she sang an American song for him and was pleased with it also. She produced a cigarette case which had been given her on her birthday and asked if he would like it since she did not smoke. He did not smoke either, but he took it with a rush of pleasure.

They had walked all afternoon and not grown tired. But at last she sat down on a stone wall and rubbed her instep. He found some Lifesavers in his pocket and offered her some. They were old friends now and he could look at her intently without self-consciousness. He jumped over the wall, and stretched himself on the grass. Her blue cotton dress was deeper than the sky. Her bright hair and the lovely up-going planes of her face were indescribably pleasing. Had she been any larger or smaller, had her eyes been any other color, had her mouth been any smaller, had she not had the direct but rather shy way of turning her head to look at him, she would not have been his girl. He threw a clump of earth at her, his girl. She rubbed her arm where it hit her, and kicked at him with the toe of her moccasin—ritualistic gestures.

She would be a sophomore in college this year, and so she would do this thing and this thing, and this. He did not understand, and was a little dismayed, so he changed the subject. But her life was very real to her. She returned again to the things she would do in the natural course of events, and at length he said, "It's all so trivial. Where will it lead?"

"Well, what would *you* like me to do?" she asked. He turned his head away and did not answer. She said coaxingly, "Isn't college much better than just sitting at home waiting for something to happen?"

He answered reflectively, speaking up to the sky, his heavy handsome face expressionless. "Education was something I longed for terribly. It was not just something to pass the time."

There she was helpless and shut-off. She was too sensitive to grow impatient, too inexperienced to answer.

"Well," she said at length cannily, "I guess I don't know as much as you. I have to make up for it in other ways."

He looked at her swiftly, amused and wonderfully tender. She did not know what he knew; she would never know what he knew, and this would not be a divider but a unifier. It seemed quite wonderful, yet he could not put it into words for her.

Now when they went down the road again, he put his arm across her shoulder and went on to say, "If you can do one thing well, you should be able to do other things well. It is all in the mind. If I were a good doctor, then why shouldn't I be a good painter too? Or a good musician?

Or a good professor? What would you think of me if I became a professor?"

She laughed. "You've got a serious look. And your hair falls across your forehead."

"When you see possibilities in one thing you do not stop there. You go on and on."

Then she suddenly asked in that civilizing voice of a woman, "But where is the common sense in all that?"

He stopped in his thought, brought up suddenly. The doctor asked him things like this, and he had his own answers. But he could not answer her in the same way. It was a shock. He wanted something so inexpressibly personal that he might willingly compromise. He wanted her to know that he would be a good garbage-collector if that would anchor his life, but he did not believe that she would care for garbage-collectors. He kept his arm across her shoulders until he had an answer ready. Then his arm dropped and he said in a firm voice, "Common sense? That's a childish thing to say. Common sense only tells us how to make money. Is that what you admire?"

"I have never been poor," she said candidly. "A lot of times it seems just plain lack of common sense to be poor."

He was angry and baffled. It sounded so civilizing and womanly—his mother had thought of these things—and yet it seemed to ignore something. With Julie, with him, walking down the road—let those things take care of themselves!

She wondered if she had made him think that she gave importance to things about which she had thought little until this minute.

He wondered if he seemed rash and unreasonable, as though he had not thought seriously on these matters.

In a moment he stopped by the side of the road and hurriedly put together a bouquet of August flowers. He presented it to her, and her eyes became bright. There was a kind of contentment on both their faces and, though they walked apart, they seemed close together.

In the village he asked her to go into the drug store for a soda. Afterwards he walked with her to her driveway. "Well, good-bye," he said.

"Good-bye," she said swiftly, anxious not to be outdone in a noncommittal attitude. He turned away and she started to run up the drive. But he turned around, suddenly desolate, and called after her, "You will come for another walk?"

She turned her head and waved, and he accepted this as agreement.

He told Nicky about the walk and the foundation of the old house and the tree which had split the rock. He even told him about the bouquet he had picked, carefully identifying the flowers so that Nicky could see them, and about the sodas. He had to tell someone, and Nicky sat there against the pillows, so alive, so identified, yet so disinterested in Julie, that Karel could talk without self-consciousness. The child looked at him with his cavernous eyes, and deeply sighed. He moved his little stumped arms as though going away and away down a long road. They sat and looked at each other, knowing the same hopes.

Mrs. Stillwell telephoned him the next day, and he went around at his lunch hour. Roscoe was out of town, and under the circumstances she needed her piano moved from one side of the room to the other. What circumstances? Well, it always made her uneasy to think of a strong man idle when something needed to be done. And what was more, she wanted him to know that Sylvia Mowes, who had sung with the Pittsfield Quartette, had offered to give a benefit song recital to raise money for Nicky's arm.

Wasn't that splendid? Individual donations had fallen off now that the summer was ending . . . it was not from want of interest, it was just because of so many demands . . . and a town like this had to be shoved, you had to have so much strength and perseverance because it went to sleep at the turn of a hand . . . but that was really human nature, yet she wondered if you found it so entrenched as in a little town. Maybe I push too hard, Roscoe says I do, but I see things the way they are and I'm confused when they're broken down into details. . . . You can't stop progress—of course you can't!—and you can't wait for it either. Now you take the Republican Party—there are well-bred people with education and ideals. Of course I listen to the others too, you've got to listen to everything, but I do not always listen right to the end, for that's confusing. Nothing is perfect—but *it must be.* When I vote I say that to Mr. Ewing. He fancies he is the political boss. If we tell him long enough something's bound to happen. But there are always small minds working, and the little boy getting his arms is just a part of that. It makes one very indignant. Small minds are talking all the time, and I tell them what I think. *You must know about that—you're a sensible boy.* That Roi Arnow. There's a bad group around him—I don't blame them, but it doesn't do any good to be with them. Poor and shiftless and, I imagine, in-bred—some old names, fine names, but gone to seed. Now . . .

Karel spoke for the first time. "He needs friends."

"Well, now, why? He's got friends. Though they're bad friends. And he *could* make something of himself."

She caught her lower lip with her teeth, and her glance moved from his face to the ring on her finger to the piano. With her heel she straightened a rug which had been disarranged.

"You see . . ." she tried. "It's foolish and complicated, but if some people here in town disapprove of something, then—well, then, what happens? Who suffers most?" Her loose double chin shook. The round eyes and round face were equally without expression. She spread out her hands. "The little boy . . ."

He felt a sudden spinning anger, a fury which suffused his eyes and blinded him. The muscles of his jaw swelled, but he did not speak. She was silent, unhappy, but she ventured cheerfully, "A nice boy like you has judgment. That's what I told Katherine. It was simply a question of making you understand how things are in a little town—any little town."

"Katherine?" he said. "That is Mrs. Wright?"

She nodded with dignity. "I wanted to keep it impersonal. I am sorry I mentioned her name."

He sat perfectly silent for a minute or two and then, although he felt as though his teeth would chatter, he said calmly, "Will the child get his arm?"

"I always keep my word."

"It is a sin," he said furiously, "to bargain this way!"

"Bargain? You're surely not attracted to a boy like Roi—a fine boy like you."

"My feelings are—no one can know what my feelings are! They cannot be put into words. If I put them into very simple words, someone would still be able to disguise them with other meanings."

She said forlornly, "Young people are always full of ideals. Older people know how to be wise. I'm sure that Roi Arnow . . ." She wanted him to finish her sentence, conjoining his words with hers. She felt so close to this boy, he meant so much to her, that she had to believe that there was a perfect meeting of minds. He stood by the piano, his back to her.

"He is very important," he said stubbornly. "Very important—as important as I am to myself."

After the first sentence she did not hear. She murmured,

"Of course," but she did not really hear for he had not said what she had been listening for.

He went out the door and down the steps, he said *Good-bye* and *Thank you* stiffly, and she nodded acknowledgment and went back into the house.

But standing unhappily by the window she watched him go, her face impassive. She watched him, and Mrs. Wright's words came with a shocking clarity. Mrs. Wright had said, *The poor boy has suffered so much, I can't allow him to add to his suffering by becoming attached to Julie. It wouldn't be fair to him—not after all he has gone through.*

She did not know why she was now suddenly so angry that she threw an inoffensive book clear across the room. For she had spoken up to Katherine Wright at the time and told her positively that nice friendships were possible between girls and boys, and she was sure such a sensitive fine boy would never have gross thoughts about such a sweet girl as Julie. Certainly she would never have if she were in his place. . . .

Always you do your best, and nine times out of ten you are slapped in the face.

As for Katherine Wright—people one knew, whose family one knew—they behaved—in the end, surely, when all was said and done—according to principles, and it was the blessing of God in an unsteady world that this was so.

He was not aware of anything closing in for he moved in his own world.

An improbable phrase . . . "closing in" . . . considering that no one had felt malice or passion or fury.

Only fear, undefined. So many small things happen. At the time one scarcely observes them. They are like small bits of conversation, suspended in air, until a hand reaches out and abruptly pulls them together.

But no one had pulled them together yet.

Everyone minded his own business. Everyone saw to that. But no one let things pass unobserved; that would be ignoring the business at hand. If nothing happened to prove disturbing, if what was remained as it was, then no questions would be asked and no answers solicited. But the watching eyes were never closed, the listening ears were never silenced.

For thirty years Mrs. Stillwell had irritated many people. She was never satisfied with the way charity was conducted here, she was never satisfied with the way the village determined its ethics and intellectual life, she poked and jostled, and then when she had created a suitable commotion, she left the confused pieces to sort themselves out, for she had by now a new and urgent concern. The shock of the first sight of that child was over. So it was nearly time for Mrs. Stillwell to grow vague of voice and preoccupied.

But that did not mean that passivity would descend. There was never any quietness under the surface. Like the sea, constant activity, weighing and balancing and concluding, went on out of sight.

What went on in all the world of small towns and in all the narrow corridors of minds and hearts? There was the social envy and the church envy and the woman's-club envy and the good-stock envy and the envy which let no lifetime friend do more than the pattern allowed. There was the control by old women and the suffocation of the young and the total fear of all things done together as a community of common interests. There were the do-gooders who were all tripped and left sprawling and the rich eager strangers who desired to absorb some of the old culture and were whipped into place and taught a proper humility. There were the cults and the fetishes—that there were no class distinctions, that a pure and primitive kind of democracy lived here (here, in exception to all the other towns of the world, for *here* was America).

But inferiority was also assumed, and although it was not good sense to remind one overtly of that inferiority, yet property-owning and lineage and morals were assessed with great care to arrive at a proper estimate. And money . . . money was also important.

And all this taking place in this cup of hills, calm, benign, beautiful.

There is the salamander which eats himself from his tail to his jaws. But that is medieval. Surely some new great light has come in. For life wishes for eternity, and one is always on the verge of finding eternity.

Then the brooding alter-mind of a village thinks deeper —the mind which affirms life in swift glimpses like the opening and closing of a shutter. Someone observes a thing acutely and without prejudice, someone labors and brings forth a fresh hope, someone sees with a freshness as though in a new world, someone holds out a generous hand and does not too quickly withdraw it, someone finds that in the voice of a stranger is a tone of remembrance and promise. The event is remarkable; it affirms. The Mrs. Stillwells have set something in motion; the Mrs. Murrays confirm and nourish it. The others question, and something falls back apace. Familiar ways had been shaken and thinking stirred up . . . And who felt it? Not everyone surely, not everyone in such a self-contained town of independent decisions. Who would go around from door to door and put his foot into the door opening and say, "Madam, what is your opinion of strange ways—*but what is strange; is a stranger strange?*—and what is your opinion of a mental stirring up?—*but have any unfamiliar words been used or sentiments which are not universal been advocated?*

Fear is seldom called by its name boldly; it is clothed

and covered and addressed as a thing of strength and virtue. Mrs. Wright's fear, for example, became more manageable when she said to herself that the experiences of such a boy, however fine the boy, however undeserved the experiences, were gross and alien and they left an indelible mark. A fine boy, but the impregnating thing had been at work, and her concern must lie with her family way of life, so imperiled and precious. It gave her antagonism point and meaning; it ceased being personal.

Old Mrs. Arnow, Roi's grandmother, was afraid. She had outlived the days of amulets, so she had nothing with which to exorcize her imaginings. In the place of incantations she could only darken the face of the unfamiliar, narrow her mind, lace up her heart.

Mrs. Stillwell was afraid—that civilization depended on one last personal gesture of the civilized.

And the doctor, who comforted himself with pessimism, saw human nature fixed in its mold, and he stared at that detested mold until his eyes watered, convinced that only by narrowing the vision and confining the expectation could fear be despised.

And George McVitty whose nerves and reflexes were conditioned atavistically, and the eight ladies who had contributed to Mrs. Stillwell's fund, and the fifteen who had been approached but had not made up their minds, remembered something never put into words, lifted their heads at a sound which never came but seemed as clear as tone.

The thing was in the air, not consciously, not alarmingly, but persistently; it was so insusceptible, so elusive, that one could only consider it a part of his own nature and so to be trusted. The world rolled up its fears, all classified, transposed, hidden, entangled, and no primal simplicity, no God-cause could speak in a language ornate enough to be heard—only in a very, very small voice which one would have to strain to attend.

No one wished to do or not to do anything. They wished just to *be* . . . the little boy, lying in his bed, and Karel conscientiously earning his wages, and Vree and Mrs. Murray and Megan and John, so anxious to be at peace with their nearest and dearest, and Julie, stirred and uncertain, Julie in whom nothing was finally shaped except in the vicarious forms of books and dreams.

Julie . . . thought and sensed and concealed and denied, and then she had to turn around squarely and look at the abstraction she was creating. She had for some time been moving so far away from her father and mother that the distance was almost unbridgeable, and yet the things which held her still were as strong as custom.

Twice she drove past the garage and saw Karel, but did not stop. At length she drew up and primly asked for gas. She did not know what she would say. She heard the meter on the gas gauge, and she heard the hose withdrawn, and she still did not know what she would say. When he brought the slip for her to sign, he was unsmiling. But as she signed, he glanced at her and she looked at him, and they smiled, each on his own account. He leaned for a moment against the door of the car and she leaned back against the seat, and there was, understandably, nothing that needed to be said. Silence was better.

That evening he came to the kitchen door of her house and asked the maid to give her a note. He was too proud to ask himself why he had come to the kitchen door. It was a kind of defiance required by his self-respect. In a short time, Julie came down to the kitchen and they went out together. Her mother would know about it. There was no subterfuge involved.

"The kitchen," she said. "How silly—why?"

He walked along quickly, his hands in his pockets.

"I don't like the front of your house. I thought I would try the kitchen."

"You're joking!"

"No. And your parents do not like me."

"Oh! They've never mentioned you!"

"Well, then, I know that sometime they will not like me."

She was silent for a time, and then she said, "Don't walk so fast. Please! I want to tell you something."

"What?"

"If I decide I want to go out with you, I do not have to sneak around—if I decide."

"Well," he said, "that is fine."

"And remember," she was saying with a touch of anger, "that I don't want to be protected from things, and I don't want it thought that I don't know about things or feel things or want just to spend my father's money!" She stood suddenly still and pounded the open palms of her hands together, her little face spirited. "I don't want to be spared things. I've never asked anyone to keep me from feeling things, whatever they are."

He turned around in the road and looked at her, his head down, his dark eyes fixed on her, his lower lip thrust out. He said, "I didn't suppose you had," and they stood there in the soft light not looking at each other, each deeply private at that moment, and yet yearning for something common.

"Listen," he said suddenly, moving toward her. "You're my age. You're the only one I know my age—except Roi. I thought I could talk to you because of that. It seemed as though you had to understand—just because you *were* my age."

She did not look at him, she looked a little to the side of him, the frown still between her eyes. "All right," she said.

He persisted, "It means that you've got to understand the things that I say—or let me show you how to understand them. It's not that I want to go back. I'm not living by remembering, but certain things are true, even when these older people discredit or disbelieve." He was walking back and forth across the road, and she, watching him, dug her hands like balls into her sweater pockets. Then he stood very quiet, his chin against his chest, a wing of hair falling across his forehead, and he sighed from the earth. Without a word, he started walking blindly down the road, not looking back.

She felt a rise of conventional anger, well-placed and respected, and stared after him. But she had said certain things, and she was honest, and she remembered them. Since they were a version of conscience, she did not dare to stand on her pride. Even what was harsh and distasteful to her temperament must be followed unquestioningly, for some destiny had brought it to *her*, not to someone else.

She went after him quickly, not running, her hands doubled up hard in her pockets. She did not know who this boy was or why he was such a part of her life. That she was a girl and that he was a boy with a commanding way and habits older than his years was partial explanation but not enough.

When she came up beside him, she said, "Stop it—now stop it. Wait for me. What's the matter?" all brisk and clear, in a manner which seemed very proper. He was eager to talk. His face jutted straight ahead, and there was great loneliness in the lips and the droop of his lids.

"It seemed suddenly as though we could never know each other, however much we might try. There aren't any words that can explain, for there aren't any words between people so different. And yet I want to know you and I want you to know me." She saw with dismay and a suffusion of feeling that the tears had come into his eyes.

She went along quickly beside him, running a little. He tried to speak, controlling his voice. "It's not that you do not want to understand—and it's not that I want to hold onto something—it is just that—that is the way it is."

"No," she said. "Maybe I can't understand one thing—but I can understand something else, and if one *wants* to understand, doesn't that count in the end?" He closed his eyes against the tears and shook his head a little. "It does count! It must mean something."

After a moment he looked at her briefly and smiled. She said in her small, gentle voice, "I like you. I'd like to be friends. But no one understands all the same things at the same time."

"No," he answered simply, and that was all. Presently he took her hand, and they walked along more closely together, their fingers lightly clasped. After a while he looked at her again, his eyes partly closed, a little mockery about his mouth. "Perhaps I like you because you are pretty and terribly protected and don't know very much."

She flushed and was hurt, and he continued to watch her and smile. Then he stopped because she did not say anything and he put his hands on her arms. "It might be so. It's nothing to offend you. It's you—and I like you."

He shook her slightly and kissed her on the forehead, and when he started down the road again, he drew her arm through his. Very well, she thought, she would not be offended, she would not draw back, she would wait and see, patiently.

All at once he felt relieved. He was not in love, but he had a friend. He would understand her and protect her and talk with her, and be a good friend and, at the same time, relieved of the need to fall in love. He felt deeply at peace, he felt how foolish and maneuvering any other sentiment would be, how unready he was for the demands of passion. That would remain apart. Without moorings one moved cautiously, or there might be sudden desolation and a sea without shores.

The long prospect of friendship swept over him and he looked at her with great pleasure, feeling how perfect she was, how utterly complete for what he wanted, and he desired nothing more. He looked at the shape of her forehead and the silkiness of her eyebrows and the little line of her nose, and the gentle mouth, full and calm in the lower lip. And the glance of her eyes and the slant of her cheek when she turned her head . . . and the quietness and eagerness, the quality of being alive . . . He laughed and he could not resist drawing her to him as they walked along, and kissing her again. His friend. Utterly right, nothing to be changed.

15

Mr. Harris Ewing, the dispenser of political jobs—who had a small insurance business and who dabbled a little in real estate and who sat on the board of the hospital and on the school board and was a selectman and who owned, through his brother-in-law, a wholesale liquor business and who controlled the jobs of Republican office-holders because no one else had been swift enough to step into the place—was a short round man who held himself very straight and always dressed fully, even to waistcoat, all the year round. And he was never out of temper, never badgered by little irritations; he was a man who thoroughly enjoyed every moment of the life he had made for himself.

He had observed Karel early, he had asked a few questions of George McVitty, simply because in his multiple capacities he was himself asked questions and he wished to know how to answer. He had contributed an equivocal two dollars to Mrs. Stillwell's fund, and promptly and jovially collected three dollars from her for the Kiwanis benefit. He knew a great many things without understanding them, and he knew the secrets of most of his fellow-villagers, wholly or in part. When you ran a political party you had to be a constable, maybe a priest, certainly healthy and able to get about.

He came into the tavern down by the river to look around, to see whom he could share a beer with, maybe to do a little business or to test wobbly fences. Newcomers moving into the neighborhood were always known here, and a little information of the right sort turned him into the very devil of an insurance agent.

But there was no one here now. Only the two boys, Roi Arnow and the foreign fellow from the garage. Roi ordered a beer and the other fellow ordered nothing, but plunked at the guitar while Roi said, "Naw! C flat. Give it here, for God's sake! Jeez, you're a round-shouldered guy!"

Ewing watched them benignly. That Arnow kid struck a mean chord. He smiled and lit a cigarette and thought of his ukelele days. He put a coin in the juke box to see what the boys would do, but they ignored it. When the Arnow boy took away the guitar and played it with love and a sure hand, Ewing's toes quivered and his feet tapped. He told himself he was a fellow who never grew old. Didn't think about age, for one thing, didn't worry, enjoyed what came along—like sitting here, beating his feet to the kids' music—did his job well, took care of the village morals and political tendencies with an unerring hand. He liked to think about himself, sitting here. He had confidence, he had vision. He knew the world was big. He had made his own choice, a big man in a little town, but that did not alter his far-sightedness or his rare command of things in a larger world.

The other boy, Lindemann, was sitting now with nothing to do, no beer to drink, no cigarette in his hand, no guitar, and didn't even seem to be listening very hard to the music. Ewing studied him. He narrowed his eyes and studied him as though he was painting his portrait. And slowly something shifted in his mind, some small earth crust sighed and slipped, and the landscape was altered.

That face was sullen. It was mean. It didn't look like a boy's under these brown-shaded lamps. Maybe he wasn't a boy. Maybe he was a lot of things that he shouldn't be, that no community wanted. Maybe Hitler hadn't been so wrong. It was exhilarating, sitting here, thinking these things, in step with the large world.

He got up and fetched himself another glass of beer and lighted another cigarette, and gave himself up to these reflections. There were very sinister things in the world and they worked in very sinister ways, and it was no good thinking that any place in the American world was safe from them. He was a big man with big thoughts, titillating himself. Hell, it was interesting! He had a sense of humor; he could be amused at himself, and still drive ahead fiercely, for the working side of his brain was eminently practical. Finally, when the time and the place and the practical man came together, he got up with his beer and went to their table. He leaned on it cheerfully. Roi glanced up briefly and said "Hi," and went on playing.

"How's your grandma?" Ewing said.

"Okay."

"Stepping out on her, huh?"

"There's a church meetin' at home."

"I heard of a job you could handle, fellow."

"How much pay?"

"Eighteen a week."

"Na-a-a."

"Lindemann, you steady at the garage?"

"I hope so."

"You a citizen?"

"No, sir."

"Why not?"

"I've been moving about. I haven't had a home."

"Where'd you say you came from?"

"Czechoslovakia."

"Ha! Russky-land. Might be we wouldn't want folks from there." He laughed amiably. The fellow looked a boy from close up. He was mildly irritated. "Don't think we've ever yet had a fellow who wasn't a citizen work in this town. Never—come to think of it. It's a fact. You're a real foreigner."

Karel did not answer him. What he felt was a disarrangement, like a tremor far under ground. He looked at Ewing who looked at him, smiled suddenly and slapped one hand on the table.

"Well, better get to be a citizen—if you can. Wouldn't want you to have to thumb a ride out of town." And he laughed in the light-hearted way that people liked.

Roi said, "Aw, Christ!" and struck at the strings vigorously. Ewing could afford to laugh. He had been a big man in a big world for a few minutes, and he had put it over smartly and competently.

"That Roi's a sad boy," said Vree, sitting on the running board and sucking his pipe, watching Roi from knee-level. "He don't *want* a spine-bone, that's his trouble. Look at the way he walks, kind of sliding and meandering along like he didn't care enough to lift up his legs."

Karel, who was painting a car a few paces away, flung down a rag in sudden anger. "Damn it, what does he do that makes all of you decide that? He minds his own business—says a word to a friend—plays that guitar—tries to keep out of the way of that grandmother—how does that make you all decide what he is and why?"

Vree said calmly, "I didn't say it's the boy's will that he's like that. He don't want a spine-bone because he thinks folks'll have no use for him *anyway*. He's a living example of our poor way of doing things. That's what's sad —not the other."

Karel went on painting and the frown deepened. He felt an anger out of all proportion to his feeling for Roi. Vree sat there, his hands around his knee, his pipe smoke curling patiently, his eyes half-closed against the smoke, waiting—but not waiting to retaliate, just waiting.

Karel finished the painting of the car. The day was over and Vree stood up.

"Come for a little bite of supper. You just open up a can and that's not good."

For the first time Karel was angry with Vree, and since he wished to remain angry, he went with him. When he got inside the door, and as Vree was getting out his pans and turning up the flame in the oil stove, he exploded into words.

"There is whispering, whispering, about my friendliness with Roi. I am disgusted. I didn't expect you to begin clucking your tongue and sucking in your breath like the others."

"Not I," said Vree mildly. "I'm not sucking in any breath. I passed a comment on a boy, not on you."

"It's the same thing."

"Don't rattle your teeth so, fellow. He makes people comment, that's all. Cause we've seen him grow up, and it's sad to see a youngster turn that way, and you wish he'd make up his own mind about himself."

Karel kicked at a chair reflectively. In this low room, with the light filtering through the dozens of green plants which stood in the windows so that the light was swimming with green, with the mounted birds on the shelves and the framed butterflies on the walls, all gentle, all at peace, he felt clumsy and beset.

Vree said, "Myself was a boy once."

"Things must have been different."

"If you remember that you're a man and not a boy any longer, that'll help a little."

For the first time Karel smiled slightly.

Vree said, "Seems like we all want to belong some place or to someone, and yet when we're young we don't want to say so, and when we're older we begin to suspect that's not exactly what we want, after all. Isn't it maybe that we just want to be ourselves?"

Karel answered fervently, "I've got reasons for liking Roi. Plenty, plenty! And when he plays that guitar I know how he feels—reckless."

"Sure. Reckless. This omelette don't stand up for anyone. Sit down."

Vree did not speak for a time. He sat down at the table and opened a napkin, and took a sip of water. He sighed and wiped his mustache and leaned his dark cheek against his big hand. "I think that Roi gave his answer wrong, that's all. That's all I mean. I didn't say a word about your being his friend. But don't think there's anything there that will prop you up or give you a big load of manliness. That's all I mean."

But Karel had painfully tightened himself inside, and all evening at Roi's he shadow-boxed with his divided responses. He watched the grandmother and Roi move about the untidy, musty room—their home, yet reflecting no ease or apparent affection; the old woman baleful, waiting to belabor without pity, obsessed by some tribal pattern which allowed no deviation by a hair's breadth. The old woman was a type he did not understand. She made him shudder, her smell, her cold heart, her set and expressionless features.

He loathed the mottled look of Roi, the elaborately corrugated brow which created a defensiveness for the small transparent eyes, the pale mouth moving, curling, rather than speaking words of sense.

When he left that night he said to himself that he was not coming back. He did not understand the house or the old woman, he did not want to learn the guitar. He was uneasy and apprehensive and out of his depth.

But, a day later, he sat with Julie in the drug store having a soda when Roi came in with a friend and stood beside him, looking at Julie. He asked Roi to sit down, and Roi ordered a root beer.

It was a strained and foolish interlacing that went on back and forth, of caution and dislike, boasting and purposelessness, edgy and hateful and yet straining at some sort of unity. At last Julie slipped off her seat in the midst of an involved account of Roi's prowess, and Karel had, slowly, to join her. Roi did not, for a moment, look chagrined; then a slow faint flush mounted and he blinked his eyes rapidly. But he was smiling at them sideways when they left, his pale eyes half-closed in their usual way, his friend grinning.

"Do you really like him?" Julie asked in a small voice. When Karel did not answer, she added, "He seems kind of nasty to me. I don't know why."

"Do you think that, or is that your mother's opinion?" he asked angrily.

"No," she answered sharply, "I make up my own mind."

He persisted against his will, "A girl does the way her mother wants."

"To a girl, he is nasty," she cried. "There are nasty people in the world!"

"And you wondered if I really liked him. If I say I do, does that make me nasty?"

They had come onto the road leading to her house, and he took her arm and pulled her down beside him on a stone wall.

"No," she said, "that's twisting what I said. You like him because you have a good feeling for people. That's the way *you* are." She was angry and a little frantic. "But what do you want me to do? I haven't lived your life. I haven't lived any life but my own. I think the way *I* think. If the same things came to me which came to you I'd be brave. But I can't manufacture experiences. I can't help it if I was raised a certain way, to think certain things. They don't satisfy me or make me happy. And I can't help it if the worst thing that ever happened to me was chicken-pox—and being lonely."

He was touched and felt a wave of tenderness, but he tried to tell himself it was not enough. "It can't be that you live off in some faraway place, making little clucking sounds that are meant to be sympathetic—sheltered round and round, bundled in, cracks sealed up . . ."

"I don't want to be sheltered," she wailed, "I can't help it. Stop it—just stop it!"

He was frantically divided in his mind. He could not allow any separation between them, and he saw this as an unbridgeable gap. He saw here the depth and breadth of difference, he saw it as a desert with no road across it. He took her suddenly by the arms and shook her very hard, using all his strength.

"Do you feel that—what does it say to you?" He wanted to find a way to build his own bridge and he was frantic and artificial. "I knew a boy in the camp like Roi," he said, still holding her tightly. "No good, you would have said. He stole from other people and whined. But they tried to make him inform against a friend. They used a dentist's drill in his jaw, they beat him around the hips and thighs till he could not stand up."

"No!" she cried, putting her hands to her ears.

"You're going to listen!"

"No—no! These are just awful words which don't do him any good now!"

"Yes, you will listen!"

She jerked herself free and started to run down the road. He sat holding his breath until his inner being was brought to a point of suspension, and then his hands came up to cover his face and wave after wave of violent shuddering went over him.

16

At the hour Nicky was to be released from the hospital, John Murray drove up in his old car to fetch him, wearing his blue jeans and his boots as he had come in from the barn.

The child said good-bye to the nurses in an abstracted way, for a change was taking place, and he had to concentrate all his attention on the next step. He came through the door with Karel, and John greeted him gravely, and the three sat in the front seat.

He wore a new plaid shirt given him by Mrs. McVitty, and his watch thudded from its place on his chest. He was very proud of his appearance, and he asked a great many questions. Karel held him on his knees and explained that the doctor had promised—a promise had been made—that when the operation had healed and he had exercised enough, the arm would be his.

The child was silent and happy, glancing from Karel to John who smiled down at him and began to whistle. Nicky watched attentively and puckered his lips soundlessly.

"Put your lips this way," John explained and demonstrated again.

Nicky tried and a small sound came. John nodded. Nicky leaned back against Karel and continued to practice quietly and privately, glancing now and then at John when his success appeared limited. Karel felt the child press more closely against him. The child was content and secure. Once he sat up abruptly and watched a friend of Tommy's pass, but he made no effort to call to him, and when the boy had gone by, he settled back again and resumed his careful practicing.

John was studiously silent. When something was said he smiled and answered pleasantly, but he did not speak voluntarily. This kind of silence made Karel uneasy. It was cool and remote. Either a man was a friend or he was not. Karel frowned in an effort to find some way beyond this silence. He watched John obliquely and did not know how to read his expression. As a younger man he admired John. He would like to look like him. He liked the thin face and the calm withdrawn manner. He imagined that women would think John attractive. He tried to understand why. He was so accustomed to seeing him through Megan's eyes that his own impressions were vague. He tried speaking of Nicky, but at the mention of his name, Nicky renewed his questions, and John was not the one who attempted to answer. He remembered that someone had said that John had been a writer, and he asked him. John looked at him with such swift dislike or fear that Karel felt a sudden flush of anger.

"As long as I'm here, I'm a farmer," John said sharply.

They were coming down the road along the ridge, and Nicky sat up in order to see the places he remembered—the hill across the valley shaped like a porcupine's back, the tree which stood bent alone in a field like a boy fishing.

"Vree says you can go down on a sled here in the winter," he told John.

"Yes," John said.

Nicky considered him with his hard round eyes. "Have you still got your harmonica?"

"No. I have grown up. I now whistle."

Nicky laughed riotously and shouted, "Whistle!"

John drove up to the house and stopped. He got out with only a quick backward look at Nicky and gave a monotone whistle as though to a dog. Mrs. Murray opened the door and ran down the walk to Nicky who stood suddenly trembling and smiling. John had not waited. He had turned into the road and was walking toward his house. Karel watched him going, wondering, alone in some lightless place where he might hide from the Julies and the Johns and all undefined tenderness. Something made John turn his head. The swift warm smile appeared for a moment, and he half-raised his hand.

The child had talked steadily. Like a little weak chicken he had followed Mrs. Murray about, telling her in a mixture of languages of hospital events of special importance. He said he had learned to whistle, and he piped on one note until he turned his white face to her and said, close to tears, that he was tired.

Karel put him to bed in Mrs. Murray's bed, although his cot stood by the window. He sat there musingly as Karel fastened his pajama coat, looking out across the valley.

"Nobody's going away?" he said flatly. "Everyone's going to stay here?"

"Later I will go and feed the rabbit," Karel said, his hands on the child's legs, watching him with great love. "But the little cat wants to sleep with you. You must comfort her. *Tante* Murray will be here when I am away."

"She loves me?"

"She loves you. I love you."

"John Murray?"

"He loves you."

"Vree . . .? Mrs. McVitty . . .? Mr. McVitty . . .?"

Karel hung the watch on a nail by the bed and drew down the shade. Then he held the child for a moment. "Everyone loves you. Because you are Nicky. Later, if you waken, you will see the beautiful moon. There is a full moon now."

The child drew down under the covers. "I do not want to see the moon," he said evenly. "Someone shot at us when there was a moon and I was riding on your back."

Karel stood there very still. That was long ago and remembered. Moonlight was treacherous. It was not a friend. This was memory. A chill went over him. Far and wide, then and now, things were remembered and how could one learn to be bolder than treacherous memory? He saw the grave black eyes fixed on him and he smiled at the child, and put his hands over the eyes to close them.

"Dream happily," he said, and kissed him again.

He sat in the dark with Mrs. Murray, his elbows on his knees, restless but held, watching the light fade over the valley. He wished to talk to her and yet he did not. To him she was suddenly old and he wanted the thing which passed from youth to youth, that understood without words and planned together some common expectancy. And yet he loved her dearly. To see her sitting there quietly in the fading light, sitting very straight by the wicker table, one arm resting on it, made him content.

He considered her steadily, the dark hair, the lines of beauty, the bright quick eyes—that is what he noticed most of all, the lively and loving eyes which seemed to be aware of everything even when she sat most still. Because he wished to speak, hear words, he said something humorously—how she never seemed to miss anything, and she looked at him with a quick expression like John's, sweet and gay.

"Well, everything is very interesting."

He answered wistfully, "Everything seems very enormous to me."

"Oh, no," she answered, and that was all.

In the silence, the wonderment possessed him again. What was Julie doing? And how did one know whether she wanted the same thing that he wanted? And did a man think about love differently than a woman? And yet of course she was only his friend, no question of being in love.

Mrs. Murray said, out of the growing darkness in a mildly ironic voice, "I am always surprised—aren't you?—at the *darkness* of the night. I don't really believe in it. I just believe in the daylight."

It was so unexpected and so firmly said that he burst into laughter.

She smiled. "Go home and feed your rabbit. And bring him tomorrow to Nicky."

He stood up, looking large in the dusk. "I would like to thank you in some way for what you are doing."

"There's no need for that. It's very natural to have the child here." She kissed him quickly. He lingered for a moment and then he kissed her. There were times when he wished unendurably to see his mother.

He turned down the road. Nothing prevented him from walking until the daylight. Nothing in life, no obligation, could restrain him at this moment. He could walk in the darkness. He could roll naked down the hillside. He could lie in the moonlight in the middle of the road, enclosed in this womb-like quiet and rest. He could. He was obliged and beholden to nothing but to the wild fierce restlessness which transformed this familiar road.

Ahead of him he saw the lights of John's and Megan's house. He had thought of Megan at intervals during the evening—when he had turned away from Mrs. Murray as old, when he had wanted to talk about Julie. And to John who was young and a man, there must be some stronger link than his silence and his spare sentences. These are the needs, and the needs do not quiet down until they are met.

He stood in the road before the house for some moments, uncertain and lonely. Then he went toward the door.

But he glanced through the lighted window before he rang the bell. He saw Megan sitting by the fire. She was alone and she was crying.

He turned away abruptly and stood frowning. Tears created in him the most instinctive drawing-back. They were always raw and grim. He stood there motionless. After a moment he picked up one of the white stones which lined the path and flung it as hard as he could across the road in blind and sheer anger.

Megan must have heard him for she came to the door and opened it. He stood there in the light sullen and distraught, staring at her without greeting, and she stood there, her eyes swollen, but smiling a little.

"I thought you were John."

He shook his head and he kicked at another white stone, but his hands were now in his pockets. He was greatly moved by the signs of tears around her eyes.

"Were you—were you coming in?"

Since he did not wish to acknowledge her tears in any way, he said, "Yes," and went past her.

She was nervous. Her hair was tousled, her lips were pale. She stood very straight as though making an effort and continued to smile as though it were an alternative to tears.

"It's nice to see you. I'm glad to see you. But I'm afraid I'm . . ."

"You've been crying," he said. "I was restless. I did not know where to go."

She laughed unsteadily. "I should think you would be restless. What do you do with yourself in this town?"

"Why do you ask me?"

She stood very straight, still smiling, her hands plunged deeply into the pockets of her blue-jean skirt. "Most boys do not read at nineteen. What does one do—dance . . . ?"

"I am no longer nineteen," he said sharply. "I have become thirty-nine. I like to read. I do not know how to dance. I cannot go to the movies for I have no automobile. But I think. I can think. I can think and remember that I have never, never been anything but a man of thirty-nine."

She flushed and turned away, her mouth trembling. "There must be some reason why I think of your age. But I won't do it again." And then she said, as an afterthought, "I think about you quite often." She said it so impersonally he did not look up. He was sitting in her place by the fire and he was bound to something at floor level with a queer perversity of attention as though no tears or disquiet existed there. He saw her slender feet pressed close together and the little bones of her ankles, which seemed to him a very beautiful part of a woman.

He said, "You sit in this house alone, and you are sad—but you know why you are sad—I suppose—and why you are sitting here. But I am suddenly at a loss. I am—I am . . ."

She sat down on the couch and put her head back, and she sighed.

"Is it your brother you are worried about?" she asked quietly.

"He is not my brother."

"Oh . . ."

He heard his words with great astonishment. He had run away from the Youngs because he could not say those words. Their brotherhood had been the warp of his life.

"No, he is not my brother."

She seemed unsurprised. She was looking at him with interest but without astonishment. She looked very young with her swinging hair against her cheeks and the slight swelling about her eyes. "Is he a relation?"

He repeated, "He is not my brother."

She regarded him intently, her dark eyes clear again for this moment. "Why is that so important?"

He could not understand. He frowned and turned away and ran his hand through his hair again and again. It had seemed for a brief moment that to say Nicky was not his brother would release him from something.

"I've told you something I've never told anyone," he said, very low.

He forced her to worry. "Did you steal him? Does he have parents who are looking for him?"

He shook his head. He had said something which was supposed to mark a climax, but it had not done so. He put his face into his hands.

"I am very confused," he said. "The child was all that I cared for until I came here. And now I see other things and I wonder about other things, and I find myself needing to say that the child is no relation . . ." He looked at her and laughed shortly. "But that does not seem to change anything."

"No, it wouldn't," she replied.

He sat there, his fist covering his mouth, his eyes on her face. "I love him dearly but I do not need him as I did. I want to go on to something else."

"But you can't leave him behind," she said, her voice without expression. "He's part of you now."

He turned away. "I know."

After a moment, she inquired, "What is it that troubles you?"

He made a wide, vague gesture. She looked at him, smiling, and asked, "Are you in love?"

"You sound like a mother," he answered sharply. She threw back her head against the couch and the light lay on the smooth high cheekbones and the sloping planes of her cheeks. He added flatly, "But you do not look like a mother."

He measured his words: "I decided I am not in love."

She was silent, but she had turned her head, and was looking at him. He spread out his hands before him and studied them. He thrust out his legs and studied his shoes. He studied the fire. Then he said very low, "She's so foolishly young. Even Nicky is older than she is. I have to tell her everything."

"Who?"

He looked at her, a little startled. "Julie."

She was silent for a moment, considering him thoughtfully. "Julie Wright?"

"Is there another Julie here?" He stood up and walked up and down, building his agitation in order to subdue it.

She looked at him then and lifted herself up slowly. He sat down beside the couch on the floor and put his head against the arm of the couch, and looked at her, past her eyes to the line of her neck where it turned into her shoulder and to the curly hair which fell below her ears. Such unaccountable parts of a woman seemed beautiful.

"I think you have confused a lot of things," she said tiredly. "Julie is a very nice girl. She's pretty and intelligent, and if she likes you, you shouldn't let her go."

"I do not know," he said in a lonely whisper. "How can she ever possibly understand the things which have made me what I am?"

"Maybe you're doing a foolish thing—locking yourself to the past, afraid of some disloyalty if you let it go."

She moved restlessly and went to stand by the fireplace. Her pallor was deeper and her hands were trembling. "That is how it seems to me."

He knelt by the couch for some minutes, and he felt something shifting inside him, shifting so that a lightness came where he had been oppressed before. He measured and turned aside Megan's words, but the shifting went on and some kind of joy began to warm and suffuse. He longed to be reassured and yet he must not be hoodwinked.

He got up slowly and he stood across from her at the fireplace. Happiness was a powerful thing, as powerful as the daybreak. He looked across at her and smiled.

"You are nearly as tall as I am," he said.

He looked at her eyes and the curved high cheekbones and the rather proud expression of her mouth and the curling dark hair. "You've got eyes like mine and we've got the same color." He smiled and looked at her intently. "And you say things understandably. Isn't there something remarkable in all that?"

She looked at him gravely and did not stir. "I'm glad we're alike." And then she said, "I'm glad you're in love with Julie."

He did not know what he felt. He asked, "Why?"

"Oh—because she is gentle—and *has* to have experiences made for her. Only you may be deceiving yourself there. And because she can love and appreciate what you are . . . why you are . . . without understanding."

He rubbed his hand roughly across his eyes. "Is that important?"

"Yes. And I think she's quite strong in other ways which might surprise you."

He turned away, walking up and down, not taking his eyes from her. "I do not really know that I am in love with her," he said, watching her.

She laughed a little. "You talk only about yourself. Perhaps she will decide some things."

He put his head down against the fireplace mantel. He stared at her, observing her as he had never done before; finding in the fact of a woman something baffling and not to be done without.

The night was very still. At a distance a voice sang and then faded. It was a radio in a car, perhaps, for no one in this place would sing alone, unprompted, on a public road, but it was sweet and eerie. It seemed as though she were listening for something, and he remembered that she had been crying. That seemed a long time ago, and he stirred uneasily and after a time asked her somewhat remorsefully why she had been crying when he came to the door.

She started to speak, and then she put her fingers over her mouth and gazed at him intently for a moment, before she turned away.

"I was waiting for John. I had decided that he was not coming home."

He could not remain withdrawn. "What is the matter?"

She hesitated for some time, her eyes wide and unblinking, gazing at the black window.

"He is terribly afraid, and I cannot reach his fear. He is afraid of all kinds of things—passing time and distracted hope and why he is not more what he wants to be. And he thinks he must do without me because I am now an impediment." She looked at him and smiled slightly. "If he explained things as they really are, I think he would have to face them. Instead he tells himself he is no longer in love with me. That is supposed to explain everything. The mind says certain things, like I am no longer in love with you, and it is taken for fact."

Karel continued to walk up and down, but he was listening intently.

"A woman, if she is loving and in any way wise, sees what is behind these things. A man—a man seems so blinded by his manliness."

She was silent for some time, and then she went on as though he were not pacing back and forth in the room. She did not seem troubled by the sound of his steps.

"I think he loves me, but he cannot say it. He thinks it will commit him to something. And he is very much disturbed by the things which the past has left undone. He is terribly uneasy when I say he was the first to help me see myself as an individual. But it is true. He loved me and opened up a world for me. He gave me confidence in myself and set a value on *me*. He is part of me—like my hands or my voice."

Karel said, pacing out a pattern, "Do something—do something then!"

She did not answer quickly. She lay quietly staring at the ceiling, and then she said, "Oh, oh!" and the tears came again.

"There are some women who have a dogged love and trust, and they live in faith." The tears came so quietly that her voice remained calm. "I think of all the dearest things about marriage—the trustworthiness and the assurance that your hopes are safe and your dreams are understood, and that when you say something which is in your heart it's not heard as something strange and unfamiliar. And that the naturalness of both of you is free and secure, and that you want your life together to be reciprocal, equal. That's a good marriage, that's the dearest thing of marriage. If that were true once, it's true now, over and beyond and above everything."

The awful pain which clamped him in the presence of suffering drove him fiercely. He pushed a chair out of the way, he kicked aside a rug which had been impeding him. She looked at him then, white and strained.

"Someone told me I was a fool, that he had never really loved me. That was the worst moment of all. But you don't deceive yourself. Not about the kind of love which replenishes and makes your spirit free and makes you think vividly and satisfies your heart. *I* know. I waken night after night, disbelieving, lying in the dark refusing to believe something that my reason and my heart say is impossible. Can I honestly go beyond that and believe something else?"

He stood looking at her, his body and his mind impatient and awkward. "I don't know. I don't know anything about these things! They're terrible to me, yet they happen . . . !"

He threw himself down in a chair. She lay very quiet, her voice moving lightly. "People talk. In kindness they talk about John and me. Out of their own kindness they tell me their opinions. It is all very wise and logical and highly probable, but I don't really hear it and I don't really understand it. I know something else—some continuity, some principle, some area of changelessness that isn't even aware of all this logic and probability." Then she suddenly covered her face with her hands. "Oh! I want him to be happy. If I never see him again—and yet I will—I will—I will."

He kicked against the log in the fireplace. Then he knelt and tidied the ashes.

"Sometimes," he said tensely, "the biggest thing you can do is hold on. It is the biggest thing in life at that moment."

"Yes," she whispered.

He laughed a little, nervously. "In my family's living room was a Schiller motto: Peace is rarely denied to the peaceful. Maybe you can say: Love is rarely denied to the loving."

He moved back into his chair, less shaken, able to look at her now.

"The day that I first saw that American convoy, all I could think was, not *Thank God* or *I'm hungry* or *Let me sleep*—but *You didn't quit, you didn't quit, you didn't quit.* I wasn't thinking how fine this rescue was—I was thinking I hadn't quit."

She laced the ribbon of her belt in and out of her fingers,

studying it. After a time she said very low, "I guess I must make my own choice—*somehow*. But I'll never be offered a choice. Not with this kind of rationalizing . . ."

"Who is given a choice?" he asked, wishing to know.

"When it's a matter of indifference—then there's often a choice. Do I sound very glib? It's because I've talked to myself so much that I am letter perfect." The tenseness came back to her face again and the little groan to her throat. She doubled up across her knees.

"Yes," he said matter-of-factly, "the stomach goes to pieces."

"Will you get me some coffee?" she asked. "There is some on the stove."

When he returned he said, "Where is John now?"

She shook her head.

He glanced at her and said in an oddly detached way, "I love you."

"Ah—you cannot confuse your feelings."

"An emotion never before experienced sends shivers down my spine."

She laughed. He smiled with downcast eyes and flushed a little.

"I love you too," she said, "but I'm not confused about it." It did not match, in any degree, what he had said, and he retreated into his own perplexity. He was overawed by what he had said and did not know how to return to it again. He sat down abruptly and leaned his chin on his fist. She watched him. Presently he got up and poured her another cup of coffee, and they sat silently with the cups in their hands. After a while she leaned back against the couch.

"Thank you," she said, and he looked at her swiftly for he did not know to what she was referring. "Why are you confused about whether you love Julie or not?"

He answered with an effort, staring hard at the toes of his shoes, "Because it is not at all the way I imagined or have felt."

"Then perhaps you are right. Perhaps she's not important to you."

He looked at her, frowning.

She smiled. "You believe in popular fetishes as much as any of us. *How one should feel.*" She considered the coffee in her cup, swirling it about gently. "It seems to me that some men's—and some women's—desires are more sensitive than pure sexuality. Then they are confused because it is not the way they have been told it should be. Perhaps that is you. I don't know." He was silent. She turned her head again and looked at him for a long time, studying his face, the deep and serious eyes, the undeniable sadness. He did not turn away. He was studying her as well. "Yet I suppose it is one of the most important things in the world: what men and women mean to each other . . . And we all try to find it the best way we can."

She lay there silently for some time, and he sat staring down at his shoes, the brooding look on his face. Finally he looked at her, with an effort, the slim body lying so unobtrusively on the couch, the lamplight reflected so that the pallor and dark hair were both filled with light, and all the conflicts of desire and confusion and wonderment rose up in him again. There had been a simplicity in his life. Where was it now? Now he wished many things, reaching out beyond his present experience to this and to her and to that. There was no peace, and the simplicity was gone.

Presently he saw that she was crying. There was no sobbing or lamentation. The tears were simply rolling down the side of her cheeks into the pillow. He could not stand that. He stared at her and sank deeper into his chair, his chin against his clasped hands, his eyes never moving from her face.

17

As the days went on, Nicky grew more and more sure that his salvation depended on his exercising. He sat in the sun with Karel or Mrs. Murray, stripped to the waist, and followed their instructions zealously. It was a game, it was power, it was the way he joined the absolute world of boys. The doctor came, and squatting down, watched him and nodded, and saw with perfect clarity what Nicky wished him to see, arms moving, complete and free, to the right, to the left, above his head.

"Well, what's Agnes Stillwell doing?" Mrs. Murray asked the doctor as she stood by his car.

"What do you think," he answered, his hands gripping the steering wheel till the veins stood out. "Contending. Because, A, some people have got to take Agnes down a peg; B, some people don't know whether it's good to give charity to strangers; why, there are those poor folks over in Hitestown we haven't taken a basket to for two years; C, some people think their own church needs it first and after that . . . Also, they always ask if he is a Jew." He sighed. "Of course some people know they mustn't ask that outright, so they talk about the Phoenicians or the

Fuzzy-Wuzzies sucking them dry. Such a private language —but I'm a great linguist, and I give 'em my plain interpretation." He thought about it for a moment. "But some people are mighty good and would give if they could."

She stood and looked at him, smiling a little.

"How did you learn the simple act of affection, Lem?"

"I? I believe what I see and then I act."

"That's not what happens. *You* see without eyes. Why don't you admit it?"

He pursed his lips and blew explosively through his mustache, and then was silent.

She stood away from the car, sheltering her eyes from the sun so that she could look at him. "John says the trouble with this town is that everyone lacks passion, has no goal."

The doctor shook his head. "Ninety goddamn per cent of them has got a goal—to be better than his neighbor. But that's no goal a self-respecting man can live or die for."

She stood silently considering this, and watching the child who sat on a mat, turning and twisting his thin little body indefatigably.

"You still haven't told me what will happen about Nicky."

He started his car and did not look at her again.

"I have ordered the arm. Don't tell Agnes."

"Lem, I've got $50 I was saving . . ."

"Keep it. I'll charge the sons and daughters of Darkness a little bit more here and there. They'll contribute. Don't worry. I'll see to that."

She said with her blue eyes suddenly flashing, "Are they always going to be this way, Lem? What do they need to wake them up!"

"What's the matter with you, Jose? You're awake, aren't you? I'm awake. What more do you want?"

"We do what we can because we've seen the child, and

love him. Would we have done it if we hadn't—just for the sake of a loving act?"

"Well, now," he said, "I'd only answer for you. Not for myself." He threw in the clutch. "Take that child out of the sun. He'll wear himself out."

The first week-end after college began, Julie returned home. The maid told her that Karel had neither come nor called.

Julie believed it was hazardous for a girl to take the initiative. It frightened men. So she had been told. So she observed. But she could not forget that she had run away from Karel the last time they had been together. She could not forget that every word he had said from the first time they had met had lodged in some place and some degree in her heart. That seemed remarkable to her. In an odd unexplained way it was as though the words he had used, the things that were unsaid or sensed or left to her discernment, all had their source in her. That most of her emotional life had been formed by vicarious things did not alter this belief. Vicarious things were often confirmations.

All alone, locked in the deep recesses of her girlhood, she had trusted only herself, had followed faithfully and bravely the unfolding of her own sensibilities, knowing well that they did not match in most particulars the pattern of her mother and father. Perhaps the reason for this lay further back, she had told herself, perhaps she was like her ancestors in some ideal, some inner life, some stern, honest, beautiful belief in the power—of what—of conscience? She had all the impulses of love and of identification.

But she lived in her own time, she used the words of her generation, although her tendencies might be only partially adapted to them. She wished that she were bold, she wished that she had some way of laying all the turmoil and tumult out on the floor and pinning it together properly. She wished she were not eighteen and uncertain at every point. And then she sensed a wonderment, that she might be in love with this experience and not with Karel.

She did not wish it to be that way. Perhaps she was cheating somewhere, cheating Karel or herself or both together. *Both together* fell most naturally into the groove of her thinking.

So she returned to her original worry. She had run away from him, and since then a week had passed. Was he staying away? Could she go and see him? She was simple in her heart like a little dog who would run to the person he loved, but she was educated to be a girl.

She decided on a compromise. She selected a book, almost any book, a book of poems, and she cut across the back country road, crossed a field, and came to Mrs. Murray's. Mrs. McVitty was there, and she and Mrs. Murray and the little boy, Nicky, and Tommy Rawlins, were sitting out in the sun. Mrs. Murray was cutting corn for canning and Mrs. McVitty was reading to the children out of a schoolbook.

Julie did not know Mrs. Murray or Mrs. McVitty very well, and she came into the circle shyly. She said that she had brought this book for Karel, and might she leave it for him to pick up. The hand stretched out, the looped tendril, the tender painless trap. Mrs. Murray greeted her with the warm bright look she reserved for the young, and went indoors to fetch them all something cool to drink. Mrs. McVitty recalled to Julie that she had taught the second grade for many years, and was keeping Nicky in line with his classmates. "Although of course he won't be satisfied without children for long."

Julie looked at Nicky as he sat on a rug, his little cat beside him, Tommy on the grass. She had never really seen him before, never really. The brown thin little body with the white dressings below the shoulders . . . oddly this body without arms did not seem incomplete. Perhaps because the child had so plainly endowed himself with what he needed, with movement. He looked at her, his head lowered, his eyes raised, thundery eyes asking the same question of all strangers. The little cat licked and arranged herself assiduously, arching her neck far back in order to reach her chest, a small world in commotion on the same rug where the child sat so rigid. After a while the child interrupted the chatting and said to Mrs. McVitty, "You're not reading to Tommy and me. Why aren't you reading?"

"We've got a caller," Mrs. McVitty said, and he looked at Julie again from beneath angry lowered lids.

Julie returned his look. He was tangible, Karel's brother; he was an expanded part of something which had been narrow before. He was a child, he looked like Karel. He had temperament and vitality and demands. She suddenly realized that he was inextricably a part of the loops and links and twinings which wove back and forth between herself and Karel, or—as she saw with sudden insight—between Karel and his human need and Julie and her need, whether or not they ever met as one need fulfilled.

In a manner her heart sank. She had no philosophy or detachment to bear her up. The suggestion that she might, after all, be without Karel left her desolate. Had she been superstitious she would have regarded that insight as a portent, but she was too healthy and direct for that. Her heart sank because she wondered suddenly how things could be made to happen which now seemed so important to her.

But the uncomplicated, the loving, has its own means. She saw the child as a child, only a few years removed from herself. After a little time, over the glass which Tommy held for him, he too saw her as small and grave like himself. Some language of his which had not been forgotten by her licked dreamily at them, rising and falling between them and encircling the little cat. Presently, without comment, she came and sat on the grass near the rug, her sneakers drawn up under her, the cat purring in her lap. She did not try to amuse him, and they remained unsmiling toward each other, but his eyes were on her continually. She made a cat's cradle on her fingers and plaited asters together for a necklace for the cat. Nicky commented, she replied. They drew together. Tommy watched with earnest eyes.

Karel looked at the book wonderingly. Julie had never talked about this book or this subject. He did not understand.

"Did she say nothing?" he asked Mrs. Murray.

"Nothing. Just asked me to give it to you."

He sat down to dinner with the book beside him. The doctor was there also and he picked it up and looked at it through his bifocals, and read aloud a poem in a flat New England voice, without comment.

Suddenly Karel believed he understood. The book was just a reminder, a telephone call. He was glad. That was good.

He felt exhilarated. In the secret little chamber of the innermost heart he felt an ease which he had never known before, a perfect calmness.

He said suddenly to the doctor, "Every night I have read your books. Every night. Now I know that it is very foolish to think that I can be a doctor."

Dr. Jarman held his fork halfway to his mouth and peered at him, and then he took his food into his mouth and chewed it. "Why?"

"Why do you ask me why? You pointed out. It would be thirteen years before I could be a doctor—if everything went well. I have no money like that."

The doctor considered his food and pushed it about a

bit on his plate. "Maybe there's a scholarship or two somewhere."

"If there is a scholarship or two I would like to use them for something else." He had bent over his plate and was not looking at either of them. "I do not want to be a doctor."

Jarman was silent for a moment and then he said rather testily, "Sudden distaste for medicine men?"

"No. It is—that things are happening—how can I put it? —I must find myself soon. I must settle down. Thirteen years would be too long. I have a great deal of time to make up. And I see that medicine does not heal everything. I am very realistic." He said it calmly, for the commotion had already spent itself within him.

"What would you want to do?" Mrs. Murray asked with interest.

"I have just begun to think about it," he said. "I might go to college if I can work in some way, and study something to do with"—he looked at them both and smiled a little—"with people. I do not know anything but people."

After a pause, the doctor said, "Well, why not?"

"Why not?" Mrs. Murray asked, pleased, her eyes dancing.

Karel took the book with him when he left with the doctor. He held it tightly between his hands. He would read every poem in it. The doctor, bouncing the car carelessly over a bad stretch of road, said, "Sociology, maybe. Anthropology."

"Perhaps it will be with children. I like children. I am being sensible, aren't I?"

"Damn relief."

In front of the Episcopal Church the next morning he met Julie. He had never seen her wearing a hat before. It made her seem strange and apart from him. But she looked at him swiftly and personally, and he said, without regard for her mother who had stopped beside her, plainly listening, and for her father who stood watchfully by the car door which he had locked, "I think the book is fine. It is . . ."

"I am away at college," she interrupted hurriedly. "I am home only on week-ends."

He stood looking at her. At college— He did not realize that so drastic a move could be made without his knowing it. Something very important to him had been realigned and represented to him in a new guise while his eyes had been closed.

The church bell was ringing and she turned away with her mother toward the door. He came up to her quickly and said with a frown, "This afternoon you'll go walking with me?"

He had not noticed her mother or her father or even, for that matter, whether Julie answered. Yet as he turned away he bowed abstractedly as though including them all.

Julie was sitting on the wall by the roadside. He did not see her until she jumped down. She was dressed in blue, her hair drawn from her face and tied at the nape of her neck with a blue ribbon. There was a flush on her face, and her eyes were very quick and alert. She said, valiantly matter-of-fact, "The maid is out. My mother would have come to the door."

He frowned and then he smiled. And then he put his arm through hers and began to run, and she ran, pulled along at first, surprised and happy. He stopped running, unbeknownst to himself, when they came into the area of his own familiarity, the fields and trees and houses which surrounded him each day.

He was smiling at her broadly. She said, "It takes three hours on the train to get here Friday nights, but I think I will do it all winter."

"Oh, yes," he said. "You should." Then he inquired, "Shall I read all that book of poems?"

"No. I will select some that you ought to know." Later she said, "After I have taught you to dance, perhaps you'll come to the college one week-end."

The thought was so startling that he did not answer readily.

"I suppose you can ski," she said calmly.

He replied, "When I was a child I skied."

She planned so calmly and gently.

When they returned up the road it was twilight. She stopped by the stone wall, and through the trees a light could be seen in her home.

She wished him to kiss her but he did not know it. He thought that it was he who wished to kiss her. So he put his arm around her shoulders and she yielded, and he thought that he had demanded something which she did not have the strength to withhold. He looked at her, not knowing what he would see on her face, and she drew his head down and kissed him again.

Now he held her tightly, and he kissed her on the lips. He kissed her again and again, his mouth on hers. She held his head so that he did not stop until she was ready. The blending was so perfect that it was hard to know where the yearning of one or the other began. He whispered, "Dearest, dearest, dearest Julie."

Julie found her mother sitting on the chaise longue in her room. She grew cold with premonition and resentment. Her mother said, "You're late for dinner, dear. What time does your train leave?"

"Eight o'clock," Julie said.

Her mother was silent for a moment. "Why did you creep away to meet him?"

Julie's voice was stiff. "I didn't creep anywhere."

"Why didn't he come to the front door then?"

Julie did not answer.

Mrs. Wright said steadily, "You were not raised to act deceitfully."

Still Julie did not answer. The mother's calmness was deceptive, and Mrs. Wright added a little wildly, "Let me say—before you accuse me falsely—it is not because people are talking or because he works in a garage that I distrust him. We're too democratic for that."

Julie turned and looked at her mother. "What is it then?"

Now her mother sat erect, and agitation leapt from her toes to the crown of her head. "There's too much concealed. You can't possibly know what will come out some day—what instability and cruelness, maybe. It is not his fault. But everything he's gone through—everything he is—is different from you—completely different. There just would be no real meeting anywhere!"

Julie looked down at her clasped hands, thinking of how joyfully they had kissed. "You talk as though I was going to marry him."

Mrs. Wright stared at her. "Oh, my God," she whispered. "Oh, my God. Don't speak that way."

Julie was mute, closed up. After a moment her mother said softly, "You are not interested in him—not personally, are you?"

"Don't *you* think I am? You seemed to think so—asking me questions."

Mrs. Wright stood up, holding herself with a visible effort.

"Julie, I will not believe it. It is a nightmare. I will wake up."

But in the daylight one stumbles as much as in the night. Next day, after a sleepless night, Mrs. Wright met the doctor in the drug store. The druggist was saying to him,

"How's that little fellow coming on? My Dorothea collected four dollars selling berries to give to Mrs. Stillwell."

"Great! He's got guts. Tough little fellow."

Mrs. Wright went out when the doctor went out. She stood on the steps, her face tense with the unnamable thing which became enlarged with concealment. She said, "Doctor, may I ask you something?"

Not medical advice, he was sure of that. She didn't trust country doctors. Yet he felt gentle when he saw a woman he had known all his life in distress.

"That little boy—are you sure this is the right thing we are doing?"

"Right thing? A child needs arms."

"Where did those boys come from? Why is the responsibility for anything as important as this not to be fixed properly?"

He was unprepared for the question. He hesitated. "I don't know how one fixes that kind of responsibility. It seems to me you do what comes to you."

Her hands were trembling and she clasped them tightly over her purse. "That is very emotional, isn't it? Perhaps it was quite the wrong thing to have happen."

He thought for a moment. "Maybe. But I'd rather make mistakes than do nothing."

Her throat tightened. "Whole lives can be changed—and not always for the best."

He looked at her with interest. "Are you afraid of these boys in some way?"

"Afraid? What a strange thing to say! Two boys—less than twenty." She went toward her car. "I do not like the things which are unexplained. To me they don't belong here. They are utterly not our own."

He could not resist saying, "Do we take such good care of our own?" but she looked at him as though she had not heard him and got into her car.

She had not really heard him. She was hearing only the jagged ends of what she might have said and might not say. If she were to say plainly what she felt or if she were to scream aloud as she would like to do, she would be yielding herself to something as unthinkable as the admission that this boy—this alien disquieting boy—might be a genuine part of her life. She drove the car very fast, and everything in her hardened, her eyes, the veins of her temples, the roof of her mouth, her voice, her thoughts.

The doctor was a little surprised when he asked Mrs. Wright that question. *Was she afraid of those boys?* It had slipped from him in a way he had not intended. He thought about it as he drove along, and it did not yield itself to an empirical approach. He was a man of science and if it did not yield in those terms it did not yield at all. But what existed must be demonstrable and, by God, this existed.

After ringing the doorbell and walking fruitlessly around Mrs. Murray's house, he hung the package from the drug store on the kitchen doorknob and returned to his car. He sat there for a moment looking at the house, so long remembered, so much a part of the landscape of his mind. She was not a woman of science. How would she put it in words? Then John Murray came up from the orchard, the sunlight on his thick brown hair. He had a basket of apples under his arm. He was caught before he could retreat.

"Megan took them for a drive," John said. When he could not retreat he became friendly and warm.

"Damn strange thing," the doctor said, "your mother's the only one I know who doesn't get things twisted. But Mrs. Cecil Truslow Wright—oh, hell . . . !" He looked at John. "Someone said that we hope vaguely, we dread precisely. Doesn't seem to me it was always that way. I once set myself a definite goal—healing. Now I wonder why. What's the matter? Too much skepticism?"

He asked his question and then he started his car. He gave a glance at John standing there in the sunlight, looking like a boy and yet with something sad and stooped and timeless in his tall body. He said loudly above the motor, "By God, I'm going to stay a skeptic, though. You a skeptic, fellow?"

John did not answer. Then he turned his head slowly. "I don't think about it at all."

The doctor sat looking at him for a moment, seeing something he had not seen before. "Oh," he said, "Sure. That may be . . ."

John smiled, sudden and winning. "What may be? Things work out. You let half your mind go to sleep and things work out. It never fails."

The doctor shut off the motor and continued to look at him.

"You don't mean that?"

John laughed. "What makes you say that?"

"Because I don't think you're a fool."

John drew up a deep sigh and held his breath for a moment. He said quietly, his glance moving away, "I'm not a fool. Perhaps I'm one of the few honest people around here." Then he looked suddenly at the doctor and smiled again. "I know what I do not want, and that's an improvement over most, isn't it?"

The doctor was not looking at him. People were very sad, he was thinking, and with all that he knew he wished that he knew more. Young men had fear and distrusted faith . . . just as he did. He rounded this thought with surprise. Fear and no faith, and when a boy like Karel was not afraid and had a kind of dogged surety that life was not merely a variation on death, who gave him a hand, who believed that he might be right?

"God," he said. "I wouldn't waste any money buying that kind of talk." He started the motor again. "Wake up. You're a bright fellow. Wake up. Start moving. Come alive." He glanced at John. "Listen, I've known you for over thirty years. Don't just stand there!"

And that was it . . . that was it, as John knew. Don't just stand there . . . Cut away. Do what he intended to do. Be free. Question. Write maybe. Ask and answer. As he stood there in the sunlight with the basket of apples dragging against his arm, he felt that an end had been reached. Right here was the end. Right here, in the sunlight. The end of what? Just the end. Like the beginning . . .

John had sat in the dark for a long time that evening, motionless. His feelings and his thoughts were motionless. Only his despair shifted and turned. Only the world outside himself offered some surety, some probability. The gentle man turning and turning and turning in the unlighted cell of his mind . . .

When Megan came out, after a time, he stood up and said he was going for a walk. Suddenly a terrible fright took hold of her. The tone of his voice shut her away. He kept his back to her. She said *Why? Why? Why?* and she insisted on knowing, there and then, what he was thinking.

"I can't go on," he said very quietly. "That's all. I can't do it. I said I was going in June. I didn't. I tried to work it out."

All her maturity, all her love and resolution and faith deserted her. She was engulfed in panic. Her fright and loss were so terrible that she believed she was screaming, but no sound came. The panic had come on her without warning, breaking through her defenses. She saw his face for a moment in the light from the house, set in misery, his eyes asking her something. All she could say on a whisper was, *No, no, no, no,* and he turned away and was lost in the darkness.

She lay awake all night, saying No in various forms. It was overwhelming darkness, the night of the soul, when no light can be found and everything is a primeval submergence into despair.

He came in the next morning and said he had sat all night on a wall in the field. He said he wanted to put certain things straight, and he stood stiffly by the table, a cup of coffee in his hand. He said with an effort, "It's not you. It's myself. But I feel as though I were dead, and everything here is dead to me. It's been dead since I came back. The war killed it, and maybe something else. We're dead together. I told you I was leaving. It's not fair to either of us to delay it any longer."

"Go away for a little time," she said, "as long as you like, but come back!"

"I won't promise anything. I don't think I could ever come back—when something is so very dead."

"That's not possible . . ." and then she stopped. All the words she needed dissolved. She was cut off. Nothing was real but this loss. She was engulfed again. She saw him going toward the door and she was lost.

He said, "I'll stay at Mother's. She makes excuses about finding someone for the farm. She can't go on doing that."

All she would say again in the barest whisper was, *No, no, no, no, no.*

He went out hurriedly, closing the door, and his steps quickened until he seemed on the verge of running.

She went frozen through the day, afraid to confirm or deny anything. When the telephone rang she did not answer it. Once she saw Mrs. Murray in the road, her hands on the gate, but she drew back, away from the window.

She tried to find her lost strength, but her weakness overwhelmed her. She could not remember what she had believed in, or where her faith lay. No action had reality. The night was very deep.

But the impulse to live is keen. Something Karel had said went through her mind. She remembered Karel. She stood with her hands on the sink, a pan of dishes before her, and tried to relate his life to hers, for in a faraway portion of her mind, all fear and grief were the same.

All the same . . . but she felt only her anguish. Her whole soul was an open mouth, a soundless cry.

She moved about helplessly from room to room. But when at length she answered the phone her voice sounded calm. Now her thoughts had a certain sequence. Some of the numbness passed from her heart. She believed if she could talk to someone who needed no explanations some of the terrible paralysis might pass away. She telephoned Karel, and when she could not reach him, left a message for him.

It was not possible to think that John would never return. She stood by the window looking toward the barn. Once she saw his blue shirt, but now, at the accustomed time, she did not see him on the path coming toward their house. It was like imagining one could live without color, sound, speech. Her world was mute and engulfed in gray.

The twilight deepened. She did not eat any dinner. She lay on the sofa. It was a dream. One's life was not rent apart in this way. She felt a terrible exhaustion. She had borne the weight of this fear for so long, and she had always believed that she would have some choice. Now her capacity to affirm, to be confident, was emptied like an overturned bucket.

She had loved him in a very uncommon way. He was her lover and her husband and her dearest friend. And the vow of marriage was an avowal of continuity.

But this was such a black night! She could not see her way.

She had no signposts. No voice spoke to her. Only her grief was loud and echoing. All she could hear was her grief.

The darkness deepened. Karel had not telephoned, but she forgot that she had called him. She stood up and walked into the dark kitchen. Standing there in her kitchen, her senses could only encompass oblivion.

She went uncertainly toward the door and out into the wide, wide gentle darkness.

She went down the road in the dark. It was a moonless dark, and the stars were very remote. They filled the sky in distant galaxies, impersonal, detached, and she needed the close and the tender. It is unlikely that there is any loneliness so deep and lost as the loneliness which feels no other heart near it.

She wished very much to believe that death was oblivion. For if death were oblivion then there was an alternative to being mistaken. If one has been mistaken in the trust and the love and the truth of a relationship into which one has built his life, then oblivion becomes requisite to the bankruptcy which follows. Here, in the numbed heart, was the emptiness which is itself oblivion, a vestibule to a broader emptiness, a nothingness which courage cannot touch.

She came to the bank of the river and stood looking down at the formless water and heard the sound of the water against a rock, a sound as familiar as the sight of the water. And she burst into tears.

She had not known where she was going. She had not meant to come here. They had sat by this river together twilight after twilight. They had not needed to talk together, for what they shared was a whole thing, and they understood it well. They saw the same shade of blue in the river; one discovered and brought to the other blue-eyed grass or robin's plantain, or the iridescent sounds of a hot day, all the symbols of that deeper communion, that natural trust.

When he had first returned after the war, they had brought their suppers here on hot days, for he had said that this place and she sitting here had been a special part of his remembrances, and he wanted the continuity which it gave. He had held her in his arms. He had said that she was a part of himself, inextricable. She wept now because some things which are shared are never yours alone. How you felt, why you felt that way, the agreement, the unspoken word and the intuition, the contentment of being one in perception, in the seeing, in the event—those things have no real identity except as something shared. It cannot be remembered except as a whole, and the pain of division is like the pain of total loss.

Surely death must be the most kindly peace. If the exact and pure vision, the precise faith which says I know what is essential and proven cannot change no matter how violent the claim—if that is true, then one does not want oblivion. If that were true, nothing could move her, nothing disturb her. The agony, the slipping foot here on the bank, was another thing altogether—is faith a vision or is it deception? How can I know what is true? I will stick to it through fear and despair if it is right, but I do not want to deceive myself. That is the agony, that is where the doubt lies. Do I trust my intuitions or do I trust the logic based on events?

There is always that indecision, the wild wonder whether self-destruction is not better than self-deception, if the cathartic of oblivion is not, in the end, the most honest means of deliverance. But what is oblivion?

The loose earth slipped, and small stones rolled to the

water. She desired it that way. She wanted the earth to move of itself so that it would shape her decision. The earth seemed to sway and dislodge itself and draw her foot after it. She dug her fingers into the bank, but they did not hold. Everything moved downward softly, there was barely a sound.

But I love him! she said aloud suddenly, as though protesting.

18

A few minutes past six, the doctor had driven up to the garage and honked twice for Karel. Karel had run down the stairs, buttoning the cuffs of his clean shirt. McVitty had strolled out to chat with the doctor, and as they drove off, he called after Karel, "I forgot—Megan Murray wants you to call her."

The doctor glanced at him. "You got you a family for sure. Nicest family in town."

Karel did not answer immediately. He had not seen Megan since the night he had come upon her crying, and he still felt weighted with some responsibility. After a moment he said, "I wish—I wish that . . ."

The doctor glanced at him again. He allowed the silence to deepen for a moment. "Fine young woman. She's got courage and she's strong—moral fiber. She won't break."

The words brought a certain relief to Karel. They lifted some unnamed fear which had sucked him. Of course she was very strong and would not break. That's why he liked her.

But *liking* was not what he had said to her. He had said

that he loved her. The meaning and the responsibility were too much. He turned away from it in his mind.

He did not want her unhappy. He was too deeply involved with his feelings to want her unhappy. His hands were suddenly trembling so much that he clasped them tightly together. It had suddenly occurred to him that he might go and talk to John.

He repudiated the idea.

He did not desire to see her as he longed to see Julie, but he wanted to remember everything she had said. It sprang from some totally subjective thing, something which had been floated out of his deepest understanding and related to all that he knew, and she had said it, not he.

And because she had said it, not he, he was thus faintly, remotely, disengaged. He could see the outlines of her sorrow, he could see it mistily with beginning and end—sorrow, as he understood it compassionately.

This was the first time she had telephoned him. Because it was Megan who had telephoned, his imaginings were stirred.

It was a startling, mature, old love he felt, and he was caught in something he only vaguely understood. This seemed to belong in the more subtle regions where his emotions were untried. He did not understand its implications, its requirements, its references. He was nineteen but he was also thirty-nine. He was a boy and a man at the same time. Yet he had to live one age at a time. He had to make a choice.

"Kinda silent," the doctor suggested.

Karel roused himself. "I am sorry."

In his mind he had gone through the motions of calling Megan, hearing her voice. Because this engrossed and insulated him, he failed to call her. He sat down at dinner with the doctor, and he asked the doctor a question about her—how old she was—and in his mind he had telephoned her. After dinner he sat down to type out a report which the doctor needed the next day.

Megan lay there for some time after she had opened her eyes again. It was now fully dark. Very possibly she was dead. One did not know what death was.

She lay there for some minutes, struggling to understand. Was this what she had desired—this dark sentience, the water lapping against her side, the terrible remote vaulting sky with its crowding stars? She did not stir. A sluggishness engulfed her. Her breath became strangled and she gasped. Why, why . . . why was it so hard to recognize death?

A long way off a locomotive hooted. It wailed for a mile or so, eerie and piercing, and through her sluggish mind ran the line of lighted cars going somewhere, direction-bent. She turned her face so that her cheek and an eye were washed by the water and she felt the water sinking into her hair and chilling her skull. Why was life so insistent? Why, why . . . held together by lapping water and a full cold sky . . . why, why life? She could still will herself to die, and she lay very still, savoring the water and the rough jagged bank where she lay. Her head ached where she had struck it, and her arm pained her.

But there is a kind of love which cannot injure and it comes when one is still. She said John . . . John . . . John . . . on an indrawn breath, and there seemed no connection between that name and death . . . no way one could willingly hurt one with that name.

The pain in her arm was very mortal. She moved a little, and the stones and sand, the weeds under her hand and the water clinging to her hair were all familiar. She sat up slowly against the bank. Across the little river was the bulky shape of a house; a lamp flared in a window and a man stood behind it. Nearby she heard a leap and a splash and knew that a fish had sprung to the surface for a moment. She remembered the time Karel had knelt on this bank and seen a leaping fish for the first time. For some reason it had overjoyed him.

She lay against the bank, her tired mind too weary to travel further. Who are my enemies? Karel had said. . . .

The sounds of the night were small but insistent, a commotion of insects and small earth animals in the grass above her, and a pebble sliding down the bank into the water. There was also the wind which stirred the dry leaves, and its chillness reached her wet side and hair. She drew a deep breath and moved. Understanding life . . . and the idea *John* . . . These might have a single meaning, somewhere in her spirit, a meaning without enemies.

After the doctor had answered the bell and remained in his office for some time, Karel heard his name called. He finished the sentence on the doctor's report and went to the office door. He saw Megan, her dark hair damply flat above her pale face, and her arm in a sling.

"Megan had a fall," the doctor said. "Pulled a ligament . . . Drive her home, like a good fellow."

"A fall . . ." Karel started to say, coming toward her, but the doctor interrupted sharply.

"Get the car."

Outside on the porch, Karel hesitated. She had not spoken and she had not smiled; her dark eyes had watched him as he walked across the room. Now he heard the doctor say, "You go on, holding to him. Let's face things as they are," and her answering, "That has nothing to do with the heart of the matter."

"What is the heart of the matter?" the doctor had asked, but she did not reply. Karel went and got the car, and returned to go with her down the steps.

She said nothing, but he was intensely aware of her as she sat beside him. He said at last in a voice that was under great control, "When you called me were you hurt?"

"No."

He glanced at her.

"You are very important to people. You must take care of yourself."

She said, "Ah . . ." and began to cry.

He sat there rigid, his thoughts leaping and disorganized. He did not know how or why he loved her in the way he did. This loving was too oblique to be in clear terms. This loving was a familiarity of the spirit, a continuing-on at one point in terms which he understood, a withholding at another point in terms which were also his own. It made him puzzled and restless, for he had not imagined that there could be many kinds of love.

She said, very low, "I remembered something you said. Then I did not want to die. I came to the doctor."

He knew, like a cold wave going over him, what she meant. He could not look at her, and he felt the cold remote fright wash over him until he realized that she was sitting beside him and that negated whatever else might have happened. It was terribly swift and painful and neither said anything through the violent journey which took place in the space of a thought.

At moments like this the heart is bared. One reads it easily in silence.

Later that night he stood all alone in his room, stood there with the harsh light exposing the old paint, the battered floor. He stood there because all the laden commotion within him reached a climax at this spot.

He had survived the death camps by his own efforts . . . and yet he knew now in the most rational way that he had not . . . That he had survived only when the degree of love and affection and unselfishness and spontaneity and liveliness had fitted together with his own refusal to die. There seemed now something wonderful and precise about it . . . and he remembered the poem which he had read the first day in this town *Those who love each other small become invincible yet.* It was like an agreement stamped on the day of his arrival, but it had taken until this moment to understand, in reality, what it meant.

In his eagerness, his emergence, his search for justice, he had been taking and taking to compensate for something. This was a glimpse. He felt that until tonight he had been a boy and that his insight had been faulty, but now he glimpsed that there was no place where the giving must not be as great as the taking to keep a balance, and that out of it a whole thing emerged.

He stood there in the harsh light, wiping his perspiring hands together, thinking of the woman, Megan, of needs and of faith. He sensed overwhelmingly that the struggle toward reality was inextricably his life, and that he would not be left in peace until it became clearer and clearer.

The doctor stopped the next day for gas, and got out of the car to stand by the pump. Karel looked at him, and he answered the look.

"She's all right. She doesn't want anyone there."

"I will go and cook her her dinner."

"No. Let her be. I still think she's strong. But then, God damn it, we sometimes leave the strong people alone too long!" He said, "Oh, hell!" as he got into his car and slammed the door.

Who knew what was strong in the world? Somehow it made the doctor very angry. It was all too elusive, too visionary. Like the boy, who had believed that life was larger than its separate parts— Now *she* believed, as far as he could make out, that love was somehow larger than the personal creatures who made it up. And it made him angry. For it took too much strength from you to prove it, and then was it worth it? *He* should be handed it to puzzle out at his time of life!

Karel bought some chopped meat and a can of vegetables and some fruit, and went to Megan's house.

She was working in the kitchen, one arm doing the work of two. Her hair was tousled and she had on no powder or lipstick. Her face seemed bare, her expression unveiled, as though whatever terms she had reached within herself were clear and elemental.

He took out a skillet and pans and went to work. "I had forgotten about dinner," she said. "I'm—that's . . ." She stood against the kitchen table, motionless, quiet, the tears going down her cheeks.

He put butter in the frying pan and opened the can of vegetables and emptied them into the saucepan and turned on the gas, and he knew that she was still standing motionless. He came and stood across the table from her looking at her.

He leaned with his hands on the table, looking down. The edge of the table made a deep indentation against her yellow skirt. Standing so quietly, one might not even know she was crying. He did not know how to tell her what he thought. But he knew that to give merely physical help was not enough. What he had attempted to give since last night must speak for itself, must go far beyond their limited actions.

He raised his eyes to her face and saw it stripped and tired. She looked at him slowly. He smiled.

"Sit down," he said, "We will have a fine dinner. Just sit down. We'll be together."

Later, when he knew that she could be alone, he washed the dishes and went home.

Megan was his glimpse into the future—what a woman's sensibilities and heart are like, a woman's not a girl's. One day he would bring to a woman his own sensibility and passion and understanding.

19

Roi nagged at him. "You only got one more lesson—unless you want a new batch. How you going to play if you don't learn?"

Karel said, "I'll pay you and then I'll come when I can."

Roi said, in a rage, "To hell with the fifty cents!"

He flung his leg over the front door of the car and threw in the gears before he started it. Karel, who had not moved, watched him drive away. Here, right here, what a strange giving and taking. Why his friendship? Why was he so important to Roi?

He kept remembering the look on Roi's face as he drove away. The next evening he picked up a sack of doughnuts and went down the road to Roi's.

In a small whirl of dust a new Chevrolet stopped, and Mr. Ewing asked if he wanted a lift. Karel said he was going only a short way, but Mr. Ewing saw no reason why he should walk that distance. Karel sat stiffly beside him, for he sensed that authority was represented in this man, and authority filled him with disquiet.

Mr. Ewing had a round head which seemed to fit poorly onto his shoulders, and he looked awkwardly at Karel, down out of the slant of his eyes. But there was an unmarred cheerfulness about him, as though cheerfulness had been determined on long ago and had proved its hard solid worth many times over.

"You decided yet whether you're going to live here permanently?" he inquired.

"No."

"It must be mighty different here than where you came from. . . . Here we've got gadgets and high speed and things like that."

"Not so different," Karel said.

Mr. Ewing looked at him obliquely, measuring him carefully. "Sure, it's different," he laughed. "You can't give me that."

Karel did not argue. He said, "I get out at the next turning."

As Mr. Ewing slowed the car and Karel opened the door, Mr. Ewing said hurriedly, "You're Jewish, aren't you?"

Karel stood by the opened door and stared at him. "I am not Jewish—I am sorry to say."

For a moment the man's expression was blank. Then he smiled a little and half-closed his eyes. "Well, some folks think you are. All the same to me. Well, so long," and he drove away.

Karel stood without moving for a moment. He felt a depleting rage. When he moved he moved with an effort, kicking a stone before him. As he saw the car in the distance, he picked up the stone and hurled it in that direction.

That night Roi showed him how to play more elaborate chords. Roi was excited. He played recklessly and happily, and challenged Karel as an equal . . . *I taught you, you're good! You're my friend . . . I'm your friend . . .*

The refrain ran through the evening. Roi turned on the radio, he brought out beer and glasses and the doughnuts which Karel had bought.

He flung himself into the old Morris chair with the sagging spring and put his legs over its arm and shouted happily above the radio, shouted in his hoarse strained voice. Karel sat laughing and smiling, eating doughnuts, listening to the radio contend with Roi's voice, observing the things about him with noncommittal interest, Roi's large hands, hanging loosely at the end of slender wrists, the thin fingers gesturing, moving, never at ease, undirected, his whole spineless appearance creating the sense that he was afraid to associate himself with anything firm and upright. Failure—always the failure concealed or flashing suddenly in the transparent blue eyes. It was a failure which was never named, it would burrow like a mole if it were questioned or addressed.

Karel was not usually aware of rooms, or where he was, or what pictures hung on the walls. But here the walls were a part of the disquiet, impregnated in some fashion with watchfulness and pitilessness. The walls were not friends to you, the photographs and the calendars and chromo-prints were ugly and impersonal, the furniture was exhausted. The house and the wall and the floors seemed more real than Roi, far more sure of themselves, identified with something implacable—like the grandmother, perhaps.

Roi started to talk about the things he meant to do. "Spud and me—the guy with the trombone—we're going to join up and make some glue. Get a singer, maybe. We got the stuff—boy, we're both great—and we can play roadhouses here and there, a week, maybe two weeks, keep moving, pick up a lot of change, things'll be happening. Brother, it's a good feeling! Sit up there on a li'l ole platform wowin' the natives. Good eats, girls, if you want 'em. It's okay."

"I thought you were always fighting with Spud."

"He's okay. Got a hot trombone."

"A hot trombone keeps you warm in cold weather?"

"Say, you're a humorist! Sure, with a hot trombone people think you're great. Management thinks you're great. Can't do enough for you. All day and all night, you can't do anything wrong."

"What if you hit a bad note?"

The long loose fingers made a vague gesture and subsided. "Maybe you hit a bad note. Maybe you sit up there on that little platform and everybody's yakkety-yakkety-yakkin, rattling their teeth and payin' no attention, but it's still better than this. And maybe the management gives you grub left over from yesterday, but I still think—I still think it's better than sitting on your ass having all the old biddies in this town beating their gums at you. That's no life. That's not even pretending."

Although the world within this room was assertive and undeniable, the atmosphere heavy with airlessness and smoke, the beer bottles and the cold pot-bellied stove and the broken-down Morris chair and the squeaky rocker cold and critical participants in their own right, the noise of the radio attempting to bully and rout the cold and critical, yet outside—outside there was another world.

Karel sat listening and rocking, his head propped up by his fist, his half-closed eyes on the black square of the window. A wheeling world of stars and other worlds, all friendly, intimate, moving in illimitable space, tender, concerned. In his childhood, a black night and a starry sky had frightened him. Now as he listened to frightened talk, as he sat in this frightened room, he told himself that fear goes, fear goes, fear goes . . . when the vacuum which nourishes fear is filled up, fear goes.

He roused himself to take another doughnut and to nod and show friendliness.

"Get a job, get a job, they all say. Doin' what? I should die workin' like a mechanic in a garage when *you* do it good? I pick up some change. I pay my own way. What's wrong with that? I pay my own way when I get two-three dates a month at a social or a clambake. I'll do better than Spud. Folks like me when I sit up on a platform. I'm friendly, got an easy word. That's true, isn't it? That folks like me?"

"*I* like you."

"See? Easy all the way around. Jesus Christ, a guy wants to be liked! You gotta be liked or you end up looking for a booby hatch. I tried to be friends with you, didn't I, right off? You a stranger here. It's lonely. So I try to be friendly. I'm not going to stick to Spud all my life. Lay a dame every night—that's all he's after. Sure, that's all right, but I've got something else in mind. Find a girl somewhere, we'll have kids—that's the kind of thing I think about. Nothing else really counts. That's my kind of permanent loving. Get married. Have her sitting at home waiting—someone who's never seen this joint or this goddam town."

"Sure," said Karel, "that's what counts."

"*Get a job—get a job.* The old woman's got nothing else to say. Sure, I'll get a job. But it won't be here. Not where folks are trying to make me just like my old man and *her* talking about me behind my back. Fine home. Fine support. Loving kindness!"

Karel leaned back in his chair, sighed, wished to be away from here, but he was held by the boy's need.

"I can't get a move on. Folks think you're shiftless . . . and you act shiftless, and there's nobody who cares whether I am or not. You know me. I taught you how to play those strings. *I* taught you. You're the first person I taught. I'm good, aren't I—I'm good?"

"Yes," Karel said, "you've been my friend."

"I needed that. I tried to be friends with you, and it got me thinking." He grinned, banging the side of the chair with his swinging foot. "Got me thinking this is my job. This is my baby. Maybe I'll go over to Springfield or Adams, and try to be a disk jockey. Maybe I'll have my own platter store." He tapped at his ear with his thumb. "I can tell what's good—nothing wrong with that ear. *Hear what he's doing there—Pee-Wee.*" He jumped up and turned the dial louder on the radio. "Listen to that! Greatest modulation you ever heard. Boy, that's being alive! Have a beer! Holy cow!"

He drew back his narrow shoulders and arched his neck, looking happily at Karel as a good host should. "Happy? Hey, I guess the old woman's got some cheese!"

"Happy," Karel said. "No cheese." He drew up a chair for his feet and listened intently. Roi leaned on the radio and shouted, "You not going to stick around this burg forever. Maybe you can be my manager!"

"Maybe," Karel said grinning. "If this is what you want to do, then do it quickly—don't delay!"

"Sure. Let's think about it," Roi said eagerly, swinging himself around to the Morris chair again. "You're a guy I'd trust. Anything you said'd go. That's why I wanted to be friends. I didn't think you'd cheat on a friend, or let him down. We could work up a trio and a vocalist . . ." A door slammed close enough to startle them, and then the grandmother came into the doorway.

She was not a large woman, but she appeared as large as doom. She struck furiously against the side of the door, again and again, and screamed, "Turn that thing off! Turn it off!"

Roi did not move. He sat there as the color drained slowly from his face, his mouth closed into a pale line. It seemed almost as though he could not move. His swinging foot was still, and only a muscle jerked in his instep as though he were tapping the air. Karel half-rose before the old woman's fury to go to the radio but she drove herself from the doorway, ahead of him, and snapped the button as she cried in her thin voice, "Decent people—decent people bring me home from a decent church meeting, and they hear that. That's all they hear—Sunday night, coming from *my* house. I stood there—the shame, the shame . . . !"

Roi had turned his head and was looking at her through narrow eyes. His large hands had become fists and the thumbs moved back and forth making a gentle sound. He said very quietly, "Turn that on again, you old bitch. We're minding our own business—and listening to our own business! Turn it on again!"

Karel sat leaning forward in the rocker, studying his tightly clenched hands, listening for something, listening intently for some hint, some kind of promise. She said, "Hah!" contemptuously, and then she turned to the beer bottles, the three empty ones and the unopened ones by Roi's chair. She kicked at them futilely.

"Bottles!" she cried. "All over my house! I told you you could never bring any bottles into my house—like your father . . ."

Roi had half-raised himself. He said desperately, "Turn that on again!"

"Roi!" Karel said urgently, "it's not . . ."

"Turn it on!" He stood up, thin and awkward, his shoulders narrowed. She turned swiftly and spryly, leaping like a young girl, and with both hands stretched before her, pushed the radio from the table.

It fell with a crash, a splintering sound of wood, of glass, of strings. For a moment Roi did not move. It was Karel who ran across the room and lifted the broken radio from the splintered guitar on which it had fallen.

Roi was a child. He threw himself on the floor beside the guitar and his face was twisted with tears. He was helpless with tears, his loose hands were helpless, he held up the box which was splintered with helpless broken strings. He tried to speak, he said, "*You bitch . . . !*" but his cry was helpless and childish.

"Roi," Karel said sharply, "it was an accident, a terrible accident. She did not mean to do it!"

The grandmother looked remorseful and dismayed for a moment, and then Roi flung the neck of the guitar at her, and she kicked it back at him.

"It's a good thing," she said. "You won't get another. Maybe you'll learn to be a man now. Get up from that floor."

"Madame," said Karel urgently, "please don't speak to him that way. He's very sad that this happened. It means a great deal to him."

"You—*get out!* Get out! Drinking here with him. He never brought anyone here before. You're a terrible influence. Making him teach you to play—making him think about that guitar. He didn't do that before—not right here, under my nose. Get out!"

From the floor, Roi wailed, "Don't you leave. Don't you leave! She can't order you around!"

Karel went up to her and looked into her face, into the dry wrinkled lifeless face, so stonily passionate, at the pale cold eyes. "Please let us have patience. He would make you pleased with him if he were happy. Now his guitar is broken, and we must find a way to get another. If he is happy, doing what he wants to do, you'll be pleased with him. I am a friend. Please try to understand."

"You want me to laugh? He couldn't do anything worthwhile if he tried. I worked for fifteen years to bring him up, and I'll still be working when I drop dead. He's just that no-good. He says he hates it here, but he's got a chair and a bed and three meals a day. He don't hate it so much."

She piled up the glasses, and with her handkerchief

wiped off the table, and stuffed the handkerchief into a glass.

"Pick up those bottles. Get them out of here."

Karel spoke with desperation. "In five years—you'll see —a job which he can do and like to do—and a home . . ."

"A home . . . ?" She darted her half-turned body and her mocking eyes and the falling comb which had loosened in her gray hair toward the boy who still crouched on the floor. "A home—you mean something would marry him!"

"For God's sake . . . !" Karel cried, but the old woman was in a frenzy of her own despair, and it seemed as though she had wound up something inside herself which could not be stopped.

"Married—*married*—him!" and the shrillness became a kind of mirth darting and looming mercilessly. "He better even be careful not to go near a girl if he don't want to get into trouble. Oh, I have suffered!" Her body spun around toward Karel in a half-dance. "I have suffered. Seeing what bad blood does—knowing it's not your own but yours brought it into the world. I'm not after trouble, and he's not going to bring it to me! I've never injured anyone in my life, and I'm not going to be injured by him." Then she darted toward Roi again, on her toes, light and airy. "But try to marry. Go on—try. When no one'll risk you, then people will know what I've put up with all these years!"

Karel caught at her arm to silence her, but Roi sprang straight up from the floor, like a ferret, sprang up straight, the looseness gone from his hands. He struck her back against the wall, and she screamed. He knocked her back and forth against the wall, and she continued to scream like a cat which had been impaled. Karel tried to drag him away, but the boy was now composed of nothing but a locked force which could not be pried loose.

He flung the old woman back and forth, and her screaming grew fainter. He was grinning and he looked beside himself with joy, sinking his teeth into his lower lip till the blood appeared, tiny pure-red drops on his lips. Karel finally hit him on the side of the head, and Roi released her so that she fell and lay crumpled on the floor. He stood with his hands out, and something as slow as old night settled on his face and his body.

Karel kicked the chair away and shoved back the table as he bent over the old woman. Roi did not move.

"For God's sake—for God's sake, what's all the racket!" a voice cried in the doorway. "Godalmighty—what's the matter with the old woman!"

A little man in suspenders and slippers brushed past Roi and knelt on the floor. A woman's voice called from the hall, "Mrs. Arnow— Is it all right to come in, Charlie?"

Charlie looked up at Karel. "Good God, you could hear her screeching a mile away. Nice thing. Look around, May. Call the police! No, get the doc first. Fine, just fine— an old woman like that."

A shudder had shaken through Roi and he moved uncertainly toward the door.

"Hey—come back here you—Roi. Tell the operator to get the state police, May. You there, come here and help straighten her out."

Karel stood against the wall, silent and watchful. Charlie shot a quick piercing glance. "You do this to her?" Karel shook his head. "He do it?" with a jerk of his head.

Karel said, "It was an accident. No one meant this to happen."

"No? Look at this room. Look at it, May. Holy Moses! *Someone* fought over it from one end to the other—*someone!*"

"Is she dead?" May asked in a small voice.

"Could as well be. Can't find her pulse."

He stood up, small and infinitely strong, no wavering, no unsureness.

"You sit down, Roi Arnow. Sit down. You sit down, too. You that foreign boy down at McVitty's?" He studied Karel for a minute, competently observing him from the mussed hair which Karel was smoothing, to the unpolished shoes. "Just the kind of people we like to have come here. Stir up trouble. Sit down both of you. Don't move." A voice called from the road and he went to a window and shouted back.

"Jessie Arnow—don't know what happened yet. Police and the doc'll be here in a minute." He turned back to the steady gaze of Karel.

Karel said desperately, "Please wait until there has been a chance to explain. It is very terrible, but there is a reason."

"Sure, two boys—strong, husky boys—beat up an old woman. Sure, there must be a reason. Did the doc say he'd be right along, May?"

The doc came in a moment—Dr. Jarman, his eyes sweeping over the broken room in the search for his patient, pausing and sharpening when he saw Karel. He knelt down beside her laboriously, opened his case, examined, tested reflexes.

"She's alive," he said. "I'll call the hospital."

He made the call and while he was doing it, the state police came.

Karel watched the doctor sitting there heavily on the edge of the rocker, and Karel listened intently. But what was said was related in different terms from what had happened. The ambulance came, and the old woman and the doctor went away. All the doctor had said was, "Blasted fools," very sadly, very unphilosophically.

Roi wept and talked shrilly. He did not try to hide anywhere. He remembered each thing his grandmother had said, he remembered each inflection of voice and each meaning behind a meaning. He had heard every word she said, and he repeated every word again and again in a voice which sounded like his grandmother's. *She got what she deserved.* He threw up his head and looked wildly around at them all—she got just what she deserved—she liked to tear your guts out. It made her feel good.

The policeman sat on a hard straight chair and took notes. His cap lay on his knees, and he knocked it off now and then, and he always restored it to his knees again without being aware of the hysterically comical picture he made. He was an expressionless man with a nose too small for his face and no special appearance of enjoying the task he had made his life work. He was impersonal; he heard the wild cries, the unrepentant boy, with no change of expression.

Charlie, who sat on the window ledge, heard and assorted and appraised and judged with the movement of his lips, the twitch of his eyebrow, the swift jerking back and forth of his feet. One of his slippers had come off on the other side of the room, and he shot an occasional sharp glance in its direction. He told rapidly of hearing the cries. His own impressions were vivid and neat, and he interpreted with equal speed and exactness the reactions of his wife. The beer bottles kicked around, the shambles, the two drunken boys, the unconscious old woman.

The old woman emerged very strong, a stern, right-living woman, not lovable, perhaps, but dependable. If she worked for you, she gave a full day's value. Everyone would say a good word for her, because one would not know what else to say. Stern, bitter, maybe, but everyone knew how she had brought up the boy. The old woman did not need to speak for herself, for she had violated no one's sense of conformity and she could be talked about with the same assurance that one talked about himself.

20

Karel did not return to the village until the next morning. McVitty saw him before he stepped out of the police car, and made the slightest motion of his head for him to go into the office. McVitty was providing gas for Mrs. Haynes, the druggist's wife, and the air seemed sullen and pregnant.

Karel stood away from the window, looking out. Mrs. Haynes's head was thrust through her car window, and she was evidently waiting with some eagerness for an answer to a question. But it did not seem to Karel, watching, that McVitty moved his lips. Mrs. Haynes drew in her head with a frown.

When McVitty came into the office he did not look at Karel. He sat down abruptly in the chair by the door and pulled out a packet of cigarettes. He asked, not looking up, "What'd they say? What's the situation?"

"They will hold him until they learn how his grandmother is. How is she?"

"I called the doc an hour ago. She's conscious."

"She won't die?"

McVitty gave the faintest shrug. "Guess it depends on

her heart." He looked up then at Karel. His brow was wrinkled deeply, his eyes were partly closed as though he did not want to look at him fully. "What about you?"

"Roi was hating her so hysterically that they agreed I must be innocent. But I am a witness if anything happens."

McVitty continued to look at him. "What happened?"

"What he said happened. Exactly. I think he lost his mind for a moment."

McVitty drew in a deep breath noisily and studied the smoking end of his cigarette.

"*You* were the crazy one. I told you to keep away from him." He sat there very quietly for a moment, and then he flung the cigarette out of the door violently. "Keep out of sight. Every time anyone sees you they'll say something to me. Everyone in this goddamn town knows every detail."

Karel did not answer. After a moment he said, "It could not have been avoided. They wanted to kill each other."

McVitty said furiously, "And you had to be there. That makes it fine. You're the boy in this town who's a stranger, and you have to be there."

Karel felt a sickness in his stomach. He did not answer. He looked questioningly at McVitty, but McVitty was watching his foot which was kicking and kicking against a chair. Then McVitty got up suddenly and went out around the back, where he could work, out of sight, until the next car arrived.

Karel went upstairs and lay down on his bed. He felt very hollow. There was no Nicky, not even the little cat. The nature of his loneliness was demeaning, for he was afraid to go to a friend. It was possible he had no friends. He was the stranger, the one no one could make up his mind about. He lay on the bed staring at the ceiling. He thought of what had taken place in reality and in the minds of others. But it led him into a circle, and he could not find a crevice through which he might creep. In the loneliness of familiar things, the loneliness of the quiet working world, the loneliness of people being themselves in daily rote, there was something less savage but more deadly than the crucible from which he had come. The boy without moral strength, the old woman without compassion, the listeners, the deriders, the watchers, the judges, shaped and diminished and reduced and destroyed because the help given must be in their own image, formed from their own concepts.

He heard cars coming and going on the road, he heard voices calling, he smelt the fumes of gasoline; the iridescence of living rose with the noon and the afternoon, but he did not move to get up. He thought fleetingly of Julie—what she would think. He thought of Megan—her arm would still be in a sling . . . although time had moved so fast . . . and he would be unable to help her.

What had happened was a profound shock, and his will was paralyzed. He thought, but it was not with his mind. He thought with his skin, his eyeballs, the tips of his fingers, with all the sensuality which in the past had brought pain and despair. Yet all the time he knew with another part of him that this was a cessation of reality, the far side of the light.

To rouse himself, to move, to stand up—always later, not now.

When Vree pushed open the door and came in, a start of joy went through him. Vree had brought him coffee and a sandwich, and Vree sat down on the end of the cot, smiling a little, the black eyes with the yellowing eyeballs fixed upon him.

"What a racket and misery." Vree pushed back his cap and watched Karel unwrap the sandwich.

Karel said nothing for a moment. Then he said, "I will not be welcome around here any more."

Vree did not answer immediately. He pulled his cap low over his eyes and swung his big foot back and forth, watching its movements. "Stick," he said.

Karel answered desperately, "I cannot stick all alone any more."

Vree laughed, a dry rumble down in his chest. He looked at Karel with a sardonic merriment. "What do you mean, can't stick all alone? You got me, haven't you?"

Karel looked at him obliquely, and smiled in spite of himself. "Yes. Thank you."

He wished that he were as small as Nicky, and could prop himself against Vree.

They were silent, but now it was a lively silence with some manner of reason. When he had finished his coffee, Karel leaned back, his arms behind his head.

"What will they do with him?" he asked.

"I guess it depends a little on what the old lady decides."

"They wanted to kill each other," Karel said again.

At the door below, someone knocked, and Vree went to the head of the stairs.

"Come on up," he called, and left the door open. He stuffed his cap into his pocket and put the stem of his cold pipe between his teeth and sat down by the door to loosen the laces of his high shoes. He was calm but he was weary. So much of the ways of the world were repetitive. It grew tedious to the soul.

John Murray came in. Vree and he nodded to each other, and he smiled at Karel. He stood very tall, looking down at Karel, the gray eyes with the dark lashes speaking with greater friendliness than his diffident words would indicate.

"How are things?"

Karel made a gesture with his hands. "I am here," and then he asked impulsively, "How is Megan?"

John looked suddenly blank and forsaken. "Megan?

She had a fall. But she is all right." It was a lost look as though he had been thrown off his balance. "I imagine they are worried about you."

"Thank you," Karel said formally. He noticed in a remote way that John had said, *I imagine*, as though he had come here on his own initiative. It carried an element of comfort, as though another friend had been added to a handful.

John sat down slowly pushing his heavy shoes out in front of him, waiting, saying nothing. He was there. He was quite deliberately sitting in this room to which he had come of his own accord. Impelled, the terrible churning of resistance over, the moment when he had stood alone in the barn, having heard the news, and swore aloud that he would not involve himself in any shock, any pity, any offer to help—that moment was past. He had come forward thus far because, when the inner turmoil had run its course, he had known that he would have to come here. For himself. For his dignity as a human being. Perhaps it was merely to sit in this room, his arms folded tightly in front of him, his head lowered, his eyes attentive. He hoped that was all. He was not prepared to do more than sit in this room, a friend.

Karel looked up at him from under a creased brow. "What was your first thought?" he asked diffidently. "That I *had* done something dreadful?"

"I didn't know."

Karel looked at him intently. "You came, although you did not know?"

"I know the Arnows." And then after a pause he said with a faint smile, "I know the village."

The three sat there, looped together, silent, very still, tight in themselves, only Vree's glance going from one to the other with a sharp interest.

"Why has the doctor not said something to me?" Karel

asked very low, and then he said with a startled raising of eyes, "What is Mrs. Wright going to say?"

John dragged his boots under him and got up slowly. "Mrs. Wright would be the last person I would care about."

But Vree understood what Karel meant, and he thrust out his lips till his mustache bristled.

After a moment Karel said, "Will the grandmother demand that he be punished?"

"People here usually take care of their own quarrels, privately," Vree offered. "They arrange something—but you can't tell. Someone may decide for her that he should be punished. It's hard to tell exactly how moral they'll be. Oh, Lord. Or maybe the law'll say he's got to be prosecuted anyway."

"An old woman was almost beaten to death," John said impassively.

"But *why?* That is what they will not ask themselves."

"Oh, *why!*" John said, pacing, his hands in his pockets. "*Why!*" He was anxious to be gone. He said, "Would you like to come for dinner?"

Karel nodded.

Karel did not know whether he would see Megan. He wished that they could all stand together, find their way free at the same time. He felt a little hysterical. He had to calm himself.

He said to John, "How did she fall?"

"Who?"

"Megan."

John's eyes clouded. "She—she just had a fall."

Karel found Megan in Mrs. Murray's kitchen, helping as well as she could with one hand. He did not know what it signified, her being there. Mrs. Murray said, "Oh, thank God!" and kissed him. Nicky flung himself against him and the cat circled him, chanting. Megan, very pale, smiled at him and stood quietly for a moment looking at him.

His confusion lessened a little. The pressure eased.

They did not talk about the Arnows or refer to the events after the first few minutes. Gradually he could begin to think. He could begin to relax, and as the evening went on one thing and another began to move together.

When he stood up to go, Megan said she would walk with him as far as her house. Mrs. Murray linked her arm with his and stood with him in the doorway.

"You won't worry, will you?" she asked. "The people who know you are your friends."

"I will not worry." He turned to look for Megan and saw John putting her coat across her shoulders. He saw him run his hand down her free arm, and then draw her toward him. His face was without expression as he kissed her cheek, but his eyes did not leave her face. A look of sheer terror came on her and she clung to him for a moment before he pushed her toward the door.

She stumbled once in the darkness, and Karel caught her arm. "It was as though he were saying good-bye," she said.

"Oh, no," Karel answered in surprise. "That is not what I saw at all."

Mrs. Stillwell sent for the doctor. He responded to the urgency in the air, even to his own reluctant desire to talk freely to someone. He came sooner than she expected.

She was sitting out on the back porch drinking a cup of tea. She offered him a cup and was unaware of his curt refusal for she had moved straight into the cause of her agitation. Her voice had the high toneless note of deafness, a condition one only heard when she was perturbed.

As he came through the door, she had begun her protests.

"This has got to stop, Lem. It's out of all reason. You've got to do something about it."

He grunted and sank into a chair. She said, "You can always count on them, just as sure as the sun comes up . . ."

"Why do you naturally blame the village?"

She stared at him with her round-marble eyes. "I've lived here sixty-five years—that's why."

"Well, I don't think he had any part in beating up an old woman, by God. But what can he do?" His eyes were slits as, hunched sprawling, he looked at her.

"Six people have called since noon, asking what I think. Each one had a different story."

"They're not interested in facts," the doctor said. "Can the boy fight rumors?"

"At the post office this morning and at the bank and the A & P . . ."

"What can he do? What can you or I do . . . ?"

She put in her hearing aid angrily and said, "I don't know *what* you're saying. What he must do is get back into their good graces somehow. It's humiliating—but I'm shaking like a leaf."

The doctor did not answer for a moment. Then he said at length, "There's no reconciling rumor and fact when no one really cares what's true, Agnes dear. If you've got moral stamina you can see it through. It dies away if you're not stampeded. It depends if seeing it through is worth the effort."

She said piercingly, almost as though she had not heard him, "Mrs. Wright talked to me for twenty minutes this afternoon. It was like an ice bath. She holds me personally responsible. What for? Julie's grown up."

He started to say, "We don't really know who he is or where he came from . . ." and then he did not go on for he could not. With his skepticism profoundly if cautiously shaken, he had nothing to say. No old adages came to his aid, no tested sentences of dignity and principle assisted him into familiar paths.

He knew that Mrs. Stillwell was watching him with worried impatience and he roused himself. He could not say to her that this was a shock for him too. He had to build up certain defenses for himself as well, before he was capable of useful action.

He said slowly, "Prejudice in a place like this is so deep that you don't see it till you're put under pressure."

She was looking at him tensely, not only her hearing aid attentive, but her round eyes and her stiff back and the folds around her mouth. And yet it might be that she was not really listening to him, but only waiting for him to speak the one word which would be exactly the word she wished to hear said.

"Everyone who has known these boys since they came has tried to settle them in his own way—by excluding or by absorbing or by rationalization." He sighed, feeling very depleted, not wishing to encounter the next hour or day or week. Let things go; what one could change was so little. He loved his apathy.

But he went on talking, for the shock of things had made him feel like a man on a jag. "It's perfectly true that we all have a prejudice against Roi. But still and yet he belongs here. In the end we won't abandon him. But this Karel . . ." He was warmed by his own irony. "This alien—of course our bad boys are only bad in a certain sense; it's the alien who really misleads them. That's important. Oh, Christ and all the angels—and that is blasphemy, Agnes, in case you're not sure."

She was indifferent. Her eyes were flashing for another reason. "There is *something* he can do or say, something that will explain to people like Katherine Wright . . ."

The doctor got to his feet, wryly patient. "No, Agnes, there is nothing. If his friends are staunch—if he has moral stamina, and these are the testing times for people who have been through earlier great shock—a crest will come and pass. That's all that will happen."

"I shall call Katherine Wright again—no, I shall write her a letter. I'll write Charlotte Boles and Mary Dunn . . ."

"Oh, Agnes, Agnes."

"And I shall talk to him this evening—straight and plain, so that he can go to Katherine—and that miserable Emma Ripley who said the worst things of all."

"Oh, Agnes, the Lord give you light on the path your stumbling feet have chosen!"

"Lem . . . !"

The telephone operators could not resist listening on the wires that morning. Nor resist dropping hints or small summaries at the end of the day. Mr. Ripley and the boys in the grocery stores, the postmaster and his assistants, the clerks in the bank and the drygoods store listened carefully, offered generalized answers that were still cautiously relevant, expressing a genuine opinion by the quality of smile, the swift exchange of look, the slight shrug or gesture. All this wove itself back and forth until there was a strong sturdy net of opinion without a visible seam, all shaped by the esoteric knowledge of the line reserved for outsiders.

If there were dissidents it was hard to number them. Yet there were many who were silent. They had the look of disagreement upon them but no solid convictions. There is something very powerful about one's own town, one's environment. In the end one could be very lonely standing on the outskirts, no matter how valiant the cause. And one can always find reasons for agreement which do not put a burden on the conscience.

McVitty had the hardest task, and he was not a man cut out to be a martyr. It is perfectly true that he revered his great-grandmother Saunders who had taken a rifle to the man injuring a child, and that he often told the story of Grandma McVitty who risked her life to save a sick horse, but there were few heroic stories of the men of his family. True, McVitty set his own precedent the day he first defended Karel. He did not know why he did so. He was evidently impelled by something which cut straight through his usual considerations.

Now he answered questions laconically. Sometimes the answers were deliberately muffled by the opening of an engine hood or a retreat to the gas pump. He was aware of a strange and furious resentment. He clung to something he called fairness—it wasn't fair to be down on the kid until everything was known—and out of some deeply submerged strata of his personality swam a stubbornness to the light. He did not know anything for sure except that Roi Arnow was no good and that the town was run by a bunch of old women and that a man had a right to stick to a good mechanic.

But he was not happy. He gave Karel another day off because he did not want him around to be stared at. He was distracted by implications, by the isolation he sensed in all this. Stubbornness fortified him, and Clara fortified him—Clara watching behind the lace curtains so that he knew when the curtains stirred Clara was with him. But there was a thinness about it which frightened him, as though the stubbornness could suddenly *go* like a paper hoop when it is leaned against.

Karel was not wholly prepared for the hesitancy of people who greeted him, or failed to greet him. He had been shielded by the instant partisanship of the Murrays and Vree. He spoke to the druggist's wife on the street, and she stared past him and did not answer. Miss Purvis was distressingly embarrassed when he came to the library, and joined someone near the stacks until she had to stamp his book. Mr. Ewing came again and questioned him about his citizenship, and with solemn good humor said that the state troopers intended to notify the FBI. It was a compact assortment of hate and distrust.

His supernormal pride rose up and he wanted to leave immediately. Only Nicky remained as he had in the past. At moments like this his first action was to retreat wholly into himself, turn away from all help, make his own world secure. Even from Vree, even from Megan, Mrs. Murray—Julie.

He faltered. He had rejected the violences of the world before and he had grown into some stature by reason of a struggle larger than a mute withdrawal. Yet this seemed to him different. One can resist racking and protracted pain, and fall to weeping with a broken finger.

He dreamed of Julie. Julie walking down a long street which seemed to have no end. And in the dream he saw her advancing, looking tired but not pausing, advancing but never reaching the end as long as the dream lasted. He wished he had not dreamed of her, but it enabled him to put something into words to Vree.

"There is no real love here," he said. "Not real love."

Vree was silent for a moment. "I'm here. Your friends are here."

It was an arresting thing to say, and Karel stopped. *I am here.* What does that mean: *I am here?* Something more than yourself. An old man whose years were nearly spent, loving and unawed by defeat. He took a deep breath, fumbling within his thoughts. There was Julie walking down that endless street, but he rejected his fancies violently.

Yet there was Vree, literal, factual in the unpressed trousers that were green with the flora of Massachusetts, rocking in the old chair, his huge feet in the high black shoes twitching up and down as he rocked. Karel sat quietly, his hands gripped tightly together, and he heard himself saying, "I only wanted one thing—I wanted to be like everyone else."

Vree, rocking more slowly, made the comment of silence.

On Friday night Julie returned from college for the week-end. The moment of her return had loomed in his mind. He believed she would be his friend if she were left alone. But the compelling pressure of rumors and glances and behavior violently shook the most trusting confidences.

This Friday, three days after the events with Roi, George McVitty had told him to take the day off. It was a cruel kindness, a barometer of George's own waverings. For an afternoon Karel would work in the garage, and then he would be whisked out of sight. For a few hours the next day he would be visible, and then the nerve at the back of George's head would begin to jump, and he would tell Karel to go upstairs again.

The nerve had begun jumping at noon, soon after Mrs. Ewing had driven in for some gas. And just at that moment Karel had remembered that this day was Friday.

He had remained by himself all afternoon, in a kind of numb thoughtlessness, as though a movement or a clearly defined conviction would open up floodgates. Just to lie there, rigid and quiet and secret, would expose him to nothing and events could move at their own pace. But after he had heard a train whistle, miles away, which might or might not have been her train, he got up and fixed himself some supper.

The next morning went by, and he worked out in the back shed on a car. He heard the noon whistle blow. A third of her week-end had gone. His throat was dry, his legs were so weak that he had to find a box to sit on as he worked.

Vree stood nearby, leaning against the wall, a coke bottle in his hand, talking idly with George. When the telephone rang and George called out Karel's name, Vree exchanged a look with Karel as he went past, a blind transfixed look on Karel's part, a wonderfully gay look on Vree's.

Karel heard Julie's voice, a long way off it seemed, a small voice, never forceful. "Karel, will you meet me at the milk bar this afternoon?"

"Oh, yes," he said, suddenly calm.

"At three o'clock?"

"Yes."

That was it—and she might yet tell him that she could not continue being his friend, but at least she had spoken, the silence had been broken.

21

They met at the milk bar and said *Hello*. They climbed onto the stools and she hesitated over her choice. He was wildly nervous and happy and uneasy, and very self-possessed. One could not have told from his expression or the calmness of his bearing what he felt.

He knew how she looked without needing to glance at her again . . . in a pink sweater and skirt, a rose-colored ribbon holding back her hair at the nape of her neck and the little line from ear to ribbon extraordinarily delicate and tender; the straight way she held herself, using her smallness to make herself erect, the swift confiding glance from the corner of her eye, the very simple molding of nose and cheekbones, the longing to kiss her, the ear and the cheek . . . She talked about something which had happened that week at college. He became intensely interested because she was talking about something that was perfectly ordinary. He listened as intently as the boy behind the counter who had turned down the radio to a whisper.

Between suckings at her straw she discussed teachers and

students whose names had become familiar to Karel. She did not give him a chance to talk, and he felt some of his tautness relaxing. She talked steadily through the entrances and exits of people. She would glance at them, nod or call out a greeting. When their sodas were finished, she joked with Ted Ewing, Harris' son, while Karel paid the cashier, and then she took Karel by the arm and turned him firmly up the main street.

This was the sort of day on which the village looked its most winning. A brilliant clear autumn day, with the bare airy lacing of boughs giving vivacity to the shadows on the Common, the white houses all shining with an improbable pristineness. They passed Mrs. Ripley's house and saw the old lady on the porch. Julie waved to her. Mrs. and Miss Dunn passed them, their arms filled with bundles, Julie spoke to them, and Miss Dunn responded, but her mother looked too startled to do so.

It was a brave and awful march down the street. Karel was only partially aware of its significance at first, but as the irony of greetings or the coldness or the exaggerated warmth or the stiffened silence or the dozen varieties of human response under stress became evident he began to realize how painful it was. He was suddenly angry, and he walked faster to turn up a side road. He did not need to endure this, and the pride which was his locked room, his high tower, rose up and enclosed him. Julie caught his coat sleeve.

"Please—please, I want to go to the Murrays!"

He said darkly, "That means we have to go clear through the village."

"Yes, please."

"I will not . . . !"

"Please!"

He looked down at her and he saw something as nervous and defiant and brave as a small animal.

"You do not need to do this for me," he said desperately.

"Please," she said, "walk to the end of the street. We've gotten this far."

She was pale now, her expression set.

"If I had known what you were going to do," he said again frantically, "I would have told you . . ."

"I don't know why I did it!" she flared at him. "If you don't want me for a friend you can say so!"

"You think that was a help to me? You don't understand anything of what I need or how I need it!"

He knew it was a cruel thing to say, but he was filled with cruelty at that moment. He walked stiffly away from her to the side of the road, reproaching himself, reproaching her, protesting most deeply against the series of events which stood like a jackal ready to pounce. She walked with her head high, the rose-colored ribbon still jaunty and springing, the pinkness of her clothes gay and confident but her footsteps uneven, one foot kicking at stones in the road.

She hesitated in front of Mrs. Murray's house, and Karel said nothing. He stood there silently, looking at her, his heart swelling. She had done something because she was his friend, and it had been painful to both, and now they hated something or felt hateful because of that. He had so often and so primitively wanted her to suffer in order to close the gap between them that now he stood making no movement, unable to deepen this moment more than it was. Now he knew he did not want her to suffer, he wanted to protect her and put his arms about her. He stood there looking at her, his dark eyes full of wonder, unable to make a gesture of one kind or another.

Mrs. Murray, coming up from the chicken house, saw them and called to them to come in. Nicky, with a basket of eggs slung over his shoulder, started to run toward them and then remembered the eggs. Mrs. Murray took them from him, and he ran in his odd stiffly balanced fashion, the little chicken with clipped wings.

Karel did not kiss him. He merely rubbed his hair. A little hesitantly, without words, the three went toward the house.

It was so secure here, with the safe sounds of dinner, the dog barking, the tractor moving in the field, the electric pump starting its labors, that the village seemed improbably remote. What had been hateful became something intimate which had to be resolved between themselves, something closer to Karel than Nicky, something closer to Julie than her home and childhood and shapen thoughts.

Karel lay down on the grass under the maple, with Nicky sitting on his legs, and Julie went into the kitchen. She did not imagine she could help Mrs. Murray, but she might. She did not imagine that she could go home, but she would have to eventually, and would have to answer her parents without great emotion, and would have to conceal her real feelings and show none of the blazing single-mindedness which had led her down the main street.

Mrs. Murray, pausing in the greasing of a pan, smiled at her. She stood there, pan in hand, looking at Julie.

"Well," she said, "I think you could sit down, and maybe have something as a reward."

Julie sat down slowly by the table, her eyes suddenly frightened. "You mean, already they're talking?"

"Not 'they.' The doctor called me."

Julie said desperately, "I wanted to show how I felt—but somehow I failed—I—I just made a fool of both of us."

Mrs. Murray stopped what she was doing and came to stand beside Julie. Julie's eyes filled with tears, and Mrs. Murray drew her head back against her breast.

"No," she said. "No." Then she picked up her pan and poured the corn-bread batter into it. She glanced at Julie and swiftly out the window where Karel and the child remained so very still. She put the pan in the oven, and remained in a crouching position for a moment. "Why are you frightened? Do you love Karel?"

Now the question had been asked, the question which Julie knew was inevitable after this afternoon.

She said pleadingly, "He's my friend. Isn't that enough?"

"It could be. But one can't always be sure."

Mrs. Murray stood looking at her, her hands busy with pans and spoons, but her blue eyes so warm, her little smile so attentive to moods and surprises that Julie sat with a swelling heart. She asked suddenly, "What will I do now?"

"About what?"

"I'll go home soon, and Mother will have heard, and there'll be a terrible row. That's all right. There's nothing she can do but be unpleasant. But I won't know why I have done it—except to break off with something I can't stand any more."

"And what is that called?"

She drew a deep sigh and the hand that smoothed back her smooth hair was trembling. ". . . The things *they* think are important."

Mrs. Murray pulled out a chair and sat down. She did not speak for a moment and then she said in an altered voice, "You said there was nothing your mother could do but be unpleasant. That's not quite so. She could make it very hard for Karel."

"How could she do that?"

"Act as though she believes the story that he helped beat Roi's grandmother. Talk about him in a way that will make it hard for him to live here."

Julie considered this, and then she said in a faraway little voice, "She hasn't much influence. People don't all like us in this town, because they think we are rich."

Mrs. Murray smiled and made a characteristic little fling-away gesture. "Oh, that! We merely envy something. We have to keep our self-respect, and everyone who has a little more—must be made to feel a little less. But remember something else. Your mother belongs to this town. So, although she must be kept in her place, she has certain rights also."

"*We*—is that the way you think too—behind my back?"

Mrs. Murray reached across the table and took Julie's hand.

"Darling child—'we' is because I belong here also. And I must try to protect Karel—for I can do that as much as your mother can try to drive him away."

"Oh, she won't—she wouldn't do a thing like that!"

Mrs. Murray went to her oven and inspected her bread. "I think, after today, she'll be really frightened. She'll think she knows what you feel about him—even though you may say you do not. Or she will decide that he has some terrible influence over you."

Julie was shaken. She stood in the door for a moment, staring at Karel's long body stretched out on the grass, and then her eyes came to his face, and her heart dissolved.

He was staring at the shifting clouds, and there was such poignancy, such dismayed wonder on his face, that she went to him.

She sat down beside him and slipped her hand in his. He looked at her with the leaping gratitude of love, bare and uncomplicated and utterly simple, and put her hand against his cheek.

The things which were happening had begun long ago. Mrs. Murray had known that this was so—that Mrs. Wright would react in spite of her will. The action had been unshaped, enclosed in her mind, until Julie, behaving as she did, released it.

Mrs. Wright had received the news of that fateful march down the main street from three sources. She had asked an explanation of Julie, and had received one, an explanation which had said nothing. The girl had looked wretched; the girl had looked in love.

She was too strong a woman to resort to any hysterical illness. As she lay in her bed that night and felt her whole body tremble, she said to herself, "I will *not* be ill!" But the next day she had a heart attack.

She struggled out of it within two days, for she had no interest in self-pity. She made it very clear to her husband and to Mrs. Stillwell and to Miss Purvis, and even, she tried, to Julie, that she did not criticize or personally dislike Karel. No, it was impersonal, the rejection of a boy who had been influenced by certain forces which, of themselves, could bring only unhappiness to certain other comparable forces. Her feeling was final and almost mystical. Someone might have spared a thought to how admirable this spirit would have been had it been fighting in a generous cause.

To Mrs. Stillwell she said, "The whole thing is impossible. He is turning Julie into a different girl. She lies to me. She was always absurdly honest before." She looked hard at Mrs. Stillwell, this figurehead of her distress, the woman who had started it all.

Mrs. Stillwell said in a voice made high by distress and indignation, "He's never lied to me!"

"How do you know?"

Mrs. Ewing was the new president of the Thursday Club. Mrs. Wright spoke to her as one mother to another. She spoke to Mr. Carver, the president of the bank. In both cases she was perfectly candid. She felt that public opinion should make George McVitty understand that by continuing to hire and house a boy so painfully involved in a scandal he was creating a situation which transcended any fairness or justice. It was not a matter of fairness or justice. It was a simple question of forestalling another scandal.

It was a queer thing to say if one examined it closely, for Mrs. Wright was implying that her daughter was capable of being involved. But she always spoke so simply and candidly that somehow one had only the feeling that Julie was a sensitive and gentle girl who needed help in extricating herself from a deplorable situation into which her kindness had led her.

She tried also to appeal to McVitty. She telephoned him and asked if she might stop in and see his wife and him that evening. He hesitated for a moment, and then he said they were going out. He said to his wife, "I'll be damned if I'll let her boss me," and Clara had beamed and put an extra scoop of ice cream on his plate.

His was the indignation of a man who felt the power of some abstract principle stirring an admired memory in his own past. It was the activity of a dignified ghost. It was an honorable attribute which had passed from generation to generation. Even when he went over and over in his mind Mrs. Wright's call, when he lost himself in wondering what she would have said in an interview, when he permitted himself to check over her account at the garage and discover that she had spent nearly $1200 in the past year in addition to buying her new car through him—even then he did not wish to retreat from his position.

It was a very fine position. It gave him a moral strength, a sense of power defying the rich and proud. He was a man who stood in a good tradition.

At times he rather wished there were others besides Clara and the Murrays and the doctor and Mrs. Stillwell to stand on his side. They were the queer ones, the rebels, whom public opinion had labeled long ago.

A day or two later, young Mrs. Eustis who had moved to the village only six months before but who was wonderfully active in community doings and winning in her ways stopped the doctor and asked him to buy a ticket for the School Hot-Lunch Concert on October 4th. He reached for his pocketbook, and then he frowned.

"That's the date when Miss Mowes is singing for the Friendly Fund."

"Well, yes," young Mrs. Eustis said, laughing a little. "It's the same concert. Did you buy tickets when it was the other? I'm sorry."

"What have you done to the other?" he asked fiercely. "What the hell's become of it?"

She had no reason to feel anything but amusement at his ferocity.

"Well, it was just decided to change. The other tickets weren't selling well, and when—well, in the last few days—we felt it was better to expand the purposes of the concert. There's more interest this way."

"And what about your consciences? Are you going to use those ten original sales to buy a hand for the little boy?"

She was young and not at all intimidated. She looked at him intelligently and said, "There'll be a fair division, I'm sure. But after all, Miss Mowes had her own reputation to consider. She didn't want to sing to an empty house."

"You may tell Miss Mowes to go to the devil, and Mrs. Wright and even Mrs. Stillwell if she had anything to do with it."

He wished that he had not lost the ability to weep.

The drivers of the milk trucks heard many things, going from house to house, and the men who drank beer at the diner heard and interpreted things in their own way. Now that it was known that the grandmother would recover, a certain formalism entered the recitals and an air of disinterest settled over the gossip. Now that Roi was released on bail and out of sight with his sister in Pittsfield, a few persons even thought that apathy might gain the upper hand, and for reasons deeply entangled in the human mind considered such a possibility deplorable. A second wind in these matters developed.

Mr. Ewing synthesized himself—himself duplicated a thousand times over. He gathered all the stories together—and no one had been more attentive than he. He gathered together all the opinions of the bank and the grocery store and the drygoods store and the milk bar and the drug store and the library and the milkmen and the Thursday Club and the tourist home and the strata of society which adhered to Mrs. Wright and the strata which adhered to Mrs. Ewing and the strata which adhered to himself—men versed in the shadings of public relations and business acumen—and he went to see George McVitty.

He came at the lunch hour, and that evening George's face was drawn and expressionless. As Karel turned out the lights, and George stood latching the door, George began to speak. He tried twice before he succeeded in making a sound. Then he said in a tone beaten very thin, "I'm sorry, but you can't have this job any more. I don't want you to argue or talk to me about it. I'm very sorry, but there's no other way. I'll give you three weeks pay and—and you'll have to get your things out of the room upstairs by tomorrow."

Karel did not answer. He stood by the closed door and the darkness of six o'clock stretched around him.

McVitty went home rapidly, feeling his stomach beating like his pulse, and his heart solid as his bones, and his mind thin as a net.

He tasted his soup and then he laid down his spoon. "I don't want you to say anything, Clara—not a word—not one word. But the boy has been fired. I don't think he's guilty, but I can't afford to let the facts concern me. Rumors touch my business and my place in the community. Don't say a word! I've *been* independent—I'm still independent. I listened to gossip and it never affected me. But I live in this town. I've got no use for Mrs. Wright. She's a snob. I held out against her . . ."

"George!" his wife finally broke it, "you're . . ."

"You sit at home . . ." his voice wound around her, high and frightened, "you're not the one who has people driving in to get gas they don't need just to ask questions!"

Clara finally cried, "You're acting little and cruel, and you care more for where you live than how you behave!"

At that moment his life and his environment assumed the appearance of the sea-serpents on ancient maps, the unknown and well known, defining the limits of the known world. It was a narrow world, and he was aware of it with a constricted heart, and deep in the chambers of his soul he saw the baleful look of his great-grandmother Saunders.

22

For some time Karel stood by the door in the darkness. He did not know which way to go. He did not know what to do except stand there by the door. After a while he moved in the only direction he knew, toward Nicky and the Murrays. But he went very slowly, for he had a whirling spiral within him to traverse from its depth to its outer edge.

The past came up like an army with guns, and for those moments his hold on his life was precarious.

There was a quickening in the air like early frost, and one felt even in the dark the clanging colors of the trees, and the sap moving darkly at the tug of the frost, and the orderly folding in and careful measuring of nature. There was nothing resigned about nature; each cold night had its own reason, the cloudy night or the night filled with stars, the night when the wind tossed the trees and rattled loose doors, the night when the rain fell more piercing than snow, the night when the last crickets troubled the silence and the river flowed warm enough for a last old bullfrog to speak once, twice, with long pauses between. All these things folded in with the night. Each night seemed linked with the one behind and before, and the continuity became more important than the details.

He would have to make some decision, go to New York or to Boston, decide if he could train himself for some profession, decide what Nicky needed. But *tomorrow*.

He thought of Julie. What possible part could she have in this moment of his life? He did not believe anyone could understand what he had not experienced, and when Julie tried she did not succeed. And then he said something else to himself . . . He did not want her to succeed, for he wanted in her something that was quite unlike anyone else, and was related to a time and a place, broad and wide and full of sunshine.

Megan's house was dark, but there was a light in Mrs. Murray's. John let him in, and said that his mother had gone to a grange meeting and that he was doing some accounts.

"May I wait for her?" Karel asked. "I'll read the paper."

"Of course."

He did not know John (however intensely he thought about him because of Megan) and between them there was always a constraint. After a moment, Karel said, "He's asleep?" meaning the child, and John nodded.

Karel sat with his legs stretched out and he glanced briefly at John over the top of the paper. He saw John invariably as Megan's husband, and since the night Megan had torn her arm, his appraisal had been affected. But now, as he glanced at him, he saw him in a flash as an individual quite apart from anyone else. Everything and everyone had a sharp separate life of its own tonight, and John was included.

John said, "I have to go down to the barn. One of the calves is sick." He turned at the door and looked at Karel. "How are things going?" he asked.

Karel answered briefly, "I was fired tonight."

John's face became very white. He stood and looked at him. He stood for a moment without speaking, then he closed the door and came into the room.

"McVitty did that? Just in that way? What did he say?"

"When we closed the garage tonight he said I was through. He was sorry."

John laid his books on a table and leaned against the back of a chair.

"He must have given a reason—after all the time that has passed?"

"Many people have come and talked about me to him. He was not happy."

John's fingers were gripping the back of the chair till they were white. After a moment he said, very low, "I detest that kind of fear!"

"He is afraid of something that doesn't exist," Karel said, tiredly.

John's voice was very cold and pale. His face was pale. His eyes were heavy as though sleepless. "It does not matter whether it exists or not. It is—it is judging a person without taking into account why he is."

Karel sat stretched out, his arms on the arms of the chair, clasping and unclasping his hands. He felt a curious deep exhaustion as though all his natural forces had been drained away, and all that was left was some small pinpoint of truth which went on in spite of everything.

" 'Why he is?' " Karel echoed.

Then John turned away and walked to the window, and walked back to the chair, and he said in a colorless voice, "*Why I am.* They would do it to me."

Of course. Each man thought of himself, and some, because they thought of themselves, thought of others as well, and it brought the sweeping love in their hearts. Now he was watching John with a new feeling; his dark eyes did not leave his face. He tried to look at him with Megan's eyes.

He supposed a woman would always love that sort of man, the face so finely made, the expression so vivid and sensitive, a sort of grace upon him, quick and gentle and obviously aware of sights and sounds and subtleties.

John felt Karel's eyes on him, and he became keenly and suddenly aware of the big form overflowing the chair.

"I do not know why I said that." He hesitated. "I suppose one thinks about those things. I have thought about you ever since that old woman was beaten. But I've said nothing."

Karel smiled briefly. "We've not been especially friends."

"No. But I wished that I could have said something, without . . ."

He wished to say, "without getting involved," but he did not know how to say it with grace. And he believed in the passionate need to preserve, even if narrowly and painfully, the himself of himself. He always said that some day he would be secure enough to give freely—some day—not now—some day, when the roof and the walls of his house were weather-tight, when the self had been fulfilled, he would have time.

He said slowly, "*I* would testify for Roi if anyone wanted me to. I knew that old woman." He stared at the lamp for a moment or two. Then he said bitterly, "But that's not what I would testify. I would say, Why should not a man do what he has to do to save himself? Even Roi. I would make their moralizing look insane." His eyes turned directly to Karel, and there was a tight misery in his look. "There's more than one kind of self-defense."

Karel did not answer. His hands shielded the lower part of his face and he watched John intently.

"You may not want to do something, you may be terribly sorry that it has to be done." John went on in a steady voice, "but you can't be held back by pity when the thing is your own salvation. And who has a right to say what is moral or not moral—for Roi? Morality and the poor old woman. Poor Roi."

"And poor John."

"Poor John?"

"And poor Karel," he added with a little smile.

John stood up and walked away, gathering up the books. Yet he stood by the door for a moment, tall and erect, holding himself with an effort. So much had been said it seemed impossible to let it go at that. And yet there was nothing more to be said. How compelled he was to turn around, how compelled he was to finish . . . finish what? He felt himself groping to a decision of some kind. *Go—go!* And yet he remained, finding an excuse for his remaining, in love with his narrow cell and the safe glimpse of freedom outside. He knew, even as he stood there, that this was an atrophy of will. He was appalled—but in a faraway manner, as the rational man is appalled by all indecision. He would do something, he must do something, he must break through. He stood by the door, turning the knob back and forth, his eyes on Karel, his eyes speaking.

Karel, still watching John intently, said, "Roi—John—Karel—it seems to me we are all trying to find how to live in peace with ourselves."

John considered the white knuckles of his hand for a long time. "There are many ways of finding it."

"Oh, yes," Karel said. "That was only what McVitty was trying to do." He studied his scuffed shoes for a moment, yearning to say what was in his heart. Presently he ventured, "Love casts out fear, it is said, but I have seen fear cast out love also."

John wished to be away, a long way away, and yet he was too kind or too polite or too held. At length he said in a low voice, a tight smile on his lips, "I am perfectly convinced that what *I* am doing is right."

"I don't know what you're doing," Karel said.

John answered bitterly, "And when you do, you will join the old woman."

Karel got up slowly, unfolding his bulk. "I don't know what you are talking about. Many times I do not know what people are talking about. They are going their own ways. All I know is that we cannot live with fear."

"I will be damned and triple damned, and hated. That will hurt."

"Who will do that?" Karel asked, pacing up and down slowly, pausing at the coal stove to give a shake, putting a chair right, always slowly pacing, for he could not sit still.

Abruptly John sat down by the door and put his head in his hands. He sat thus, and the silence was very round and infinite, going out along the starry way and into day-break somewhere else, and rounding back in the silence of this place where only the fall of coals made a fretful little murmuration.

"I do not know where I fit into any world," John whis-pered, at last. "All the old things are coming back into the world—the utterly drab and commonplace—and I am through with them. And I don't see where the future is. And yet inside me I have a whole sublime world—a whole world to live in—but I'm the only one who knows it is real."

Karel was very quiet. He felt a deep compassion. He said, without looking up, "No one lives to himself alone."

"That is not true," John said passionately. "We're born and we die all by ourselves, and in the interval between we must follow the line of our own salvation."

Karel lifted his head to look at John. "I am telling you what I have seen. No one lives to himself alone. Maybe it is a hard fact—but then it is a hard fact."

John was silent for some time. "Let me say something," he said at length in a low voice. "I know that some things are an integral part of my life. I know that. There's a part of me which can't imagine leaving the things I have grown with and loved—there are times when I think I must understand them better and so find my strength. But I cannot—I cannot. Myself I don't know—myself I must find out. What am I—who am I—why am I? Why am I so unhappy? Why am I pulling away? Why will I go crazy if I do not have myself to myself? I have to know many things—many things—before I know myself!"

Karel raked the fire and put coal on it. He moved the coffee pot over the blaze. "And yourself you are taking along with you—where?" He spoke sadly, tentatively, for the complicated sorrows which a man gave to himself seemed more burdensome than anything he had known.

John said, "I don't think women suffer this way. I think they adjust themselves. I don't think they know much about this kind of misery. My wife will—my wife is very strong—she will always be able to keep her life together. If I knew what I really needed—I would follow it any place."

Karel was silent for a long time. He watched the coffee boiling, and he poured out a cup for John and for him. Then he drew up a deep breath and he said hesitantly. "Do you know why her arm was hurt?"

John's reaction was delayed. Then he looked at Karel wildly. "She fell down. She told me that herself. She fell down."

Karel looked at his closed fists, and he pressed them hard together. The silence was not peaceful. At length Karel stood up. "I may leave this town also. But now I am not so sure that I will find anything new—anywhere else. It may look different, but I think it will be the same. I think there is only one me and it goes where I go."

Mrs. Murray said nothing when she heard Karel's news, but her lips grew thin. At length she said he must come into her house with Nicky.

"I do not know what I must do," he said. "I must think. If you keep Nicky, that is very fine. . . ."

When he left, John was still sitting silently by the door, his chin against his fists. He did not look up.

After a moment John said to his mother, "You understand that I am going the first of November even if you have to be left alone?"

She did not answer for a moment. Then she said, "You've told me."

"I haven't changed my mind. I've simply tried to be patient."

She went to the open door and stood looking out. "Why do you say that so violently? Why—when the boy has just gone?"

He did not stir. No element of him seemed to move. Only his heart beat loud enough to be heard. He whispered, "Neither you nor she nor he nor anything can make me change my mind."

Karel saw a light in his room, and found Vree lying on the bed smoking. The place was bare. Vree said, "I moved your duds. You're going to live with me. I told McVitty exactly what I thought. I didn't spare him one semi-colon. I punctuated it just right. Now I feel better."

Karel hesitated.

A shadow came into Vree's eyes.

"Can't you come? I counted on it."

Karel smiled at him. "It is within myself . . . something unsettled."

Vree was silent, then he said, "It seemed to range me up on the right side."

Karel laughed. "What friends!" He went with Vree.

"It's not that I'm such a good friend," Vree explained. "But I've got my thumb to my nose, and I got to keep it there. There isn't anybody can make me do different. There isn't anything I got to lose. There isn't anything I'm latched onto. Why, I am completely free, and it's got to be plain."

But the pressures started. McVitty seemed goaded. It seemed necessary to him to pass on every item of gossip to Vree, to disconcert, to wound if that were possible, all in a dull noncommittal voice. Folks said Karel was really a Russian spy, and the FBI was interested.

"Wouldn't surprise me a bit," Vree answered placidly.

Two of the selectmen were wondering if Vree's rented shed was not a hazard which should be condemned.

"It'll last," Vree said.

There was new talk, quite urgent, of passing the zoning laws which had been long debated. Then an eyesore like the shed would have to go.

"It could stand a little paint," Vree said. "Guess I'll buy a couple of gallons."

There was also talk that Vree was getting old, a little incompetent, the county might begin to take an interest. A rumor like that could spread fast. Vree had nothing to say.

It made him white-hot with rage. It weakened him diabolically. Two of the women for whom he had worked many years stopped him and asked him solicitously about himself, advised him, seemed unimpressed by his answers, said, "Well, we all get old, Vree, and there comes a time when it's better for other people to handle our affairs."

"Thanks. I'm not interested." He said it rudely. Rudeness would not help him in the end, but it was necessary to him to speak freely.

Karel was aware of this. John Murray had been watching with an intent concern. When Karel came down to the barn to help with the sterilizing, John said, "Don't stay with him. It'll work badly for both of you. I heard someone call him a nigger. I've never heard that word used about Dunnigan before."

"I'll go," Karel said.

"Where?"

Karel was silent. As he swung the cans back into place he said cautiously, "I'm not proud and I'm not afraid any more. A year ago I would have left immediately, police or no police. Now I want to know what will be best for the future. I have written to colleges but it is late. I must also have a job." He hesitated for some time. "It is too late now to make mistakes. But I'll leave Vree's."

John was watching him intently. "You're not bitter?"

Karel shrugged. "That is a luxury. But I am amazed at injustice." Then he looked at John, and the dark eyes were very calm, very aware of John. "What is happening is mechanical and fearful and I feel compassion for everyone —including myself."

John's expression clouded. He withdrew and leaned against a post and lit a cigarette. His narrowed gaze remained on Karel. "You have been balked all the way. You have suffered all kinds of cruelty. Now you're finding it in unexpected places. That must be a real shock."

Karel did not answer. He gave a quick half-smile.

"You're not an idiot or a fool. It makes me wonder what you really do know about human despair."

"I cannot show you my heart," Karel answered sharply. "I wish that I could."

"I think you do not know," John said stubbornly.

Karel rolled the last of the cans into place. "And I think that the spirit filled with life can be indestructible. That is something I learned."

John regarded him with listening eyes as he leaned motionless against the post.

Vree would not allow Karel to leave at that time. Vree was determined. The tears came into his eyes. Karel knew then that he could not leave. He sat down at the old table by Vree's window, with the kerosene lamp at his side, and resolved to lay out alternative plans for the future. Vree played an old hand-winding phonograph, first an old record of Caruso, then an old record of Harry Lauder, then a new record of a tenor singing "Rock of Ages."

He played the last one several times until it became a refrain and Karel wrote to Julie, half-listening to it. Vree was adding some especially fine pressed flowers to his collection, and when the music slowed, Vree would be delayed for a moment in winding the machine. But the refrain succeeded in maintaining its calm stateliness.

Karel put in the letter to Julie what he saw as the practical side of his life. If he could not be a regular college student, he would go to Boston or to New York, find a job and study at night. It would take longer that way to reach a career, and he did not have time to waste. He had decided to study sociology. His mind circled easily around that decision. He sat staring at the letter to Julie, his heart melting. If God had given him Julie, then God would surely know how to take care of them. It was a child's thought. It cut through the maze.

The doctor climbed up the stairs of the shed and sat down in front of Billy, the stove.

"I've kept away from you," he said to Karel. "Had to. But I thought I'd tell you that Mrs. Arnow's leaving the hospital."

"That is a stone off my mind."

"But there's something else. She's going to prosecute."

"What will she prosecute? All the things that went on before?"

"She's a self-righteous old woman." He contemplated his twirling thumbs. "And what I might say to you would be beside the point. How are you feeling?"

"Why do people want to know that?" He smiled.

"Well, how would a fellow like you feel?"

"Amazed. This happened—but it need not have. That happened, but it need not have. People mutilate themselves without reason."

The doctor gleamed at Karel. "As a doctor, I would say fellows are always hacking away at themselves."

"So one watches it—and one is amazed."

A day or two later the doctor called Mrs. Murray.

"Tell the boy it's okay. All clear."

"What? What has happened?"

"The old lady's not going to prosecute. That Mrs. Fellowes she works for has talked her out of it. And the police say it isn't worth pushing a case if she's not going to cooperate."

He paused at the other end of the wire and then he added on a tired heave of voice, "In some ways this makes it worse. Roi's now a poor misguided kid, and Karel is the bad influence. Someone's done a thorough new job."

"Well," said Mrs. Murray, "that won't break his bones."

"If it would just break his bones, I wouldn't mind. But she's found something to talk about. She's got something people can fasten on to. She dotes on Roi now. It's a great conversion. It'll be mighty convenient for some people this way. No legal trouble. Just a nice settled conviction of who was wrong. I wish I knew who had turned the trick."

"Lem, don't be so tired."

"I've got reasons to be tired. I'm a poor old misguided fellow who's lost his protective coloration."

The doctor was right. Now that the distastefulness for legal action was past, many people might have their cake and eat it too. The quiet and the thoughtful people were silent. Others were certain that ostracism could be made effective, but how it could be accomplished was not clear when the object of it seemed unaware of their intent. But on the other hand unexpected people came to his defense. Miss Purvis found her voice during library hours, and firmly declared her independence.

"No one can prove a thing. I'll just believe what I *know* about that boy."

It was bold. It reverberated.

Others said, "The boy mustn't go away. Not now. Not under these circumstances. Not as though it were a witch hunt."

Mrs. McVitty never let a day pass that she did not say something pleasant to Karel.

Mr. and Mrs. Wright were frantic when they realized that Karel remained after losing his job. Mrs. Wright telephoned Julie and told her not to come home that week-end, but Julie returned just the same. Mrs. Wright wept, for it is a terrible thing to have your immutable world shaken out of your grasp. Julie wept, for she knew no other world than this, but its confinements had dissolved, and what lay beyond was mist-enshrouded, courage-dissolving.

Mrs. Wright said to her husband that a girl of Julie's temperament—her *new* temperament—would glorify self-sacrifice, would become a martyr simply in opposition. The boy must be really *exposed*—his weaknesses exposed. Mr. Wright said, "How?" with no pleasure.

Mrs. Wright did not know the answer. She was not an evil woman. Perhaps the most she could do would be to drive him away. Then she could set about repairing the damage he had done. A village, more aroused than it had been, would consolidate pressure, would naturally and effectively squeeze out the undesirable elements—something she could not do by herself.

Julie came to Mrs. Murray's where she did not find Karel. She stood in the center of the kitchen, a small shipwrecked figure.

"I hate them," she said. "I hate, hate, hate them."

Mrs. Murray said calmly, "Then you won't be clear-headed about what you must do."

"I don't know what to do anyhow."

"Well," Mrs. Murray said, "you're a woman. I've found women are very much needed."

"Am I a woman?" Julie demanded. "He doesn't think so."

"Oh, nonsense. What do *you* think? That's more important."

Julie was silent, standing there in the center of the kitchen, her hands over her face.

"That I love him," she said very low. Then she looked palely at Mrs. Murray. "But I don't know where I fit in."

Mrs. Murray sat down by the table suddenly and rather wearily.

"All I know," she said, "is that we can't leave that to someone else to decide. Women like us are seldom given a place voluntarily. Scarcely anyone says outright we're needed. You just have to learn what *reciprocal* means, and do something about it."

Karel felt that he did not have very much time. But he was determined that he would not run away. He would wait to find out which college offered him the course best suited to him, and he would stand where he was until he found out. It took courage, and he could not afford pride.

Vree said, "You sweat out something, and folks begin to forget. Anyway, they get so's they're not thinking about it all the time. Give 'em a pleasant word, and it'll get better day by day."

"Maybe. But I think there is a real hate here."

A postcard came from Roi. *Got a swell job in Albany. Keep your eyes peeled from now on. Be seeing you, chum.* The postmaster handed it to him with contempt.

That same evening Bert Miner, the constable, came and arrested Karel as a vagrant, with no visible means of support.

"Then I am too!" Vree cried.

"Oh, shut up, Vree. You've got a sockful of change under that mattress. Everyone knows."

Vree did not have enough money in his pocket to pay the fine. There was no jail, so the constable and Karel sat in Vree's shed until Vree telephoned. He made three calls and then he reached Mrs. Stillwell. She said breathlessly, "You come right over. Oh, my goodness, my goodness, I never heard of such a thing!"

The constable was a man with an iron upper lip. Only the lower part of his face moved slightly when he talked.

"Okay," he said, "that's all for tonight. But tomorrow you'll be a vagrant again. You better quit."

Vree asked very coldly, "Who reached back in his mind and fetched up this law?"

"Oh, what do you care? Every now and then they dust off the whole kaboodle."

"Not so long as I can remember." Then Vree said to Karel, "You'll have a job tomorrow."

Karel had stood very still when the constable came. He had sat in complete silence while they waited for Vree. He had said nothing at any time. Now his rage was appalling.

He said nothing but he walked up and down, up and down, until one was exhausted from watching him. His face was flushed and his eyes were full of pain and something darker than anger.

"You could always spot it when people were stupid before. Figure it out now," Vree urged, sitting on the edge of his old chair, alarmed by the pain on Karel's face. Karel did not answer.

"Eat some dinner," Vree ventured, but the pacing did not slacken.

"I'll make us some coffee that we can have later," Vree said, not making a move.

Karel looked at him so speechlessly that Vree tightened up. He became a small closed man, feeling only one emotion and constricting it to a hand's breadth.

The Murrays heard by the next morning. Most people who made a point of village news had also heard. Megan came down to Vree's, and found Karel alone.

"It was a stupid thing to do," she said. "You'll get friends this way." She sat by the window looking off across the lovely valley. "Oh, dear, dear Karel, what do you think of us . . ."

It was not a question. It was spoken with great sadness, and he looked at the sadness on her face. She was someone very beloved and meaningful to him. He could feel and observe and love her, and yet feel no need to cross the room to her. He sat, his elbows on his knees, looking at her, suddenly calm and secure.

"Mother says she would trust you to take John's place on the farm. Will you—would you take that job?"

He hesitated and then he shook his head. "You have done more than anyone else."

She looked at him gravely. "Why won't you come?"

"I must bring an end to all this, find what I can do with my future. Stop being helpless—even if I make a mistake." He smiled at her. "I might borrow money from you to go to New York."

"No," she said quickly. "Not yet—not at this time."

"Why?"

She hesitated. "It's my feeling. It's not time for you to go yet."

He smiled again. "It is something mystical?"

"No." She turned away, and stood by the stove watching

the steam spiral up from a pot. She moved restlessly, standing at one window and then at another. "I feel as though John will not leave me as long as you are here. As though, perhaps, watching you, his life is widening for him."

He was silent, and she said sadly again, "It's unfair to say that to you. I suppose each one of us must end fear in his own way."

He said softly, "I really want to stay here now for many reasons. If I go to New York, perhaps I will get a letter that I should have gone to Boston or to Cleveland. I do not want to make mistakes. I do not want to guess at things any longer."

"What if Bert Miner comes back again tonight or tomorrow?"

"Oh, I would go to jail. Now I would not be so disturbed."

She smiled. "It would be for ten days. You might miss an important letter."

He laughed. "Vree would answer it for me. He would make a better impression than I would."

She said finally, with some desperation, "What shall I tell Mother?"

"What I have said." He touched her arm. "It's getting all right?"

"Yes." She colored slightly. "In love, we make so many mistakes. Need we? I want a chance to rectify. Will I get it?" She looked at him suddenly.

He spoke rather severely. "You are the only person who really makes me sad when you are sad."

She smiled, and the light came into her face again. "I am not a sad person naturally. I am very fond of life." She moved restlessly about the room, and he stood by the door watching her, aware all over again of how common and shared each feeling was, how he understood hers and she his, how all of them—all of them wanted the same thing, though in different terms.

"When is Vree coming back? I don't want you to be here alone if Bert Miner returns." She stood for a long time in forced concentration before the framed butterflies on the wall.

"I don't know." He put his hand on her arm. "I will look after myself."

"Perhaps. Let me talk a little longer. I've got no one else to talk to." She smiled somewhat apologetically. "What is it that goes on in us this way—making us misjudge a situation? I've talked to John a great deal too much. I've pleaded and pointed out. But he needs to work out his own way. If I can conceal my feelings, be wise in some way—God knows how—be as nearly dehumanized as possible, intruding nowhere—but I suffer . . ."

"Megan . . ."

She looked at him for a moment. "John thinks I am strong. It seems an irony to me. Oh . . ." Her breath was caught in a deep sigh, and she stood silently looking across the steep slope outside Vree's western window to the hills. "But I have learned a great many things. He says he can never return to what is past. Yes, we make ourselves anew. What is permanent belongs to the present. We reclaim. I could not believe in anything if I did not think it had continuity in one form or another. May I make us a little tea? I should like to be busy."

She took down the teapot, and measured out tea which Karel handed her. She asked, "Have you heard from Julie?"

He shook his head.

"Oh, you will. I think this must be harder on her than on anyone. She knows what her parents are doing."

"Is it her parents?"

"They're a kind of bleak natural force."

He mused, "And if I talked to them, what would I say? That what happened is not at all the way it appears." He smiled ruefully.

"Yes, but that is Julie's job. To do for you. It is not a bad thing to discover that we have to give what the other one needs . . . not what we want him to need."

"Megan—Megan—dear Megan . . ."

Vree came in a little later, hurrying up the stairs. He said, "Doc Jarman told Bert Miner what he thought about most things in general. He did a fine job. He covered the ground! Said you were his secretary; you typed reports for him. He said you were going to type a report for him tonight."

"Am I? Good."

Megan got up to leave.

"What else can they do, Vree? Can you think of anything else?"

"Oh, they don't plan. They just fumble. I haven't got that kind of mind. I think some of the kids down at the diner are getting excited. They're Roi's friends, and it's been exciting for them. They don't want things to get dull again."

23

Vree was beginning to look like an old man. It was in his thought not in his bones. He had listened to so much and said nothing; he had shut himself into the dark defendable house of his own being and, for many days and nights now, had been watching through the white apertures of his eyeballs, and he felt the strain and the weariness. It was not that he was an old black man or that he was an old man or that he was a poor man; it was simply that he had been seen by others in one fashion, and he had seen himself in another fashion, and both ways of seeing were very strong.

What makes life so vivid? Who says you're old and broken and thrown aside? Those who observe and preside? But who are they to know?

He wished to go into the hills where the natural purgation of his whole life had taken place. Nicky went with him, and he showed Nicky all the small details of the autumn in the hills, the tracery of roots laid bare, the lovely drifts of fallen leaves in which the small boy rolled, the quiet held-breath watching of a delayed red-and-black caterpillar, hurrying, hurrying to find his winter home. They gathered flowers to press for the album Vree was making him. They went up into a high meadow by a brook to eat their sandwiches. Vree told him more stories of Billy, the kerosene stove. Billy had come with him last year, so that he might camp higher up in the woods, and watch the squirrels and chipmunks at their preparations. Billy was very real to Nicky. As real as the foxes and mice preparing for winter, or the wild ducks who had flown with their lone wild cries over his head.

They returned late in the afternoon when the coolness of the evening had begun, Nicky dreamy-eyed with the multiple and varied world of Vree.

Vree said they would have some cocoa which was waiting to be heated, and he propped open the door downstairs while he managed an armful of wood for the old stove. They went up the rickety stairs, Nicky clever as a puppy now, undaunted by their height.

Nicky went to sit on Karel's bed. Vree had broken several sticks across his knee and crumpled wads of paper and had laid out the cold cocoa for Nicky to admire, when he heard a sound and felt a premonition.

He laid down the sticks and the wads of paper, and he went to the open door above the stairs. There it was in the stairwell, the way he had known presciently almost the moment before it happened, a crackle, a blaze, a flame shooting up. He shut the door hurriedly, and then he stood with his back to it, looking at Nicky. Shutting the door was all right, but that was not enough. And he had only a moment, a fleeting spiraling moment, to wonder, to inquire.

He looked at the window—the hill dropped away at that point and there was only the lovely and dreaming valley which had been his heart's delight. The child sensed or heard and said, "Vree?" in a thin voice which might become frightened.

"Never mind," Vree said. "Just a little accident. Somebody must have dropped a match down there by mistake, and it blew up when we opened the door. Think you can manage the stairs quickly—real quick—quick as me? I can't come for a minute . . ."

There was a lifetime of something to be preserved. Sentimental and foolish, but life, as most see it, is composed mainly of symbols, and he had collected symbols—not because he was of the unhandy color of black but because his education had stopped too soon, his overalls had been patched all his life, and it was expected that into this mold would be poured a certain man.

He took out the book of pressed flowers, the framed butterflies. He took down the mounted birds, his children, his little brides, his sister sparrow and brother finch. He was a man a little touched in the head by all the visions and realities he had made out of the stuff of his day-by-day, and to lose these would be to succumb in some measure to the negation wished on him by others.

He took Nicky to the door and tied a handkerchief around the lower part of his face and saw him start down the first step. The flames were crawling up the far timbered wall; not for a few minutes would they come near the stairs.

Nicky said, "Billy!" and Vree said mechanically, "Yes, Billy," and turned back. Nicky looked behind. Billy would be forgotten, and Billy was the dog-part, the pony-part of his life, the living thing which had been his companion. Each story had been part of the wit and wisdom of Billy.

He stumbled back, and Vree did not know it. He took the wire handle of the stove between his teeth. When he came to the stairs they were hotter, but he sat on the top step, and he lowered himself step by step, sitting down, jolting from step to step until he was near the bottom where the heat was growing intense. Then he stood up and jumped the last two steps and steadied himself against the wall. The stove swung terribly against his teeth and he wanted to cry out. But why should he? He was deeply proud. It was a moment of manhood when the untried becomes the tried, full of significance and glory.

He ran at a trot to the sidewalk where Billy would be safe, and he lowered it carefully and separated his teeth. His jaw ached, he raised the stump of his arm and rubbed his mouth and jaw against it. A man was running toward him, and Miss Nolle, who lived next door, was standing with her body half out the window screeching, *Fire!* Nicky shrieked at the man, "Vree is there!" as the flames suddenly came to life. The man started toward the shed, and then Nicky saw Vree.

A minute later Nicky heard the siren summoning, summoning, demanding the help which was too late.

Karel and John and Megan came within fifteen minutes. Miss Nolle had taken Nicky into her house and telephoned. She gave him milk and cookies, she wanted to put him to bed, give him an aspirin, give him dinner, call the doctor, she wanted to do something. But he would not let her.

He had seen the end of Vree and that was all there was to it. He had seen it as he had seen earlier things on a railway siding, in a German camp, in a German woods, and the differences were negligible. He sat with tears rolling down his face, his eyes fixed in agony, his power of speech gone.

Vree had come down the stairs once and laid his mounted birds near the old stove. But he had gone back for the framed butterflies and the book of pressed flowers, and Nicky had seen him start down a second time, the flames roaring, the stairs cracking and collapsing. Vree had lain in the doorway, his neck twisted, the books scattered about him, the glass on the framed butterflies splintered. Then the cuff of his old trousers had caught on fire. That was what Nicky seemed to think of more than anything. The fire creeping around the trouser cuff, although the man who had come running stamped it out, and dragged Vree away from the shed onto the pavement.

There was the trouser cuff charred and there was Vree dead.

Nicky forgot the old stove. He forgot all the present. He was five years old again, and his mother-Vree was dead.

Karel carried him in his arms to the car.

Was anyone not shocked? There was not a person in the whole town who was not shocked, not even the boys, the friends of Roi whose nerve-ends and mind-ends and blood had been excited and titillated and churned and reached an ejaculation point, and set a rag fire, intended to threaten Karel who was the culprit. The fire would smolder and frighten and feed excitement so that the terrible dullness of days could be postponed for a time. Maybe as a libation to Roi, who knows? For, through Roi, what was not even true could be talked about, magnified, made true through dull evenings.

No one knew who did it. No one volunteered to inform. People sat very tight and quiet behind their shaded windows. No one wished to make a move. No one quite dared, though the fire chief made some mechanical inquiries. It was only spoken of in low voices by the majority everywhere . . . although there was not a person in the whole township who did not know about it before nightfall, and the newspaper reporter from the county seat came to interview Nicky.

Mrs. Murray would not let Nicky be seen by the reporter, and she spoke with a sarcasm and bitterness that was not like her.

A great many flowers were sent to Vree's funeral at the Methodist Church, but not many people came. They were embarrassed. The flowers were a compromise, as was the eulogy written for the paper by Miss Purvis which ended with a verse by Countee Cullen which did not really invoke Vree at all.

Mrs. Murray had handed John the paper, and after he had read it, he threw it to the floor and walked out. He walked out and on and down the road, and he walked long into the dark.

Nothing wiped out cruelty. He could find no purgation for cruelty.

Face to face with it he was sickened and terribly frightened, and it was impossible not to relate it to something within himself. He hesitated and tore at his soul and questioned and found no answer because he wished to find the dividing line between cruelty and necessity.

He believed they were two separate things; he could not see where they fused and became one. What is necessity at the deep end of entrapment? What is failure? Is it breaking a heart or beating an old woman or setting fire to an old man's shed? Everything was not cruelty that appeared so; some things were necessity. The hairline he would find—or he would be cruel. In what way might one have come to terms with the old woman? Was beating the necessity? What way had there been to come to terms with yourself when faced with the deadness of do-nothing, think-nothing, be-nothing? Was it by burning the old man's shed?

He slipped past the third question, but it was with him, phosphorescent, eerie, the nearest, the most painful, the most demanding.

The village remained appalled. "Every effort is being made," the county newspaper said, to find the culprits. But perhaps there were no culprits . . . Someone uneasy in his own mind at all that could be opened up in *any* small town, *any* place, *any* hemisphere, suggested that it might have been spontaneous combustion in old rags which Vree had been careless about. But Miss Nolle screeched her objection.

"He was the neatest old fellow I ever knew. And you can't talk away that young fellow I saw running away and laughing."

"Who was he?"

"That I couldn't say. I saw most his back. Looked like a Dachee back, but that I wouldn't ever swear to."

It was fortunate she had not seen the front of him. She had her indignation safe and sound and it propped up her own fears—a poor old woman living alone with mean boys abroad—but she didn't have to tell for sure on someone in her own town where she'd have to live for the rest of her life. If events, abstract and implacable, proved it a Dachee, then that would be destiny, it would not be Miss Nolle.

If it were a Dachee what would they do? Prove it? Perhaps, but did anyone really think so? Surely there would be a settlement some way, something not too clear-cut, that could melt into time and be mostly forgotten by Thanksgiving. Much better. Much more homogeneous.

Mrs. Stillwell had a stroke. It seemed a futile and inappropos thing to do, and one or two people—the doctor, Mrs. Murray, Mrs. Wright—felt a twinge of impatience or, let us say, an emotion that was not strictly sympathetic.

Mrs. Murray said, "Yet her feelings are so right. Who else in this town ever cared enough for world peace to make us listen to speakers month after month? Who else cared enough for girls getting equal chances with boys out in the world as she did, making us listen to people who said women had to get out of the kitchen. Well, who cared enough for Nicky, in the first place? I love and respect her."

The doctor said bitterly, "She's the living, breathing symbol of always the right thing, always mismanaged—

always right, always mismanaged. Sometimes I think she hurts more than she helps."

Mrs. Wright said ironically, "It is as though she felt that the sympathy had gone away from those boys, and she had to do something about it."

Mrs. Stillwell lay in bed and for several days she would not speak. It was this last event which had been too much. Children struck at through the death of Vree. Not only had she always loved children, but the child Nicky had a multiplied meaning for her. And back of him was Karel. For the child would not have had meaning without Karel who saved and brought him here. Vree would not have had meaning without Karel and would be an old ruminator, safe in his shed. What was Karel?

The issues were so enormous, so enormous . . . Overwhelmed, dismayed, she had retreated. It was not something to be faced.

But in the quietness and silence of the bed, one turned thoughts over and over, and sometimes, under those circumstances, there comes a little light.

Karel was frozen into hate. He could not look at a face in this town, a house, without a cold and murderous rage. He hated everyone, everything, in wave upon wave of hate. He felt nothing but the chattering racking inner excitement of a remembered past, a convulsive loss of control when he was composed of nothing but chattering teeth and icy terror.

The doctor sat in Mrs. Murray's kitchen every evening that week, in a dogged wordless desire to forestall, to be at hand for something he did not bother to name. He was the man who had locked the door after the horse had been stolen. He believed desperately that he might have prevented the death of Vree—How? was not answered—and now he wished to guard the locked door behind which he had hidden his two boys.

Once Mrs. Murray said to him, as she sat motionless for a change, "The boy has an immortal soul. That means he can love and endure." He did not hear her. She persisted. "This kind of thing is the boy's test. He survived terrible things before. Now what is he going to make out of a test that's even more crucial in many ways?"

The doctor did not hear.

She went on stubbornly. "He's an exceptional boy, he's a real innocent. He hasn't had to compromise the way most of us learned to do when we were his age. He can see things with really fresh eyes."

The doctor did not bother to answer. He watched Karel walk up and down the kitchen, his face colorless, his skin cold. When he spoke to him, Karel would turn on him blindly. He sat in a hard chair by the lamp, the light shining on his stiff veined hand. He kept his eyes on it with a flickering interest, for he knew that the pulse must be racing. Dangerous for a poor helpless old man, ringed around with helplessness. There was nothing he could do, and now his pragmatism did not seem worth a lifetime's cultivation.

Karel's emotion was a fearful thing for it sprang straight up from itself, intact and terrible. The nightmares of Nicky were his nightmares, the flames which had eaten around Vree's trousers were the methodical day-by-day, night-by-night flames which had consumed bodies. Two things were the same. They would go on and on in everlasting night. Darkened in hatred the daylight eluded him. Clamped with hatred, his own power was stripped away.

When he had been drained and exhausted, the hatred suddenly crumpled.

He drew an exhausted deep breath, and he became aware of others. The doctor did not ask for subtleties—blast it to hell!—that's not what he wanted! The boy had no sublety, but the doctor rocked back and forth against him nonetheless. He had to get up from the kitchen table and the nightly vigil, and he did not properly understand how the boy had compelled him to do so.

All these events, all these people—everyone he could name—even the anonymous setter of fires—tampered with, interfered with, changed the boy's life. But it was not changed. That was the strange part. In the end it was still intact, and that was not easy to accept. Next, he supposed sadly, all the people who had not learned anything would have to face up to this, and then they would shift on their tracks to something else.

"What is he going to do?" John asked the doctor as he stood by the doctor's car.

"Damnation—how do I know?"

John was compelled to ask Karel. He asked him as they drove in a new fence post.

"I am going away. Your mother says she will take care of Nicky."

"Where?"

"I am waiting for a letter. Wherever I can work and train myself."

He looped the wire over the post and John nailed it down. How open and disclosing is the human face, like a mist that is shifting, showing the near and the far. John looked out across the road, into the little woods which ran down to the river, to the edge of sky above, to the wheeling hawk and the clear blinding day, to the sweet smells and the sweet sounds, and his eye took in the sight and the sound and the smell all in one moment as though it must say something to him urgently, without delay.

"They'll think they've made you go away," he said suddenly. "Stay here and I'll give you a job on the farm."

Karel stopped and looked at him. "But I want to study."

"You can do that too." John listened to himself grimly.

Karel sat on his heels preparing the ground for another post. The earth flew up from under his hands and lay on his fingers and arms. The brittle leaves under his heels had a wry noise of their own and he shifted his feet as though he did not want to disturb them.

He asked abruptly, "*You* give me the job, not your mother? You would be here?"

John had not expected that question so soon. After a moment Karel sat back on his heels and looked up at him, the dark eyes extremely wise and guileless. It was a question which acted for John as a great gulf. What had been shifting and changing inside him could have been played with for a long time. It could have grown and been secure and very private. It could have become a small room instead of a cell, unknown to anyone until he chose to open the door. He could have continued in that small room for many weeks, uncommitted, allowing more light to filter in, letting things drift into a new state, always reserving the right to change his mind.

But he had been asked a sudden question, and Karel knelt there looking at him, oddly impersonal, and yet the eyes, warm and even a little gay, never left his face.

John felt an explosive burst of anger which shattered that small inner room beyond redemption. He heard his answer, the answer which might have been dreamed over for weeks until vague intuitions became convictions. He heard himself answer, "Yes."

"That's good," was all Karel said.

John felt a terrible bloody rage, something wild and terrifying as though he had been looped around and around by an inexorable rope in the hand of God. He felt a surging primitive fear, and he stood there for a moment, his boots driving into the ground, his fists clenched on the top of the post.

He cursed softly over and over again, monotonously, as he wound up the wire and picked up the clippers. Karel crouched very still, still as an animal, his hands barely moving although he was working. He was deeply compassionate, for he sensed the reason for this violent commotion, and he knew that one could say one thing too much or too little.

John said something dark and unintelligible, like a command, and Karel looked up. John saw the expression of his face, and he cried, "You don't know half as much as you think you do. Stop interfering."

Karel did not answer. He worked quietly. John said violently, "I can do whatever I want with my life—whatever I have to do!"

Karel's hands trembled but he took the mallet and drove the post deep into the hole.

"Oh, yes," he said softly.

"What? What did you say?"

"I said, 'Oh, yes.' "

John turned away and there were sudden tears in his eyes. "Why is this—what is this—I didn't want it this way."

"Remaining?" Karel asked diffidently. It was a moment before John answered.

"The other things."

Karel shook the post to test it, and gathered up the tools.

He said merely, "I do not know enough about farming to be responsible for it all alone."

They walked toward the barn, not together, for John kept several paces ahead. As they came to it, Karel asked quietly, "Why is it running away if I leave, but not if you go?"

John did not answer. He hung the wire against the wall, and he put the tools away where they belonged. When he looked fleetingly at Karel his eyes had the peculiar veiled look, but he smiled a little, almost pleadingly, so that the question might, perhaps, be put aside for another time.

John sat on the stone wall in the field where he had spent a whole night once before. The twilight was colder, the dew had a touch of frost. He was huddled, he was deeply alone.

What majesty we give to pain when we should feel only contempt for the degrader, the diminisher.

What explained the enormity of life, what simplicity, what sure defense?

Not self-pity or bitterness or rebellion or despair—they offered no superstructure, no creativeness.

There was unselfed love and humility and grace. When they filled the spirit then it was audacious and found a reason for its hope and found a purpose and a strength and a way and a place, and a reality to the hidden and longed-for.

It was only an intimation, but it gave great range to the vaulting sky, it extended the depth of the hills, it remarkably enriched the sound on the wind in the dry leaves.

Early the next Saturday morning, Julie came to the door. She picked up the cat in her arms and fondled her and stood watching Karel make the coffee. He smiled at her, but he said nothing. After a moment he came over and kissed her on the cheek.

"You won't go away?" was all she said. He smiled a little and hesitated but did not answer.

She sat down in a chair still holding onto the cat. There are many bewilderments not put into words. There are desires and the undefined hopes that become so real they are organic and cannot be cut away except as an amputation.

"I wanted to come to the funeral, but the dean wouldn't let me."

He smiled at her. "Your mother was there," he said, as he broke the eggs for the omelette. Nicky came into the kitchen and then Mrs. Murray, and Julie felt lost again, for there was a unity and familiarity here which had grown without her.

Nicky leaned against the table looking at her, the dark circles under his eyes. She got up and selected cups and plates for the breakfast. It might be the wrong china, and then she would be more lost than ever.

"Tante Murray," Nicky said weakly, "she is taking cups and saucers."

Mrs. Murray replied, "She is helping," and then she said, "You sit here, Julie, and fix the toast," and Julie was, for a few minutes, safe.

Nicky regarded her for a moment and then he said, "Vree is dead. I saw him dead."

Karel came and lifted him to a chair and crouched beside him with a bowl of cereal.

"There are other things to remember about Vree," he said softly. "Do you remember how he found the baby otter by the brook? And how he showed you the fox's den? And then there are the flowers you can recognize by their leaves." He talked on and Julie listened to the sound and to the intent even when her mind strayed from the words. She loved him very dearly. All of this merely intensified her love.

She said suddenly, "My parents are setting up a scholarship for a Negro child. In Vree's name." No one answered. Mrs. Murray paused. Then Julie said flatly, "It's nothing. I'm ashamed that they think they can do it."

"Oh, it'll be a reminder," Mrs. Murray said calmly. "*That'll* be good."

When breakfast was over Karel came to Julie, put his arm through hers and drew her into the sunlight.

"What are you going to do from now on?" she asked still fearfully.

He looked down at her and put an arm across her shoulders. "What am I good for?" he asked gently. "I have great hopes in me, but that does not earn a living. I must start somehow very patiently and plod dutifully, and then I will be fit to be a householder."

"I don't know what you mean," she said, her heart cold.

"I do not know how to do anything. I must study, start at the beginning again. Start afresh—altogether."

She shook his hand off her shoulder and went apart from him. She leaned against a tree and began to cry.

He watched her, and the invariable misery he felt at such times closed his throat. She cried because it suddenly came to her in a great ocean of despair that her deepest and most innate longings bore no relation whatever to the only life that she knew. She would never fulfill the thing that her mother wanted of her and yet she had no preparation for any other. She had always reserved a small expectation that her family way of living and being would, in some manner, be hers as well. Now she had to face herself and what she wanted. And there was no clear way, no one to help her.

Karel came near and sat on his heels at her feet, breaking blades of grass and chewing them, not looking up. He saw her little feet in the brown brogues and the tense way her ankles supported her, and this he found more touching than any part of her small body flattened against the tree.

He said in a constricted voice, "I love you. But it does not seem as though you and I as persons are very important in that. It's a third thing we make together. That is why I say things to you and am unkind. Perhaps if we get ourselves out of the way, then we will find what we want in common—and want with each other. But I think we are too different still. We have not quite come together."

She took one thing out of what he had said. "You love me? I love you."

She did not move except to look down at him. He remained quite still. At length he said, "There is such a long way yet—such a very, very long way."

Then she cried out with a little anger and struck her hand against the tree.

"Loving a person means wanting to be with him, wanting him to become the very best he is able, wanting to help him be his very best, wanting him to succeed in everything he does—wanting to be with him."

He did not answer, but he was very happy.

One evening, just before dinner, the doctor came along. He blew his horn outside Megan's house, and when she came to the door called, "Come along!"

He drove slowly down the road and turned in at the farm gate. The kitchen light was shining, and Mrs. Murray, to whom he had telephoned, came to the door when she heard him. He looked at her and he shook hands with her suddenly.

Nicky was under the table, attempting to make a house for himself and the dog and cat. Karel could be heard in the basement shoveling coal for the stove skuttle. Mrs. Murray called him and he came up with the heavy skuttle, and nodded to the doctor before he shook some coals into the cook stove.

Mrs. Murray went to the table and coaxed Nicky to come out of his house, and held him, a wan little boy, in her arms. She held him with great tenderness and ease in spite of the long legs dangling against her, and then she moved back a chair with her foot and sat down, kissing him on the cheek.

"Guess what has come," she said.

He looked at her swiftly, and Karel stopped shaking out coals, and both, he and Nicky, turned their eyes toward the doctor. But Nicky turned back to her again, and buried his head against her neck. He was trembling.

The doctor unwrapped the package and lifted it out. It had been so long expected, had acquired so much the nature of a symbol, that to see it now, in dimension, form, left one with a sense of unreality.

The doctor sat down on a chair near the door, and waited. In a moment Nicky got down from Mrs. Murray's lap and went to him slowly. They went about their task with economy of movement and no speech, and the child watched every action of the doctor, and the aluminum and leather arm.

Mrs. Murray and Karel did not stir. Even the animals crouched under the table watching a situation, a state of mind, with round yellow eyes. The doctor took it off and made adjustments, he put it on again and told Nicky to stretch out his arm.

He stretched it out, an appendage which resembled other appendages, a normality of length, a conformation in a world of conformities, and yet—a divine event. He lowered it to his side and he lifted it again. He lowered it and lifted it, and he turned a white ecstatic face to the doctor and to Karel. The doctor gave him a handkerchief to grasp between the two metal fingers, and he showed him how to bend the elbow. At length he gave him the cat to hold, cradled in his own arm against his own breast.

The doctor could not stop smiling. Nicky was his ewe lamb, his little chick, his fine boy, his wise man. Nicky sat on his lap, moving the metal fingers, reaching out the arm, touching the table, the shining look of pure joy on his face even when he momentarily frowned. The little boy's arm, which some had imagined could be kept from him. Keep the wind, keep the sun . . . !

The doctor looked at Megan and she smiled at him.

There was Megan who had remained intact in one fashion, and there was Karel who had remained intact in another, and he thought of Vree who had not been broken until they threw him on his neck. And even then—how did one know? And John, who was looking at Megan with no expression on his face, but looking at her steadily, and the child, and Jose Murray, and the girl, Julie, of whom he could have no impression except that she sat here at ease and seemed to belong.

Julie sat very still on an old footstool. All her safeguards had been taken away. She had no real home. But as she sat there watching the child she realized that in the end nothing had reality but one's deepest sense of life and its truth and its potentials. And the loving heart which gave this expression.